THE BIKE COP

in

The Greater Weight of Evidence

James H.K. Bruner

To order additional copies of this book, contact:
Xlibris
1-888-795-4274
www.Xlibris.com
Orders@Xlibris.com
768553

Dedication

This book is dedicated to my first fans for storytelling, a truly captive audience (at bedtime): Meredith, Seamus, Julia, Sally, Teddy, and Faith. Thanks for the encouragement. The more adjectives that were added, the quicker sleep came. To my wife, Gretchen, thanks for believing in me and helping with edits and ideas. Let's do more! Love you guys!

JHKB Amelia Island, Florida
March, 2018

Acknowledgements

I would like to acknowledge Ken Sukhia, an attorney's attorney and the Department of Justice's former U.S. Attorney for North Florida. His advice and tips on the prosecutor's role were invaluable. Thanks to Lisa Soininen and Chubby Whitten on Damariscove Island, Maine, Cousin Johnny Barnes and bro-in-law Bob Schwarz for their suggestions and encouragement. Thank you to John Martin and the management at the best hotel on the eastern seaboard, The Colony Hotel, Kennebunkport Maine. Finally, thanks to Katrina Vega and my mystery editor at Xlibris for their excellent insight and confirmation of worthiness.

CHAPTER 1

In the good old days in this small Maine seaport, it was safe for an eleven-year-old boy to fish alone at five in the morning. Who could predict that this day was one of the last of the good old days in Port Talbot?

The young fisherman had only left a note to his parents saying that he had gone fishing. The parents, three hours later, would only smile upon his industriousness and perhaps look at the tide chart to see if their boy was wise as well. In the good old days, being a kid alone and riding bikes, fishing, or skipping stones across the water at the beach was normal, especially in quaint Port Talbot.

The Port, as most fondly referred to it, had lobsters, fish, and in the summer, tourists who were attracted to its coastal village charm. Striped bass the size of bed pillows also came to visit. They came in from the depths of the ocean to feed up the creeks and estuaries on the falling tide in the warmer months, creating almost unnatural possibilities for fishermen to land trophy fish out of small creeks.

The stripers, like the young fisherman after them on this early morning, were also wise. The morsels that these monsters fed on could not withstand the pull of the outgoing tide that occurs over a six-hour period in this part of the northern hemisphere. By proper timing and swimming against the current, the bass were treated to a moveable feast.

The tides in Maine cause coastal landscapes to be in constant flux. High tide ushers in a nine-foot of rise of spirit-lifting blue water that, like clockwork, immediately starts to recede. It recedes six hours later to reveal a brownish-green muck that has a foul fragrance to most tourists. It is the smell of home for the locals who believe the low tide was also beautiful even though the mud resembled sewage and decomposing sea life. This change in tide brought transformation that, while only temporary, was profound enough to actually drive down the value of adjacent real estate. At least in the good old days it was so.

How the cyclical revelation of low tide and the temporary brilliance of the high tide paralleled life was lost on Digger as he cast his line upriver toward rocky outcroppings. Like a clock, and life itself, it would move too fast when you needed it to be slow and peaceful; and when it you needed it to move along, the tide took forever.

Digger didn't realize how good he had it. At eleven years of age, rich kids really don't dwell on such things. All he knew was that the night before, he wound his alarm clock, much like one would wind friction cars on Christmas morning, and set it for 4:30 a.m. When it clanged with decreasing urgency, he jumped to the window to check the seas and skies and punched the air with approval. He didn't marvel about the extreme privilege in viewing the ocean from his bedroom window or getting on his Schwinn Orange Krate bike with the sissy bars. Nor did he think much of grabbing Zebco's latest fishing rod and tackle box chock-full of expensive stuff. Off he strode with both items balanced in his hands, grasping the bike handles with the tips of his fingers. Like a jouster from the Middle Ages, he rode his bike in the dark down to the Port Club docks where his other steed awaited.

He mounted his twelve-foot fiberglass skiff, which had the name *The Seahorse* emblazoned on its transom. Digger threw the mandatory life jacket, called a *kapok* in the good old days, into the bow and crossed the plank seats to get to the stern where the little three-horsepower engine was cocked in the air, drying out from yesterday's adventures. Observing the starting protocols: gas valve on, air valve open, lever to start, and yanking the pull rope with the black rubber handle, he was off. In the silence of this hour, the engine's noise echoed off the banks of the Talbot River and the clubhouse itself as if to signal that Digger is taking charge and dominating the space. His steed, the *Seahorse*, would take him wherever he wished.

While the wealth that undergirded Digger's activity was off his radar, the freedom he had was not lost on the young sailor. No accountability, no concerns; only the fleeting notice of lobstermen who shared such industriousness. Digger's industriousness had earned him his nickname early on. *Digger* had been bestowed upon him for his determination to get fishing worms as early as four years old. It also allowed his parents to distinguish between the father, David Adam Davenport Sr. and David

Adam Davenport Jr. As he was wont to do, Dr. Davenport jested during introductions that Digger was a nickname given so the father's creditors would not come after the wrong Davenport.

Digger reeled in another empty cast and thought about how great it would be bringing in a trophy bass to the Port Club docks; how it would impress his buddies who were, at this moment, soundly sleeping in their similar ocean's edge cottages built back in the age of, well, industriousness.

The line got fouled. *Drats!* That was his best Rebel lure. He looked at his position in this estuary: twenty feet off the rocks, up a river tributary, hidden from the port's activity—a perfect spot for his hunt. At this crook in the creek, he could see the cupola of the Brigantine Hotel and not much else of civilization. It was amazing really that the grand hotel's overflow parking lot bordered this part of the tidal creek. In another decade it would be taxed as prime waterfront and ogled. For now it was simply a gravel parking lot with a great view at high tide. He pulled again on the rod.

At this depth and location he shouldn't have snagged the ubiquitous black seaweed. That could spell certain death to a prized lure. Only rarely could one slowly and gently pull in the clump of seaweed to free up the hook. Usually the seaweed's grasp on the terra firma below won the tug a war with the angler.

"Double drats!" Digger muttered, having been taught not to swear. He rarely let a curse word fly like his friends, but he didn't give them grief when they swore. He ignored the expressions and used his somewhat outdated vernacular anyway, only to find that in many cases his friends started using the hokey words, too.

Digger shifted into seaweed recovery mode. It was a technique almost as deft as landing a fish. But this clump on the line was different. Seaweed shouldn't be twenty feet away from the rocks. It grows on rocks. His hook was hung up where only muck should be. He vowed to come back at low tide in old tennis sneakers to retrieve this spinner if he couldn't get it free.

With only a thirty-pound test line, he carefully reeled in and noticed that his boat was the only thing moving toward the area where his line disappeared. High tide in these creeks meant a depth of only eight to nine feet. He felt with the sun rising he might be able to see what was fouling the line. As he reeled closer, a brazen seagull dive-bombed where his line entered the water. *Shoot! That seagull came away with a good size pollack in its beak!*

Birds were a good omen to fishermen. His father, known for stupid puns, had called them *beak-ons* because they signaled that something was lurking below with their beaks. "Beak on!" said Digger, smirking and thinking of his dad and his dad's story of fishing with Mr. Steingut in the Bahamas, where his dad, casting with live bait, had caught a seagull—or rather, in midair the seagull had caught his dad's minnow, hook, line, and sinker. Dr. Davenport would relay the story like a true fish tale—with enthusiasm, grandiosity, and pride as he explained what it was like fighting a beast in the air: the zigzagging, flapping, squawking, and the dramatic conclusion of Mr. Steingut pulling a shotgun from under the gunwales of the boat and blasting the bird, which showered the boat in pinfeathers.

There was clearly fish activity going on in his area of the hang-up. Birds were now circling overhead as if lining up for a meal. *Man oh man! To get this hook free and join the feeding frenzy*, thought Digger. His boat now directly over the fishing line's point of entry, it was time to put down the rod and revert to the ancient fishing technique of pulling in the line hand over hand.

Digger's tender fingers were being creased and burned as the line seemed to slowly come back to him. Even at eleven years of age, Digger knew when a thirty-pound test line would snap. He wisely played the line, just under its breaking point. "Yes!" It was coming up … and was dead weight. Hauling slowly, he realized this was not a clump of seaweed, which would resist and then break free and come easily until you hauled the mass of black and green stringy pod-like sea vegetation to the side of the boat and tried to lift it in. Often, if one were successful at loading the seaweed in the boat to untangle a lure, one had to be careful of hidden hitchhikers that would abandon their vegetative universe when the clump hit the deck of the boat. Crabs having hissy-fits would start scurrying about the deck with pincers cocked open and pointing up in the air as if to say, "Where are you? Who disturbed my home? I'm going to reach up and snip the crap out of you. Where are you?" Understandably, they would have a serious attitude problem.

Digger knew instinctively now he was not dealing with that headache. Was it a trap? A lobster trap? Couldn't be. No, not up a tidal creek. And a trap would not be slowly rising as this load seemed to be.

His first glimpse revealed a white mass of cloth with schools of fish darting hither and yon as the mass slowly surfaced. He thought he had hooked a sail or a tarp. "What the heck?"

As the hook tugged at this mass of white cloth near the surface, Digger first recognized buttons as if on a white coat. Double-breasted no less. And then the mass rolled as if through some act of inexplicable sea physics. It had tattered flesh caused by the feeding of the multitude of swirling fish, like what he remembered of seeing a partially decomposed seal. The scene wasn't particularly new to him as a young fisherman, but what threw him back off the bench seat of the boat and onto the deck was the sight of the flesh bound tightly by a shimmering silver wristwatch.

Digger's mind flooded immediately with the realization that this was not a seal or a fish. This was the body of a half-eaten human that he had to think clearly about on how to handle. He didn't realize it then, but it was something that would forever rock the safety and naiveté of his youth in the good old days. It instantly scribed an effect upon him that would follow him for his entire life—as time would tell.

Chapter 2

"David Adam Davenport Junior!" The proctor called out in a mocking, hoity-toity English accent. Digger stood to the glare of his fellow freshmen at the University of New York. It's not like such an upper-crusty-sounding name should throw his colleagues into a tizzy. They all had bougie surnames that read like the passenger list on the Mayflower. Or in some cases, the Amistad. They had they maintained such a list on the slave ship.

"Mr. Davenport, you're assigned to Sheffield House!"

He strode to the side of the great hall where other Sheffies lined up to welcome him with the traditional handshakes: firm grip, eye-to-eye contact sort of thing, the social ritual taught by all the blue bloods' dads.

This was no NBA team pick with high-fives, butt slaps, and knuckle raps. This was the University of New York: future titans of industry, if one got As. Senators, if one got Bs. Judges, if one got Cs. And if one got anything less, one got nothing.

Sheffield House had the ivy, leaded glass windows, and the fireplaces so grand you could walk into the fire box, which was a real pain because to make them worth the effort, you needed four-foot logs and a kindling temperature only reached by burning a small forest. So passé had the fireplaces become that they served better as goals for indoor broom hockey.

Digger had decided on the University of New York after having been recruited by their crew coach. Unlike other members of the crew team who needed the boost to get in and afford the school, Digger had his choice of Ivy League, and his parents didn't even bother filling out the annual financial aid forms filed with the government and universities. His EFC (Estimated Family Contribution) was "all," meaning 100 percent. What brought him to UNY was its campus's waterfront location in the heart of the world's most desired city, and its criminal justice program. The program was unique. Their sweatshirts read: "UNYQ—The University of New York, Queens Campus."

The Queens campus was a short subway ride from the main campus but worth it. Here the university had decided to build the best criminal justice program in the world. Queens was a perfect training ground for fighting crime. There was no shortage of cadavers, clinics, and cops. He knew from a young age that catching fish and catching criminals were what really excited him.

UNYQ's criminal justice program was not merely a two-year degree type of rent-a-cop training. The university, like most ivies, had a general liberal philosophy at the main campus on Manhattan, which held that criminals need coddling because their crimes are not behavioral choices but rather uncontrollable and ingrained urgings spawned by an imperfect society or a failed government program. But at the UNYQ campus, it actually had a top-notch, forensically-focused criminal justice program. Sure, the Crim-psych courses indoctrinated the students with the usual blame-shifting rationales. Let's face it—there weren't many college kids into catching criminals. After all, smoking pot was criminal. How could you smoke pot, which was rampant in the seventies on college campuses, and have to bust fellow partiers?

Nonetheless, the forensic physics, chemistry, and anatomy courses were free from the spin unless such science helped to vindicate the wrongly convicted. That was one of the more active clinics offered in Digger's program, The Vacation of Judgment Project. It was as if the goal was to vacate all convictions. Students, using their newly acquired forensic powers, would work in cooperation and on-site with the ACLU and Amnesty International attorneys to try to reopen criminal cases across the world. The non-Crim students thought the Vacation of Judgment Project was a fancy term for turning on and tuning out. In reality, it was a highly coveted program that introduced students to criminal elements (while innocent … possibly … they were still unsavory) and their defense counsel, who were pro bono attorney do-gooders, often bowing to white guilt.

Attending his Advanced Forensic Anatomy lab class, Digger was reminded of his earlier forensic field training at the age of eleven. A naked, bilious, and gray cadaver was rolled into the lab in front of fifteen to twenty students. This bashing of the students' sensibilities on the first day of class with the grotesque sights and smells was certainly some sort of institutionalized hazing by the professor. Even though the Crim majors were a small and dedicated group of select individuals, they all groaned and gagged as the room filled with the reek of death shrouded in formaldehyde. Many instantly recognized the smell from high school days with fetal pigs, nematodes, and for those who came from a well-heeled prep school, furry distilled calves.

As the groans and yakking lessened, and the appreciation of the presence of a dead human with tattered flesh grew upon the class, Digger remembered the scene: flesh whitened like parboiled chicken meat. It could have been the Brigantine Hotel Chef he caught with his hook eight years ago. Although this cadaver was naked, if you put on the white double-breasted coat and black and white check pants and black soft-soled shoes and chewed away some of the fingers and facial features, they could be spitting images. The eyes were a dead giveaway … literally. Both cadavers had nothing but sallow sockets. Digger couldn't be sure what happened to this one's eyes. He knew what happened to the chef's eyes. He was an eye witness, literally, to the feeding frenzy.

Chapter 3

He couldn't put it out of his mind, even as the lab professor droned on, how at eleven years of age he used the Danforth anchor and line to secure that morning's catch so long ago. He remembered that he had taken several minutes lying on his back on the deck of the *Seahorse*, stifling gags and wretches and lying low in the boat, hoping the partial body of the human would not reach up or do something Hollywood-like. In the bottom of the boat, as much as he resisted, his mind kept being called back to a reality of sorts by birds circling overhead and by their dive-bombing at his ghoulish find. From his vantage on his back, the birds looked like they were after him. He had to act. He stood up, waved back the gathering flock of flying predators, and examined the catch. Fish also continued to act brazenly. Apparently in their food chain this was a link of uncommon taste. What was with their focus on the decedent's eyes? Lost in the fascination, Digger watched small, silvery fish dart frenetically as they fed on the eyes and lips of the bloated body. Occasionally and absentmindedly, Digger would wave off the impatient birds swooping in for their share as he was mesmerized by the scene.

He slowly began to take control of his sensibilities. He looked to the water's edge and saw that the tide was flying out now, just when he needed it to be slow. Both he and his newly acquired bloated ecosystem would be high and dry in muck very shortly. He reasoned that it would be better to bring the body to the town dock than to cut it loose and speed at one or two miles per hour for help, leaving it to be consumed and left on a mudflat. He ginned up his courage and prepared to roll the body in his anchor line, which was attached to the bow of the boat. Coast Guard rules of having an anchor on board had finally paid off.

He took the anchor, placed it on the now-floating chest, and simultaneously pulled gently on the fishing line. This caused the heavyset man to roll. In the momentum of the roll, Digger let the fishing line out so it would start to spool around the body. He figured between fishing line and anchor line, this guy was not going to get away. But another sight of the rolling cadaver threw Digger back on the bottom of the boat again—the sight of the back of the poor fellow's skull. It was missing, and only white, mealy meat was there, much to the delight of the crowd of flashing minnows. Digger regained his composure and deduced this guy had taken a blow to the head.

He used his oar to reach the anchor line draped on the other side of the body, pulled it up, and placed it on the man's back, causing him to roll again. He repeated this several times and secured both the fishing and anchor lines. Then he started up the engine, put it in gear, and realized that as he went forward, the body gravitated toward the back of the boat and the propeller. He soon recalculated his options and turned the engine completely around, a trick available only to small, three-horse engines, and pushed the lever to one third speed. Now as the boat moved in reverse, the body floated toward the bow of the boat. And so he towed the body downriver toward civilization in reverse.

He encountered some difficulties in the falling tide. The body would at unpredictable moments submerge and drag on the bottom, slowing Digger to a precarious standstill in a falling tide. He looked at the kapok in the bow and concluded this guy needed some flotation. He stopped and hauled the dead weight to the side and took the kapok. Lifting the bands of anchor rope off the body shoved the kapok between the belly and the rope. The compressing of air and its escaping through the corpse's mouth caused the chef to involuntarily speak in a guttural whisper: "Hep maaah!"

For the third time, Digger was thrown back on the deck, where he looked up at the sky. *This is too much. Did this guy just speak?* He peered over the gunwale. The body floated quietly, not moving at all except as jarred by the marauding seagulls. *Must of have been the way the air escaped through the throat and nose.* Gradually, he resumed his extraction operation.

He approached the bridge in the Port. This was the epicenter of tourism. It gave the landlubbers the closest and cheapest way to be on the water and get the photos of the river and the lobster boats and seagulls hovering over the nearby fried clam take-out windows. The bridge was still a drawbridge from Port Talbot's shipbuilding days. It had the weather-beaten shingled bridge tender's shack, which was no longer manned full time. You could make arrangements hours in advance to have it opened if needed. It was one of those bridges that moaned as car tires went over it. What made the tires moan was the fact that the deck was nothing more than a crosshatch of steel screening that allowed you to see down to the water under the bridge. It was these screen panels that would get drawn up when needed for taller boats to get through. Digger and his friends liked throwing pennies on the bridge when boats would go under … brats in the good old days, criminals by today's standards.

As he approached the bridge in reverse with a flock of seagulls dive-bombing the partially floating hunk of flesh with the orange floaty, it interested even the most distracted morning tourist. The traffic, which could be standstill on this bridge, was remarkably sparse, but the foot traffic was rather heavy, and now began pointing in his direction as he came closer to the bridge. From the vantage of the bridge, it soon became clear that the item being dragged was a human body with arms and legs. Screams started coming from the bridge, and people started running and pointing. The people running across the road to see that side of the bridge caused cars to screech to a halt and the drivers to exit the cars, leaving their doors wide open. People came running from the adjacent gift shops and small restaurants to see what the commotion was all about. The Port was about to witness an event that would become lore for years to come.

As Digger approached the bridge, he looked up at what seemed to be hundreds of onlookers who were collectively looking aghast. Some were shielding their or their children's eyes. Some stood with their hands covering their mouths, and some were even gagging. The seagulls now engulfed the gawkers on the bridge.

He yelled up to no one specifically, "Get the police! I'm going to the Port Talbot Marina!"

Replies were yelled that he couldn't distinguish as he entered the echo chamber under the bridge. He looked up and saw a surreal scene of frowning faces, some retching, others batting at the seagulls, but all were looking down through the steel decking of the bridge. He couldn't help but notice that the underwear of the women wearing dresses was showing. He made note to tell his buddies about this leg of the trip. It was all too fleeting now that the river was forced through the tight confluence of the bridge.

His juvenile thoughts were interrupted by sirens. It was as if the town was completely in scream mode, with sirens wailing from every direction.

The Port Road was on his left, Ocean Avenue on his right. On the bridge was an officer with binoculars. Suddenly a boat with sirens came tearing up the river, violating the speed limit. Digger had never seen a boat with blue lights and sirens nor one violating the no-wake zone. He wondered where they kept that rig. Upon closer inspection, it was actually someone's lobster boat with a siren and previously unnoticed rig of strobe lights attached. Chief Nickerson was at the helm.

Digger thought Chief Nickerson, a local celebrity, was chief because he looked like an Indian chief: red, ruddy skin, wise eyes with crow's feet, and a crow's hooked nose—a man of few words. Digger thought that the mountain face on the New Hampshire license plate was the spitting image of Chief Nickerson.

Years earlier, Chief Nickerson had carried Digger in his arms, put him in his police car, and taken him to the hospital, sirens blaring. Digger had been hitching a ride down the Brigantine Hill, balanced on Toby Brown's bicycle handlebars. He got his foot caught in the spokes of the bike and was catapulted to the pavement. Then his driver, Toby, ran over him. Chief Nickerson had come on the scene, yelled at Toby for laughing uncontrollably as Digger cried and moaned, and took Digger off in his cruiser.

The chief was coming to his rescue again. After the dock hand, at the chief's direction, had used a net and an electric lift to pull the body up onto the dock and the EMTs had strapped the remains to a stretcher and hauled it off, the chief turned to Digger. "Son, do you think you can lead us to where you found this body?"

"Yes, sir, I hooked him behind the Brigantine parking lot."

The chief and the district attorney drove to the gravel parking lot behind the Brigantine Hotel with Digger sitting in the back of the cruiser. Digger jumped out of the car and waved the officers to follow him down onto rocks. When the officers arrived, slowly picking their way over the rocks, Digger pointed out to the mud flat. "That's where I hooked the body!"

The chief started climbing closer, huffing and puffing and taking it slowly over the seaweed, but Digger was already scampering across the rocks to a different place.

"Chief Nickerson?" Digger called excitedly. "There's some blood over here!" he yelled as he pointed down at the rocks.

The chief yelled back, "Digger, don't touch anything. Hold up there, we're coming!" The chief clicked his radio. "Dispatch? Unit 1 here. We need a photographer and a forensic team over behind the Brigantine. We've got a crime scene."

"Ten-four, Chief," crackled the dispatch in return.

Digger started to follow something with his head bent down like a bloodhound with his nose to the ground. "Digger! Freeze!" bellowed the chief. "We got this, son!"

"But Chief, there's a blood trail here," he said, pointing down.

"I said freeze, Digger!" the chief barked again as he surveyed the tree line and adjacent bushes. Digger sat down and waited for the DA and the chief to climb over to where he perched himself. The chief spoke calmly. "This is a crime scene, Mr. Davenport. The perpetrator could be watching us right now. I need you to stay close to me. I have some help on the way, and we are going to get you home."

"I'm sorry, Chief. I got caught up in following this trail," Digger said, pointing down. "It leads to this area here and this rock."

The chief looked down. "Don't touch it, son!"

"No, sir, I won't, but doesn't that look like hair there along the edge?"

"Yes, son, it does." The chief looked up. "Jack?" The chief called over to Mr. Butterworth, the district attorney. "We got something here!"

CHAPTER 4

The memory of that grisly scene jarred Digger back to reality in lab class just in time.

"Mishter Da-wen-port, tell our colleagues vy dese arms vill not move?" asked the professor, who was wearing a white coat and sporting a goatee and an authentic German accent.

Digger responded perhaps too eagerly. "This condition is caused by rigor mortis."

Cocking his head to the side, the professor said, "Of course you dummkopf! It tiz vigor mortiz! What causes da vigor to mortiz?"

The class laughed at the obvious toying the professor was doing with Herr Da-wen-port. Digger kept his composure even though he was beet red and retorted, "Yes. I'm sorry, Dr. Schtein. The muscles, within three hours of losing a fresh circulation of oxygenated hemoglobin, issue an enzyme called ATP, which causes the cell walls of the muscles to become impermeable and inelastic. When this occurs in each cell of the muscles, it is impossible to move the appendages for about thirty hours, when other decomposition processes loosen the musculature."

The professor looked impressed by the explanation, and yet Digger thought he might be upset with Digger's obvious overemphasis on the German pronunciation of the professor's name, Stein. Thankfully the professor decided not to engage Digger further and moved on in his lecture and demonstration. Digger seemed to pass this test as he had on so many occasions.

CHAPTER 5

In fact, Digger's life from all accounts was a charmed existence. Bouncing between his family's winter residence on Lake Placid in upstate New York and the summer home in Port Talbot in Maine, it may have not been quite jet-setting, but certainly fortunate.

Living in Lake Placid for nine months of each year put him in a strange category of youth. Not quite townie, but not ski tourist either. Just when the locals could let loose in the warmth, which finally comes to Lake Placid in May or June, Digger was headed to Maine for the summer, leaving behind the feeling with some of his schoolmates that their way of life was not good enough for Davenport. Likewise, he was an outsider to the locals in Port Talbot. He was mere summer folk. Nonetheless, Digger's friendly disposition and good sense of humor allowed him to build friends in both locales. It also helped that in Digger's oceanside community there was a large number of families who also were only summer folk. That the Davenports' ancestors had settled New England in the late 1600s and were the architects of the Industrial Age in the 1800s and frolicked up and down the eastern seaboard during the Gilded Age of the 1900s also added to Digger's acceptability among all groups. To the outsider, it was like the Davenport genes were touched by God himself. There were only five people on earth who knew the real truth about Digger's genes. His parents, being two of them, had debated among themselves how and when to reveal the secret map to Digger's gene pool. It was always later.

Living in two places, each of which had multiple social structures within themselves, had differing effects as Digger aged. Summers in the Port in the preteen years, he was almost exclusively hanging out with friends who were likewise up for the entire summer from winter homes in suburbs of Philadelphia, Washington, Richmond, and, of course, Boston. This meant frenetically pursuing leisure activities of tennis, swimming, sailing, golf, and fishing. While at sailing lessons at the Port Club, the summer folk children would sail by the "other boat club," the Talbot Yacht Club, where the locals were also learning to sail in the same simple small sailboats designed by a local lobsterman. The Port Club gang would comment among themselves what freaks those kids from the other boat club were because they would be in T-shirts with heavy metal bands or some pop culture icon displayed, wearing gym shorts and Converse High Top sneakers, or barefoot; while the Port Club kids would be in Lacoste shirts, tennis shorts, or faded madras shorts with top-siders, Fred Perry tennis sneakers, or Tretorns.

In the younger ages, the class warfare could be brutal in the summer community. One time Digger and his summer buddies were slowly navigating their three-horsepower engine skiffs up the river against the tide. Even though the engines were screaming at full tilt, the boats only inched forward. The boys slowly came around a bend in the river into full view of the Talbot Golf Club. At the edge of the river below the clubhouse were about ten caddies, all local boys of the same age, who were smoking cigarettes and lounging on the bank of the river, waiting for golfers to arrive. Upon seeing the Port Club kids come around the corner, they got up and started yelling obscenities and throwing rocks at the boats.

At first the boaters thought to turn around and run with the tide to escape. But whether it was pride or stupidity, they pressed on and tried to steer to the far bank to get out of reach of the incoming rocks. This worked until the caddies got the brilliant idea of using their golf clubs to fire old golf balls at the boats. The caddies started with nine irons, which caused the golf balls to loft high and drop down on the boats. The ten-year-old skippers could watch and divert from these incoming missiles.

Then as the boats slowly started getting some distance from the marauders and were at a point of no return for fear of having to run the gauntlet yet again, the caddies changed weapons to three irons and wood drivers. This made the balls whiz directly at them with no time to anticipate direction. Some balls actually skipped across the water. The boaters could only lay flat on the decks of their boats and steer the tiller handle of the engine with their feet. Golf balls were banging off the engines and sides of the boats, causing the caddies to whoop and cheer. Finally, the golf pro came out of the clubhouse and yelled at his caddies to cease fire.

When Digger and his buddies saw this, they stood up in their boats and taunted the townies, calling them white trash, scum, retards, and other such labels of the day. One of Digger's friends, Bradley from the Philadelphia area, mooned the retreating caddies. Mooning was a new form of offense in that day, which involved 'dropping trou' and bending over to reveal the full moon of one's buttocks. Bradley had explained how they did that at their sports events in Philly when the TV cameras were panning the crowd.

What was particularly ironic about the clash with the caddies was that most of the caddies would carry the clubs of the fathers of the boys they just had bombarded and would do so acting as complete gentlemen and truly grateful for summer folk. Likewise, the boys in the boat would have parents who would turn to the caddies' parents for help with their homes, boats, cars, and dining choices. Thus at the dinner tables of the families from each group, the families of the other group were usually talked about in thankful terms. Yet in the younger years, skirmishes were being waged.

So it was against this backdrop of youthful hostility between the factions that one summer Dr. Davenport, who had for his own geo-political reasons maintained memberships at both yacht clubs, enrolled Digger in the sailing camp at the one for locals, the Talbot Yacht Club. Dr. Davenport felt it was important to remain friends with the folks who taxed and maintained his property and ran the local government. With Digger's love of boating and good-natured disposition, he put up little resistance at thirteen years of age and agreed to start making friends with the locals.

The sailing instructor at TYC was Bobby Doolittle, the oldest of the six Doolittle boys each of whom were legendary sports figures in Port Talbot, except for Rusty Doolittle, who was overweight and the same age as Digger. Rusty was also in the sailing class and had to endure the prodding of his brother. Digger and Rusty became good friends, as did many of the other local yokels in the sailing program at TYC. Some, however, remained resentful of the summer folk in the teenage years. It would take more maturing for some, and for others the resentment never lifted.

As Digger grew older, his skiff, the *Seahorse*, and the knockabout sailboats were traded in for bigger and faster boats and cash to finance the higher level of fun. The Davenport motto was: "Get a trade ... always get paid!" Thus, Digger was encouraged to get summer jobs early on, even though many of his summer friends did not. This would solidify his friendships with the local townspeople and start to be a natural wedge in his relationships with the Port Club friends.

The whole thing about getting a good summer job was applying early and, of course, getting out of school or college earlier than any other competing students. This is what the T-shirt shops, restaurants, hotels, and marinas looked for in a tourist town.

Chief Nickerson of the Port Talbot Police Department in Lincoln County was no different in trying to staff his summer police force. The fact that Digger could start earlier than anybody was a key factor indicated on his typed job application, but so, too, was his listing of the college curriculum at UNYQ, which was clearly devoted to criminal justice, a key factor. The chief had also received a call from the town supervisor, Tom Bradford, reminding the chief of how important the summer folk were to their livelihoods and that hiring one of their kids might be a nice gesture since they had just reassessed the waterfront properties to fund the police department's cruisers and new boat, among other projects.

Chief Nickerson debated the candidates in his mind. Charles Branson's son, Chuck, had applied along with twenty other college kids. Nickerson knew he would get grief from his old friend Branson for not hiring his son, but Nickerson had a bad feeling about the boy. Chuck had been implicated in some criminal activity back in high school and drug activity currently.

In the chief's mind, Digger Davenport was the best candidate, especially in view of the young man's performance as a witness at the trial for the murder of the chef from the Brigantine a decade ago. Digger's testimony as an eleven-year-old was somewhat controversial—not just because of his age and the ability to tell right from wrong and the truth from a lie, but more so because of the youth's own involvement in finding evidence.

Some had questioned whether Digger should've towed the body to the town dock or left it in the mud. The chief and state police had sided with Digger's decision, but there were detractors who argued it disturbed the evidence. The buzz about Digger finding the body and bringing the police to the rocky coastline upriver behind the Brigantine Hotel had taken years to subside.

It didn't help that when Digger was leading the officers to the site, Digger was actually the first to identify the murder weapon, a jagged rock the size of a brick. The chief liked the young man from that episode right up through his testimony at trial. The kid was smart and had guts. The chief called the telephone number on Digger's application.

"Sheffield!" the voice answered.

"This is Chief Nickerson of the Port Talbot Police Department calling for David Davenport."

"Just a minute, sir." The chief heard the phone clank against something and then he heard in the distance, "Digger? Digger! Dude, you're busted! There's a cop on the phone for you!"

Digger ran to the hall phone. "Hello, this is David Davenport."

"Digger? Chief Nickerson. How go things in New York, son?"

"Oh fine, sir. I'm sorry about the idiot who answered the phone."

"Not a problem. I should've never identified myself as a cop on a college dorm phone line. I hope it doesn't cause ongoing problems."

The chief plowed on. "Say, I'll be brief. I got your application along with about twenty other kids … ah … applicants, and wanted to discuss it with you if you have a minute."

"Sure, Chief. I have plenty of time."

"You and I go back a few years, ever since I picked you off the pavement after that bike accident. Then, of course your help on the Brigantine murder case when you were in what, sixth grade?"

"I was in fifth grade, but all I can remember was you yelling at me to freeze and stop scrambling over the rocks because it was a crime scene!"

"Yes, and you were observant and took orders pretty well. And it is because of this history and your demeanor and your educational pursuits that I would like to offer you the position of the Port Talbot bicycle patrol officer."

"Fantastic, Chief! Thanks so much; I accept! I'll do my best to make you proud of your selection."

"That's fine, Digger, but hold on. Let me tell you some expectations."

"Yes, sir."

"First, it's a minimum of forty hours per week and a salary of a hundred-fifty dollars per week, and you'd be on call for anything that comes up. No overtime. Is that understood? And oh yes, there will be a background check."

"Understood. Not a problem."

"Next, you are a *peace* officer, not Eliot Ness. You understand?"

"Yes, sir, I understand. All sugar, no stick."

"Exactly! Are you okay to start June tenth at eight in the morning?"

"Yes, sir. I can start even sooner if you like."

"No, that's fine. It's a couple of weeks before the tourists get here. You'll get sworn in, issued your bike, uniforms, citation book, et cetera."

After the chief asked for Digger's clothing measurements they concluded the phone call. Digger went bouncing down Sheffield's dorm hall punching the air and hissing "Yes!" repeatedly. He was the next Port Talbot bicycle patrol officer at nineteen years of age.

CHAPTER 6

Digger's first day on the job was simply to get his gear, get sworn in, and then walk the beat in Talbot Square, which was the epicenter of the quaint seaport. As agreed, he was assigned to bicycle duty, which was put in service only during the summer months. The one holding the position was commonly referred to as the *copsicle*. He had prepared himself to handle the jokes, but because he loved the idea of being paid to ride a bike in the town and grew up exploring by bike and boat, it would not be a problem.

The chief had met him at 8:00 a.m. at the station to swear him in and show how the two-way radio worked. At the chief's swearing in ceremony, he pulled open the top drawer of his desk and grabbed a tattered little black book. "You 'Epis-cop-aliens' accept King James version?" the chief jested as he emphasized the syllable *aliens*.

"Yes, sir," replied Digger, not taking the bait over the mispronunciation of his church.

"Good. Put your left hand on it, raise your right, and repeat after me. You swear or affirm to uphold and enforce the Constitution of the United States and the charter and ordinances of the State of Maine, so help you God?"

"I do," replied Digger.

The chief shook his hand, reached for another drawer, and pulled out another booklet, green and crisp. "Here's the other bible—our ordinances and criminal code and that stuff. Pay attention to the ordinances. Your retailers downtown know 'em better than their own attorneys. Loitering, parking, dog crap ... smoking," the chief paused and sighed as he picked up his Camel straights ... like the word had triggered the urge to light up.

Squinting and cocking his head sideways to duck the initial puff, he said, "No hero stuff, Digger. Just look clean and sharp, and call on this radio if anything comes up. You won't even get a citation packet for two weeks. We used to issue them right away, but the new guys would get ticket happy. I want you to develop the art of persuasion. The uniform itself does most of the work ... and this," he said as he pawed through the drawer and raised a badge. "How's badge nineteen?"

"Perfect," said Digger. "It's my age. I'll be able to remember it. This summer, anyway." The chief rolled his eyes.

Digger looked at the green booklet and hesitated before speaking. "Ah, Chief, this ordinance book is five years old."

"Yeah," said the chief, "we had money back then to print them. Not much has changed, though. The law is the law. Your bike is out there. Here's the key to the lock. Good luck!"

The chief abruptly headed out to his unmarked cruiser, which, but for the searchlight on the driver's door and the simple bronze plaque on the bumper that simply said "Chief," looked like any middle-aged person's car. Digger had been in that car or its predecessor twice: once to go to the hospital, and the other to go show the chief the area where Digger had hooked the Chef's body. Digger was glad the incident didn't get discussed at all.

He walked over to the dispatcher's office behind three walls of glass and nodded at Mrs. Wentworth. She motioned him in the side door, took off her headset, and stood with a hand outstretched to congratulate him. "Digger, welcome aboard!"

"Thank you, Mrs. Wentworth," he replied as if she had just given him cookies at the back door.

"Oh no, Digger, it's official now. I am Patty to you from now on."

Rodney Wentworth, Patty's husband, was the best carpenter in Lincoln County and was always over at Digger's family home on Ocean Avenue, keeping the monstrous shingled "cottage" looking crisp. They also attended the same church together. Patty had been Digger's Sunday school teacher.

"I told Rodney you were being chosen for one of the summer slots, and he agreed with the chief ... for once!" She rolled her eyes.

"Did the chief brief you on radio use?" Knowing better, she shook her head and immediately added, "Look, you press this here and say who you are. First name is fine, but when you're around people in a stressful situation you can also refer to yourself by badge number. It's code to let me know you're in a situation and that you rather not let your audience know that you think it's a difficult spot. You just say, 'Unit 19 to dispatch.'"

"Gotcha," said Digger. "Nice!"

"It's slow right now," Patty added. "Just get out there and be a good will ambassador with the retailers and day visitors from Boston and the rest of the Mainiacs!"

As Digger started to ride his souped-up twenty-one-gear Raleigh mountain bike, which was custom painted black with the word *Police* emblazoned on it with reflective lettering, he thought about being sworn in. How simple it was, but how huge, legally and personally. No photos, no parents to congratulate him. Just get to work. He patted his breast pocket, hoping he hadn't forgotten the little green citation book. *Five years out of date? Shoot! Dogs could crap legally wherever back then. You could smoke anywhere five years ago.* He knew he'd have to go to the library and get the new ordinances to supplement the book soon.

Chapter 7

Downtown Talbot Square was bustling with activity even at this time of the season. Memorial Day had passed, and that marked the official date for retailers and restaurateurs to get up to Port Talbot and start getting ready for the season, which started more like the last week of June. From the end of May to the end of June was nonetheless an exciting time in the Port for high school and college kids in search of jobs, living quarters, and love … in reverse order.

One could start on June 5 as a dishwasher and by June 25 be a cook at a different restaurant. Or one could start living in a yurt on a back road and move into dorms at one of the resort hotels. The search, placement, and move-in was like applying to and being accepted into college. If one got accepted to work at the Brigantine, it was like getting into the Ivy League. You got a package: the dorm room, the laundry facilities, three squares in the employee dining room, and training. The female hires could even try out for the Blue Dolphins water ballet team that was entertainment for the guests. Employees had a beach down in front of the monstrous building, which had a commanding position on a bluff overlooking the ocean. The look of a Brigantine employee was distinct: Connecticut prep—pinks and greens for the girls. The guys could be a little scruffier, some pinks and madras, but also some north Boston browns and blacks, and drab clothing from those who worked in the kitchen.

Just across the bay you could see the Abenaki Hotel, another ivy job placement with the package. There were three other grand hotels like this from the Gilded Age in the Port. The staff from each would often have volleyball competitions with keg party mixers to follow. So June was an exciting month, watching the new talent roll into town. The local youth would go to Talbot Square and simply hang out to see the new blood flow into the town's arteries.

Digger Davenport, standing six foot one inch (or six three wearing his black baseball cap emblazoned with the word *POLICE*), surveyed the flow of traffic slowly moving thru Talbot Square. So far so good. Bike locked to a lamppost, he was free to walk a beat. *A beat! What a trip! Me, walking a beat. I better not start swinging my whistle or something cliché.* He did, however, stand a little taller as he thought about his position.

He stepped into Mr. Ruge's pharmacy. Alex Ruge, wearing his light blue smock that said "I *am* a health care worker," looked up and said, "Well, well, well … finally! I can sleep at night!" And looking around to a smattering of customers who were paying no attention, he pretended to speak to them, "Justice has come to town! Hallelujah!" He reached down from his perch, an elevated drug counter, to shake Digger's hand. "Congratulations, Digger. Glad Nickerson picked you. I heard competition was stiff this spring. The lobster lobby was pushing for their own kin."

Digger, not being sure of the reference, ignored the comment and said, "Thanks, Mr. Ruge. It's an honor to serve."

Alex came from around the counter and took Digger by the arm much like he ushered folks at church on Sundays. "Here, Digger, is the soda cooler. I know you would never think you'd hear me say it after chasing all your shoplifting buddies out of this thing, but you, sir, may help yourself anytime you want. Just wave at the cashier and go! We take care of our men in blue."

"Thanks, Mr. Ruge," Digger said as he slowly extricated himself from the love fest.

But as he left, he had to squeeze through the Out door as the most beautiful college-aged brunette came bouncing through the same door.

She smiled up at Digger and said in the most bent southern twang, "Pah-don me, Offisuh, the mistake is all mine," as they squeezed uncomfortably close to one another.

He was savvy and saucy enough to say, "No, ma'am, pardon *me*," as she zipped by … and then double-looked back at him, realizing he was speaking in her native tongue. She beamed and giggled and turned to head for Alex's medicinal perch.

Digger was still reeling from how cute that girl was—mesmerizing blue eyes, freckles with a super tan, and totally prepped-out: oxford blue and white striped, button-down type shirt, but instead of buttons on the collar, it was curved collar points. *Classy dame!* he absentmindedly thought as he looked in the pharmacy window. Was that a smell of alcohol he had detected as they brushed by one another?

A honking horn brought his mind back to Talbot Square. A traffic jam had formed at the crosswalk next to the pharmacy. Getting through Talbot Square, a simple two-lane road with very few street-parking options, was difficult even in the quietest of times. But here was a car that had just stopped in the crosswalk and had no driver in the driver's seat but did have a beautiful sandy-haired coed with a wide-brimmed sun hat in the passenger seat trying to wave on the cars behind her as if to say "Move on! Don't bother me."

This was a scene—Digger's first scene. The cars couldn't go around because that would force them into oncoming traffic. Digger cinched up his pants, straightened his hat, and came toward the vehicle, which was a VW Bug convertible, its top down and the back seat loaded with suitcases and a cooler. Digger approached, confident every car in the line-up expected some justice to be poured out here and now.

"Excuse me, Mizz." Digger used the new moniker that the professional women preferred in that day. Not Miss and not Missus but a contraction of sorts: Ms. "You're in a crosswalk and are holding up traffic," he stated calmly as he pointed behind the VW. The young lady held the top of her hat as she quickly spun toward his voice and looked up. Her smile, the sunglasses, and the half shirt tied at her waist as if this was Hee Haw Junction, caused Digger to pause for a second.

"I am sorry, Offisuh. We had a medical emergency, and my friend, Janie, had to seek assistance."

Digger stiffened. "Emergency?" He looked around.

"Yes sir, Janie had to see the doctor regarding some urgent personal need," the passenger said as she pointed toward the pharmacy.

Digger assessed this to be a reference to the young lady he met in the door, regarding whom he would like to impress, as well as this one with the hat. But he also had to solve the jam. Digger coolly pulled the whistle out of his breast pocket, walked into the crosswalk, and held up the palm of his hand to stop cars in the other lane of traffic. He gave to two short bursts on the whistle, which made all of Talbot Square his audience.

He turned to the young lady and said in the sweetest southern style and without mocking, "Ma'am would you kindly move the vehicle to round front of the pharmacy while your friend receives her necessary attention so these patient saints can get by?"

She responded, "Oh my gosh! You are just the sweetest thing in the whole wide world. I'd really love to do that, but I can't drive a car with a shifta!"

At this point no traffic was moving in either direction. Digger ran over to the VW, saw the keys in the ignition, waved the cars he had stopped to proceed, squeezed into the driver's seat saying, "May I?" put it in gear, and made an immediate right turn in front of the pharmacy where a coveted parking spot had just opened up. Digger bounced out of the car as if it had never happened and jumped out into the crosswalk again to wave on the long line of cars and hold up the pedestrians who had gathered and would exacerbate the problem if they had started trying to cross at the crosswalk because state law required all cars to yield to anyone at a crosswalk in tourist trap areas. So Digger waved on the patient line of cars and held up the pedestrians. The crisis averted, when Janie came out of Ruge's Apothecaries, Digger approached the southern belles. He knew the drill: These folks were the lifeblood of this fishing village, but they were also law breakers.

"Ladies it is my pleasure to welcome you to the greatest place on earth," he said, taking off his hat like John Wayne or Tommy Lee Jones the sheriff and bowing slightly. The girls visibly swooned over this gentlemanly conduct.

"Oh, Offisuh," lamented Janie, "I had to go to the bathroom so badly and needed some Solarcaine for my sunburn from our trip up from Richmond. We couldn't put the top up because of all this luggage! I just fried!"

Putting his hat back on slowly and looking at the girl with the hat and sunglasses, Digger continued to play along with the emergency theme, "Our medical emergency services in Port Talbot are nothing but the finest. Let me guess. Are you on the way to the Brigantine?"

They squealed with delight at his kind handling of their obviously dumb parking stunt and his keen insight as to their destination. "Yes! How did you know? Please tell us where's it at." They chortled in cadence.

"By the way, I'm Margie, and this is Janie. Thank you for your kindness. We had not experienced such friendliness on our trip up here."

Digger continued the conversation, pulling out a notepad for directions, suggesting to the onlookers: *See? I'm reprimanding these rebels. Don't worry.*

This might even look like a ticket. "Do us all a favor, ladies. Use the parking spots, or at the very least pull out of traffic!" Digger paternalistically warned them as he handed them the directions to the Brigantine.

Just as Janie and Margie were finished eating out of the palms of Digger's hands, along came a very handsome local boy by the name of Chuck Branson, whose dad was probably the richest local in Port Talbot, all gained from lobstering and transporting. Some riches were also gained from harvesting and marketing sea urchins to the Japanese, at least until the urchin beds were picked clean by Branson's men.

"Heya theyah! How you doin' girls?" bellowed Chuck. The coeds squinted as they checked out the muscle-bound local and twittered imperceptibly. "Fine, thank you!" replied Janie. Chuck, like a lion eyeing his prey, replied, "You young lovelies must be headed to the Brigantine."

The girls looked at each other wide-eyed and giggled. Janie said, "What? We got signs on our foreheads?"

Chuck spoke up, "No, no. It's just that that's where all the attractive young debutantes go to work."

Digger was starting to feel uncomfortable. Here were two horned elk bucks about to clash. *What does lobster boy know about debutantes?*

"So you got to meet Diggy, the Port copsicle. You better watch out for him. They'll give him a ticket book in a couple of weeks and maybe even a whistle. And then we citizens are toast! Yessah! It's gonna be wicked bad."

Margie, sensing the testosterone in the air, didn't mention how well Digger had already blown bursts into his whistle.

Digger spoke up in a forced Maine accent. "Ladies, allow me to introduce Mr. Branson, a true Mainiac, from lobstah delivery in the summah to plowin' snow in the wintah. Chuck has you covahed. Yessah! Wicked busy!"

"Dispatch to Digger," cackled the radio on Digger's belt.

"Uh oh, it's Commissioner Gordon," said Chuck, raising his eyebrows as he faced the girls. "Where's the Batbike, Boy Wonder?"

Digger ignored the cuts and turned away. "Digger here."

"Digger, can you get over to Mrs. Milliken's? That fat coon cat is stuck again."

"Ten-four," said Digger. He blushed as he turned to the ladies and said, "Duty calls. I hope your summer is profitable and safe. Until we meet again ..." and he shook their hands, nodded toward Chuck, and said, "Mr. Branson, good day."

Chuck replied, "Good luck chasin' tail up a tree." The girls couldn't help but giggle a little.

Digger quipped, "Yeah, it'd be a lot easier if I smelled like lobster bait." Chuck glared.

As Digger left for his bike, he heard Chuck say, "May I show you where the Brigantine is?"

Digger sighed, "Honestly, Milliken's coon cat? Dang! That was bad timing. I better get an earpiece for this radio."

CHAPTER 8

Digger rode back to Sow Hill, where the Police Station sat on top of the biggest hill in town. The hill was also the site of the water tower, which sailors used as a point of reference out in the Gulf of Maine. Apparently, the site was where a pig farmer had been located in the 1700s. It was wonderfully ironic to the hippie generation that the police station was located on an old pig farm on top of Sow Hill. It was an exhausting climb, even on a twenty-one-speed "Batbike" as Chuck Branson put it.

He and Chuck had quite a history through the summers growing up. For some reason, Chuck never liked him. Was it Ocean Avenue? Or was it just being from New York State? That actually offended a lot of folks, even as far away as Florida. What was so bad about being from New York? Since going to UNYQ, however, he started to get an eyeful of the pushy New Yorker with "da accent" and the "Yo, Adrian" attitude, as Rocky Balboa the boxer in the movies would put it. But that type was rarely found in Lake Placid, New York. If anything, LP was like a New England town. But that would be news to Chuck Branson. To him, Digger was no different than the pushy tourist who'd wear the Naugahyde sandals with the white-chicken-meat legs, baggy shorts, wife-beater muscle shirt, and the crisp, white baseball cap cocked sideways that had either some ghetto designer's logo or a simple Yankees logo on it. Digger laughed to himself. *Yep, got to love those New Yorkers.*

Digger's ride to Sow Hill gave him time to rethink the day's events. High on the list were the Virginians and the confrontation with Branson. But what kept nagging at him was Alex Ruge's comment in the pharmacy. His police job had been lobbied for by the lobster lobby? *Hmm.* The only thing that came to mind was that every morning down at the Chat 'n'

Chew Diner, the lobstermen would gather for coffee and breakfast before launching out. They could park their pickups behind the restaurant and walk to the docks from there. They fondly referred to the gathering place as the Bite 'n' Belch.

"Hey, Mrs. Wentworth, er … ah, Patty, who's the lobster lobby?" he asked after locking up the bike in the garage at Sow Hill and putting his radio on the charger in the back office. Patty pulled off the headset and came out of the dispatcher's cage.

"Where'd you hear that term?" Her head corkscrewed a quarter turn.

"Alex Ruge said the lobster lobby was pushing for their own candidate for this job," Digger stated plainly.

"Eew! That Alex Ruge is the biggest gossip in the entire town. He's like one of the hens at church. What's worse is that his pharmacy is like a beehive. The bumblebees with nothing better to do come in for their daily dose of Alex's honey. I swear Reverend Brad has got to do a sermon on gossip!"

Digger just stayed quiet, realizing he'd just tapped into a vein.

Patty obliged. "The lobster lobby is none other than the singular personage of Mr. Charles Branson Sr. of Branson's Seafood Distribution, Inc."

Digger wrinkled his face, thoroughly confused. "Why would Mr. Branson lobby over a bike cop job?"

Patty came closer to Digger to emphasize the importance and hush-hushiness of the information she was about to impart. "Don't you dare talk to Chief Nickerson about this," she said as she squeezed his shoulder, "but this year's summer temp position was a tough call for him because Mr. Branson wanted his ne'er-do-well son to get the job. But Chief bucked the lobster lobby and picked the best candidate."

Digger was about to explain his run-in with Chuck Jr. when the chief came bounding up the front stoop and into the office. Patty deftly floated into her cage, and Digger spun around to say, "Hey, Chief, how goes it?"

Chief's steely eyes penetrated Digger as he asked, "You always jump into strangers' cars without permission and drive them?"

"You mean today in the Port?" Digger asked.

"Yeah, Alex Ruge said you were directing traffic."

Digger stole a glance to Patty.

"And you jumped into some girl's car and drove it over to a parking spot! Is that right?"

"Yes sir, that's right," Digger replied as if it were his dad reprimanding him about something he had done wrong.

"Did you have the owner's permission?" Chief asked, preparing a trap. "I had the passenger's permission," Digger offered lamely.

"You *did not* have the owner's permission to drive their car and yet you did? Unbelievable, Mr. Davenport! I've never had a carjacking bike cop on my payroll ever!" Turning to the dispatcher, the chief sarcastically added, "Patty! Put an APB out for a carjacker in a Port police uniform."

Digger didn't know whether to laugh at this sarcasm or what. APBs— all points bulletins—were radio alerts issued for robbers and murderers that were sent to not only the entire Port Talbot force but also the surrounding towns on their frequencies, as well as the state troopers' frequency. Patty responded with half of an "Aye, aye" salute.

Thinking quickly, Digger spoke up. "Chief, our code allows us to take such steps as are necessary to ensure the safety of the public. This includes the use of private property without consent. I assessed the situation to be of such a danger that such action was required. May I explain the risk factors that were at play?"

The chief gave Patty a "get a load of this" look. Patty responded in kind, nodding her head in an approving manner, meaning, "This kid is sharp."

"No, you need not give me the risk factors," said the chief. "I'll grant you that you probably did the right thing—getting the car out of the lane of travel so traffic could resume to move smoothly. And trying to have the passenger move the vehicle with a standard transmission when she can only drive an automatic would've been worse!"

"Chief, were you there?" asked Digger coyly. Patty was all ears for this one.

"Son! I am everywhere! You don't get to be chief for a generation without being all-knowing. Say, how'd Mrs. Milliken's cat fare today?" he asked, abruptly changing subjects.

Digger replied "When I rode over to her house, neither she nor her fat cat were anywhere to be seen. I let Patty know and continued on my beat downtown."

The chief just nodded his head okay then added as an afterthought, "Do me a favor, will you? Keep the peace with Junior Branson, okay?"

"Sure thing, Chief, no problem."

"I don't need my rent-a-cop getting all huffy with the Lobster King's son." The chief moved into his office and closed the door.

Digger looked toward Patty and rolled his eyes. She nodded her head approvingly in a look that said, "Yep, this is the way it is."

Digger stepped out the back door of Sow Hill wearing his civilian clothes and hiked into his car, a hand-me-down from his dad, a black Jeep CJ-6. He had a short drive to the cottage on Ocean Avenue but long enough to think about whether the chief was watching him and whether Mrs. Milliken's cat was a ruse to get him to disengage from Chuck Branson. If so, that would be pretty creepy. Surely he could trust Patty to be straight with him.

He rounded the bend and bam! There it was: the ocean, framed by craggy rocks and rosa rugosa bushes with their little green apples and pink and white rose-like flowers. *Could there be anything more beautiful than this strip of the earth?*

As he drove Ocean Avenue westward, most cottages were on his right. The Ocean itself was on the left. Only three properties with houses were on the ocean side: Senator Whitten's, Davenports', and the church property, which included St. Peter's Church and the minister's rectory. Digger pulled in his driveway and paused to take it all in. He never grew tired of the view or the extreme good fortune his family had to live this lifestyle. He was thankful that he was born into this family and that his parents had instilled a spirit of gratitude in him.

As he pondered his lineage and the day's activities while he looked out over the ocean, he could not help but think how fortunate he was and *yes!* The Brigantine waitresses he had met today. He wondered if they had settled in and would they be at Disco Fever at Ship's Pub tonight. At least during the summer proper, it was the best place to be on a Monday. The girls got all decked out in discotheque clothing and wanted to dance.

Digger wondered whether his new position would put a crimp in his nightlife. What if he saw open container drinking in the parking lot? Or someone relieving himself. Surely the chief didn't expect him to bust everyone.

CHAPTER 9

"Aren't you the policeman?" Janie asked with her twang.

"Yes, ma'am at least I play one on daytime TV," Digger replied lamely as his heart raced a little when Janie approached. Her blue eyes framed in a tan face with freckles and dark, thick, shoulder length hair caught him every time. Her oxford shirt unbuttoned that was one button too many also tugged at his eyes.

"Hey Margie, look who I found!" she said, genuinely and openly rolling her eyes toward Digger in a gesture that said to her friend, *Get over here. Can you believe he's here?* Digger was gratified by the blatant body-speak that was occurring silently.

Margie sidled up to Digger, "Business or plezhah, mistuh lawman?"

"Strictly pleasure, I assure you, Miss Margie," Digger said in his southern gentleman way. He wasn't sure why in the South they called all the women by their first name and put a "Miss" in front of it—even if the woman was eighty years old and married.

Margie melted to his side at the sound of Dixie diction. "Oh, you're a regulah charmah I do say."

Digger played along with the repartee. "Let me put my money where my mouth is. Can I buy you belles something at the bar?"

Janie jumped on the offer even though her tan hand bedecked with gold jewelry was holding a full drink. "One fifty-one and Coke, suh?" she said with a slight slur and a fluttering of her baby blues.

Digger made a quick assessment of this girl: So very pretty, very slight frame, seemingly intoxicated already at 10:00 p.m., and double-fisting 151 rum? That's just shy of Appalachian moonshine! Maybe there was a connection.

Margie asked for Perrier with lime. "I'm the designated driver," she said cheerfully and then added pointedly as she moved with Digger toward the bar, blocking Janie's earshot: "Again!"

This confirmed that Janie was a bit of a lush. As Digger approached the bar, Rusty the red-haired bartender bellowed, "Capt'n Davenport! Permission to come aboard, sir!" as he rang the tip bell like it was tolling a change in watch on a schooner. Like Pavlov's puppies, all the barflies buzzed with approval whenever the bell rang. Digger and Rusty high-fived over the heads of the patrons on stools. Rusty was a local yokel that Digger had gone to sailing school with at the townies' yacht club. They had some fun memories together; picking on the girls in their class, capsizing the boats on purpose to freak out the instructor, pirating a fellow sailor's rudder off his boat on a quick pass-by in open seas—the usual bad boy stuff that the girls thought was great.

"Rusty anchor, boy!' Digger replied in an authentic Maine accent. "How you doin? Yessah, wicked good!" Digger loaded up the vernacular to chide the local boy playfully. It wasn't as if Rusty was a numbskull. Far from it. Rusty went to Bowdoin College, also rowed crew, and was pre-med.

"What's your poison, Mr. New York City Slicker?" asked Rusty, getting him back on the Mainiac slight.

Digger pushed through to whisper to Rusty, "Give me an NA in a mug, and that sweet young thang over there wants a 151 and Coke," Digger said, wincing after using a mocking southern accent. "And this young lovely would like a Perrier and lime."

Rusty, too, winced at Janie's drink request. "I'm not charging you for Snow White's Roman Coke because I'm just passing the rum over the top of the glass. She's already lit."

Digger erupted. "That's it! Snow White! I knew I had seen her somewhere!" he said as he turned to Margie and added, "She looks just like Snow White in Disney's movie. The hair, the eyes, the body ... She is the spittin' image! Can't you see her in that blue and white gown with the poufy cuffs?"

Margie rocked her head back in laughter, agreeing and added, "But she's no G-rated princess, I assure you!"

Digger turned back to Rusty as the drinks were being handed to him. "Man, that is perfect, Rusty ... Snow White!" Digger handed a twenty-dollar bill over, indicating to keep the change. It was a ten-dollar tip. Rusty nodded sincerely and gave the ship's bell a hearty ring which caused the chorus of barflies to hoot and holler instinctively.

Digger handed the mocktail to Janie and watched as she sipped it. She said, "Much obliged, Mr. Digger!" showing no sign of any dissatisfaction with the alcohol-free drink. *Yeah, her taste buds are dead.* He rotated away to check the place out. Janie was contentedly slurring her way through some conversation with a hopeful Brigantine busboy.

Margie blocked his exit. "A New Yawker? Where in New York? I love midtown," she asked as if New York City was the only place in New York.

Digger was kind. "I'm five hours north of the city in Lake Placid."

Margie gushed approvingly, "I love Placid! I've tried to ski Whiteface Mountain."

"You mean Ice Face?" Digger interrupted. They both laughed approvingly at the misnomer. Skiing in the northeast part of the United States was notoriously icy compared with the West.

Digger and Margie migrated to a table away from the dance floor and enjoyed getting to know one another.

Digger shared only a bit of his family history. The whole story was overwhelming. They talked about church stuff. Margie was raised Baptist but started attending Janie's youth group at the Episcopal Church in Richmond. She said the boys were cuter and went to the private schools in town. Digger shared how he was the acolyte at St. Peter's out on Ocean Avenue at the 8 and 10:00 a.m. services.

Margie commented that not many college-aged guys were comfortable talking about faith in God, and most were downright atheists. Digger led her through his thought process on why he believed in God. Margie concluded, "Sounds like you approach Christianity much like someone might approach a craps table in Vegas: Odds for eternal life are better if you cast your lot with the Christians than gambling that there is no hell."

"Exactly!" said Digger. "Plus what is the downside? So I behave ... follow the commandments, et cetera ... and then poof! I die and was wrong. I end up feeding worms. No heaven ... living a grand charade! Nonetheless, the mistaken belief made me be respectful of others, avoid nasty behaviors, follow tried and true principles, and ... I mean, I'm no choir boy!" he interjected.

"No, just the acolyte," Margie added.

All of a sudden they heard some shrieks coming from the dance floor and the music stopped. Margie shot up instinctively and ran toward the scene on the dance floor, calling Janie's name. Digger followed, wondering why she was so sure Janie would be in that particular direction. But sure enough, as Digger got to the center of the crowd, there was Janie on floor with a nasty gash on her forehead and blood everywhere for three feet around. The busboy was rubbing his jaw. Just as Digger was going to get into Dragnet mode, Rusty came barreling thru the crowd like a snow plow, deflecting people out of his way. He put a white towel on her forehead and scooped her to her feet. She provided very little resistance and looked almost as if she thought she was being romanced by someone.

Rusty spun around to find Margie. "Last call for Snow White," he said to her. "Time for her deep sleep. Can you get her out of here?" Turning to Digger, "Hey Digger, can you help on this? She's got a minor contusion, no stitches necessary, but she needs to lie down and put direct pressure on the wound."

Digger readily consented and took Janie into his arms. He asked the crowd on the dance floor, "What happened?"

The busboy replied, "We were dancing, and then all of a sudden she just passed out. I tried to catch her, but her head hit my teeth and knocked me back."

The crowd moaned and started chiming in with negative comments. Rusty, who was now wiping the floor, looked up at Digger and gave him a serious look that said, "Move it please." Digger nodded and scooped Janie out the door into the cool sea breeze.

Margie said, "Over here!" pointing to the VW Bug, top still down. Digger stopped in his tracks. "Wait a minute, Miss Southern Baptist girl! How can you be the DD when you can't even drive a stick?"

Margie looked embarrassed for having lied to Officer Digger earlier. "I'm not that good at driving a stick," she explained. "I didn't want to try to move that car in that traffic jam!"

Digger didn't care to make a big deal out of it and simply hissed, "The obstructress of justice!"

The busboy, who had been trailing them as if he had some interest in this event, piped up, "I know how to drive a standard transmission!"

Margie stopped, spun toward the kid, and said, "Jerome! Whose ID did you borrow to come here? Your license isn't even valid at this hour!" Turning to Digger, she added, "Do you think, Officer Davenport?"

Before Digger could figure out what to say after being outed as a police officer, Jerome turned on his heels and said, "Okay! Good night," and ran back toward the entrance to Ship's Pub. Margie and Digger both started to laugh as they continued toward the car.

"I'll tell you what. Let me lay her down in the back seat of my Jeep. I'll follow you in the Bug, and we will both put Janie to bed."

Margie came over to Digger. Standing on her tiptoes, she reached over Janie, who was snoring in Digger's arms, and kissed Digger on the cheek. "You are a true gentleman," she said.

Digger was awestruck by the gesture and wished he didn't have the sack of potatoes in his arms. He lamely replied, "The South doesn't have the corner on the market of the only gentlemen."

Margie, added in faux twang, "Oh, Rhett!"

Picking up on the *Gone with the Wind* reference, Digger carried on, "Frankly, Margie ... let's go!"

As Digger followed Margie in the VW, he saw that she was not kidding. She was a lousy shifter which made her more endearing to him. His mind was racing. *Was this the beginning of a new summer romance? That kiss was awesome and natural. A bit forward, but A-OK!*

Janie moaned in the back seat as they headed for the Brigantine dorms. Digger checked Janie's awareness, "Sorry, Janie, Jerome the bus boy left us!" Janie slurred something incomprehensible. Digger tweaked it. "He seemed like a very nice young man."

Janie slurred an unmistakable reply. "Daddy, you like any young man as long as he's white. I loved Willy! You never should've done it. I'm sorry. So sorry, Daddy." Janie's whimpering trailed off. "I shouldn't have ..."

Digger remained silent, hoping this window into Janie's obviously painful history would close on its own. Soon snoring sounds emanated from the back seat as he pulled into the staff parking lot. His mind quickly flashed to when he brought Chief Nickerson to this very spot at eleven years of age. Just to the left was the tidal creek, the scene of the murder he helped discover nine years earlier.

Carrying Janie up the stairs of the girls' dorm, the place where all the Brigantine waitresses and chambermaids stayed, was a breeze because she was so light. Digger knew he was in the Promised Land. As a youngster he and his buddies monitored the girls' dorm from the surrounding bushes. He couldn't wait to tell of his gaining access.

Margie motioned him to the correct bed to place Janie down in the dimly lit, slightly musty room. A couple of dorm mates in skimpy T-shirts arrived at the door to see what the commotion was all about. One left as quickly as she arrived, simply pronouncing, "Janie's blotto again! Show's over."

Margie rolled her eyes as if to say this was her lot in life. "Come on, I'll walk you to your car," she offered.

Digger reached for Margie's hand and gently pulled her back from heading toward the door. "No, really, it's okay. I can find my way." His tug brought her willingly up against his chest; he cradled her in his arms and kissed her. Margie responded by clutching Digger's back and shoulder blades. Digger whispered, "I don't think boys are allowed up here."

Margie hushed him. "You're not a boy. You're an officer of the law on official business."

Digger stood his ground. "No. I gotta go. I really like you, Margie, and want to do this right."

"Absolutely, Officer. You have the right to remain silent." She leaned in to kiss him.

Digger gently disentangled from her and whispered, "No, really. I have to get up at seven thirty!"

"Ugh," she said, dropping her hands down to hold his. "I have tomorrow off."

"Perfect!" said Digger. "I do, too. How 'bout brunch at the Laughing Gull at 11:00 a.m.? It's walking distance, and it's the best in town."

Margie exclaimed in a loud whisper, "My first date of the summer of '78!" as she bounced up and down next to Digger.

He stepped back and said, "You could come to church at ten if you want. I ring the bells at 9:45 and 9:55 then lead the minister down to the altar. He does all the talking. I just take an inventory of who's there."

Margie started sidling up to him again, "You check out the babes, don't you?"

Digger stammered and snickered. It was so true.

"I sure could make some points with my mom and dad when I tell 'em I started my day off at church. You may see me there, Mr. Davenport. Now get out of here before I conduct a citizen's arrest and unlawful imprisonment!" she said in a husky whisper as she pushed him out her door and shut it.

Chapter 10

Digger wondered why he continued to serve as an acolyte. That Father Brad specifically asked him to do it was a key factor. Reverend Bradley Smith—or as Digger had coined the nickname, Dad Brad—was a great minister: connected to worldly cares, yet full of wisdom on how to view such things in view of the ancient teachings of the faith. Being an altar boy was just a natural extension of all the churchy stuff his parents enrolled him in through the years: Vacation Bible School, Student Diocesan Convention Delegate, and choir boy. None of the activities really had any special meaning to him unless there were other friends involved. That is, until he went away to a week-long mission trip during spring break in his senior year of high school.

It was in the dusty barrios of Guatemala City that Digger saw miracles in living color. Lame walked, blind saw, strange behaviors were cast out. He tried to use his innate forensic and analytical skills to explain it all. But then he himself, during an altar call, was hit with an overpowering invisible force that caused his knees to buckle and laid him straight out on the dusty floor of the revival tent. As he lay there half conscious, he could hear music and foreign language being spoken but was unable to move and was at complete peace over the odd situation. It was here that he heard a soft inner voice: *Digger, you are mine—set apart for a good work. I am with you.* The physical feelings accompanying this event were undeniable: goose bumps down the neck, an inability to move, and a slight hyperventilation occurring where the air taken in was icy cool in this sweltering city. The Guatemalan pastor explained that Digger had experienced a powerful move of God—that he had been slain in the spirit.

Explaining this to Dad Brad months later up in Maine, Digger was met with skepticism. He quickly learned that some Episcopalians frowned on this type of event. All he knew was that there is something very real, very present about this thousands-of-years-old religion. He kept active, always knowing or hoping the event would occur again.

"Oh God our help in ages past ..." sang the worshipers at St. Peter's as Digger started down the center aisle, lifting high the crucifix and gliding in time with the processional hymn. Reverend Smith followed, purposely keeping the hymn book closed, perhaps to impress his congregants that he knew all the words by heart.

Digger tried to be professional by not rubbernecking as he proceeded down the center aisle. But there on the left in a yellow sun dress and straw hat with a matching yellow swatch around it was Miss Margie. She bowed like a pro as the cross came by. Digger did a little head nod himself to acknowledge her.

Once situated in his altar pew, he couldn't keep from looking out at her as the service progressed. He also saw Alex Ruge, Rodney and Patty Wentworth, and in the very back, his mom and dad. The pews were populated with many other good family friends. Senator Whitten was front and center with his extended brood. Digger made sure he didn't gawk at the political celebrity.

After church, Digger stood out front as the faithful filed out. The church had a commanding view of the Bay of Maine from the mouth of the Talbot River on the south, 180 degrees to the north, where the one-mile bell buoy tolled incessantly. Eventually, Margie emerged from the stone church and curtsied as she shook the pastor's hand and bee-lined for Digger.

"Mr. Davenport! You look good in robes. Are you sure you don't want to trade in your police uniform?" asked Margie.

Patty Wentworth, the dispatcher, who was close by, piped up. "Oh no he does not! He's *our* police officer. I shudder to think what we'd get if we had to replace him." Digger introduced the two and snuck away to get out of his robes.

Upon returning, he found Margie talking with his parents. "David, I'd like you to meet Margie George from Richmond. She's a pre-law student at UVA." His mom introduced him using his formal name.

Pretending to have never met Margie, and to goof on his mom, Digger hammed up his introduction by kissing the back of her hand. Mrs.

Davenport gasped. Digger elbowed his mom and said, "We're old friends, and we're having brunch today at the Laughing Gull."

"Well, son," said Mrs. Davenport, "if that spot doesn't have the southern fare that suits Miss George, you bring her back to the house. Isabel can whip up some grits and ham with biscuits and gravy." Margie thanked Mrs. Davenport, and Margie and Digger sidled away from the church crowd.

At brunch Digger asked about Janie. Margie explained that Janie had to work breakfast, lunch, and dinner, and her wound had healed enough to require only a Band-Aid. Digger deftly asked about Janie's dating history in Richmond, alluding to her sleep-talking last night in the car as he drove her home.

Margie stiffened and urgently asked, "What did she say?"

Digger played it down and changed the subject. "One thing's for sure, she'd better get ahold of her appetite for booze. It's not safe for someone as pretty as she is."

CHAPTER 11

The summer had started with a bang: exciting job of authority for a college kid and clinching a relationship with probably the town's prettiest summer worker. The *copsicle*, as the townspeople affectionately called Digger, was eventually issued the citation pad and had issued tickets for only the most blatant of violations—usually parking. They were easy to write up. Very little confrontation. The offender was off in the buying zone in one of sixty little knickknack shops. The car didn't fight back. Plate number, make and model, rip and slip under the wiper, and move on—a mere brush with the law.

Digger's most confrontational activity occurred at night in keeping the teens from skateboarding and drinking in Commodore Park. Digger would come riding in out of the shadows with a blue strobe light on the bike, turning the scene into a choreographed scene that looked like a cross between Blue Man Group of the future and cowboys and Indians of the past. Most teens would scatter and yell some choice words: "Here comes the pig rig!" or "Cheese it! It's the fuzzicle!" Some punks would stand their ground, keep smoking their cigarettes, and assert their rights. These kids had already been involved with the family court and were only months away from another civic lesson, inside the criminal court.

Digger had earned their respect because he grew up in this town. He knew this age group had nothing to do at night. He made sure there was no skateboarding, drinking, or drugging. Other than that, he'd talk with the kids. They all wanted him to tell the story of the Brigantine murder. It was legend in this age group.

Digger put his time in and improved the summer police program as well. He printed up new ordinance booklets for the other officers on the library copy machines. He wrote memos to the chief suggesting new parking signs and paint lines for Talbot Square, which the chief approved and sent directly to the public works department. The chief had approved the blue strobe light for the bike. That little doohickey even made the weekly paper with a photo of Digger writing a citation in a dark blue glow.

Digger kept dating Margie. Digger's buddies, who didn't have to work in the summer, complained that they could never hack around with him like they used to. It was either Margie or work. They used to water ski at sunrise when the ocean was calm and take their Boston Whalers to the rocky outer islands to look for *fruit de la mer* (fruit of the sea)—anything that might wash up on shore like whale bones, or a set of seal teeth that looked like lion's teeth when all the flesh had been picked clean, lobster traps, or brightly painted lobster buoys.

"Digger, dude, what's the matter with you, dude? You don't come to the Port Club anymore. You're never at the beach unless Margie's with you, dude!" lamented Peter Hill, one of his best friends, whose winter home was in a suburb of Philadelphia. Peter's family was tied to DuPont way back.

"Petah!" Digger replied in his exaggerated Maine accent, "You gotta grow up, boy! Life's awaitin', dude!"

Peter reached over to slug Digger and put him in a headlock. "Why don't you set me up with that other Virginian, Janie?" asked Peter.

"No way, man," replied Digger, "She's trouble. She turns to mush with only a little alcohol."

Peter jumped in, "Exactly! That'll grow me up right quick, dude!"

Chapter 12

The Brigantine Hotel was folklore: the semi-famous guests, the lobster served for all meals including breakfast, the waitresses who would join the hotel's water ballet team for shows in the evening, and the murder that took place ten years ago. Of course controversy wasn't sought by hotel management and was deftly squelched. So it was a mystery why the bellhops were all African American and were made to wear red vests and white gloves. They were brought each summer from south Florida and were given separate but equal quarters under the hotel in the basement near the quarters of the cooks, dishwashers, and busboys.

This area where the men stayed was aptly called the dungeon. The long hall ran the length of the hotel and accommodated maybe thirty men, ranging in age from seventeen to sixty. Each door on the hall opened to a large room that had four separate sleeping quarters divided by closets and bureaus. The two areas furthest from the door had two windows. These quarters were for the ranking employees of the service area they operated.

The oldest two, Erastus and Ethelred (known as Red), had the windows. These two had seen a lot, having worked at the Brigantine for forty years. It was rumored they had real estate holdings in the Caribbean and stock on Wall Street. Red could often be seen reading the *Wall Street Journal* at the bellhop desk near check-in.

Erastus invested his money in dogs and ponies and other games of chance. In fact, Erastus was at the poker table with the chef the night of the chef's murder nine years ago. If anyone could tell the story of what happened that night, it was Erastus. (Or as the college boys called him, Rasta-mon.)

The other black men living in the bellhops' quarters were Reggie and George. Reggie had about eight seasons under his belt at the Brigantine. He was tall, thin, very dark-skinned, and had greased-back hair with a part. No white person could know what it took to get Reggie's hair to do what it did. It was "relaxed 'n' shellacked," as Reggie himself would put it.

George was a newbie to the Brigantine but was quick to endear himself to everyone. He had charisma and knew how to communicate with the guests and work staff. The waitresses loved him for his wit, forwardness, and zero chip on his shoulder for being an African-American or for others being white.

Those who took the time to find out would discover his mother was white. She raised him in Palm Beach, Florida, and had taught him to play tennis and golf with the elite. George's father was from Hialeah, a poverty-struck barrio outside of Miami. George bounced between the beach and the barrio all his life. He medicated the conflict with eating and had become self-conscious because of his weight. He would bristle at his nickname from the dishwashers and busboys who would call him Georgie Porgie puddin' 'n' pie. They would inflict this invective partly out of jealousy because George was truly a ladies' man with some of the white waitresses, making far better time with them than the dishwashers or busboys who shared the women's skin color could.

Jerome, the busboy from North Boston, asked, "Georgie, you going out tonight?" This was part of the normal dinner conversation in the "zoo," the employee dining room, on any night of the summer.

"Man, I don't have to go out to have fun. My fun is set up ahead of time right here at home," said George as he put a plug of tobacco chaw in his cheek like the manager of a baseball team.

"Who you romancing tonight, George, you lucky dog?" Jerome pined, ignoring George's gross habit.

"My suitors prefer discretion, my man. No need creating scandals for these fine young lovelies."

"You're not breaking taboos of the deep south … are you?" fished Jerome, who was referring to dating one of the Virginians.

"Certainly not Margie. One, I'd get shot by her cop boyfriend. Two, she talks too much. Now Janie—she is my kinda girl … putty in your hand!"

Jerome was hurt by this description. He was two years younger than Janie and had been trying to date her since the beginning of the summer.

Jerome had been her designated driver, grocery getter, anything she asked. But he liked her so much that he was unwilling to take advantage of her inebriations. Janie had played clueless to Jerome's chivalrous designs and seemed to use him relentlessly through the summer.

"George, do me a favor and keep your hands off Janie, will ya?" Jerome asked in the deepest, manliest voice he could muster.

"What we do in darkness will never be revealed. Besides, Poindexter, you're hired help, not even in the running," replied George.

Jerome couldn't control his voice and yelled at George in a boyish pitch, "Don't you dare touch her!" Jerome couldn't believe his own reaction. He looked around the hushed zoo and got up, grabbed the plasticware, and threw it disdainfully into one of the gray buckets as he exited the dining room.

George yelled toward Jerome, "Full moon on the beach tonight! Yes suh!" adding a little southern twang and then spat into a Styrofoam cup.

Jerome was especially upset that he had to go home to Bradford, Massachusetts that evening to help his dad. Jerome lived relatively close to the hotel and would frequently go home the night before his day off.

Chapter 13

The hotel had its drama within its walls but also had drama with its frequent vendors from outside. The linen delivery guy provided a case study in his own right: chipper, always whistling as he carried tons of laundry in and out—uniforms of workers, tablecloths, and linen napkins. Housekeeping on site handled bedsheets and towels only. The girls were creeped out by Larry the laundry guy. He knew their names. "Hi Jessica!" he'd yell across the parking lot at a waitress twenty years younger.

She'd instinctively wave back, thinking a co-worker or (better yet) a guest had recognized her. When she saw the source was a wiry forty-five-year-old launching the greeting from behind a stack of folded tablecloths wrapped in cellophane, she shuddered and muttered to herself, "Who *is* that guy?"

Larry knew their names and their sizes. The hotel provided them to Larry's laundry on a print-out for uniform rental, cleaning, and coordination. On occasion Larry could even approach a waitress or busboy or bellhop and ask if a particular item left in a pocket was theirs. It was a little odd how well Larry followed the course of his uniforms.

The one vendor welcomed by all, however, was the lobsterman Chuck Branson. He was handsome, quick-witted, and had a deep Maine accent—not a common combination because the drawl of the accent is anything but quick. Chuck offered what everyone wanted: lobster for the tourists, and on the side he did a brisk business in marijuana sales for the wait staff and kitchen workers throughout the area. A truck that carries refrigerated foods like lobsters is commonly known as a "reefer truck." Chuck gave the rig a whole new meaning.

Chuck's greatest fans were the waitresses and housekeeping girls. He was tan and did a wife-beater tank top T-shirt justice. The girls would stop in mid-sentence and nod toward him as he went about his business of carrying large wooden crates, busting at the seams with dripping seaweed and glints of orange and black claws and tentacles of the live lobsters. Occasionally he could be seen at the loading dock sharing a beer with the chef after a hectic lunch. His shiny black pick-up truck was well known for its size and for the pumping music.

Chuck was well entrenched in the Brigantine community. He could enter the dungeon hallway to visit his friends and "customers" and not raise an eyebrow. After all, he usually was the life of the party.

That evening was no different. It was a payday Thursday. Chuck had filled his pot orders through Reggie, who had become a trusted wholesaler over the last few summer seasons. Chuck had made a delivery to Reggie that afternoon: a cooler with a chilled boiled lobster on top. The cooler had gotten the interest of Reggie's roommate, George.

"Yeah, I like lobster. I'll eat that bad boy, but I'm more interested in the dessert underneath him," Georgie said to Reggie with a little wink.

Reggie put the lobster on a hotel towel and said, "Here," as he handed him a bright orange, fully cooked, and yet chilled lobster.

"Never you mind about the dessert. You're not on the list of dinner guests," Reggie quipped. He thrust his hand deeper into the ice and retrieved a large heat-sealed white opaque plastic bag that had the words Knuckle and Claw Meat emblazoned on it. Reggie hated lobster, so handing George the twelve-dollar lobster nestled in the shaved ice was getting rid of a problem in his book. He needed to get down to the other business in the so-called knuckle and claw meat package.

Over by the girls' dorm, perfume and Carole King music was wafting out its windows. Payday Thursdays had that effect. It was the early stages of evening preparations. Most of the waitresses were still hustling in the dining room, but those who had it off were getting ready to go to Talbot Square. Janie was alone in her room, listening to some Patti Smith tune that seemed to connect to her soul: a dark tune about being dead to the world lost in some addiction or affectation and done in Dylanesque talk-sing. Janie's shades were drawn. She was all dressed up with no place to go. Her choice of music didn't match her preppy pink and green attire, but it fit her emotions perfectly. Her driver, Jerome the busboy, was gone for two days.

"Jerome, where ah you when ya needed, you cutie?" she muttered to herself. She'd had a DWI in Richmond and knew better than to drive.

"This is payday Thirsty!" she mumbled and laughed at her wit. Margie would be mad at her again for starting to party so early. She lit up another cigarette while one still smoldered in the ashtray.

"She can't get mad at me if I'm not here. Ha!" she said defiantly to no one. She heard some gravel crunching in the parking lot below her window. She lifted a corner of the shade and saw Martha the mild-mannered if not mousy muffin maid headed to her car.

"Hay-ay Marthaah! You going into town?"

Martha looked up and squinted. "Janie, is that you? Yeah I'm headed through town. You need a lift?"

"I'll be right there!" Janie threw down the shade, grabbed a sweater, put on some espadrille shoes, threw back the rest of the tumbler of Jack Daniels whiskey, grabbed her purse, and headed out the door saying, "Bye, Margie!" She didn't notice that she had knocked the perfume over on the table when she grabbed the sweater. She had soaked her Lilly Pulitzer Bermuda styled canvas purse on the table in a puddle of Jontue.

Janie and Margie's friendship had become strained through this venture to Maine. Janie, who had everything materially, was not doing well emotionally. Margie, who was from humble roots, was being treated royally by Mr. Copsicle. Janie, in a moment of jealousy, mumbled as she headed down the stairs, "It ain't right."

In the parking lot she approached Martha's sensible sedan and hopped in the passenger side.

"Thanks so much for the lift, sweetie. I'm just going downtown for a bite." A lie but plausible.

"Is your Bug not working?" asked Martha, genuinely concerned.

"Oh no! I just like getting the exercise, silly!"

Martha had first gotten hit with the whiff of Jontue perfume. *Too sweet*, she thought. Then, on Janie's exclamation of "Oh no!" Martha was hit with a whiff of sour mash whiskey. She could identify it only as alcohol. Martha stiffened and pondered how Janie, by leaving her car and riding with her, was getting exercise. It clicked pretty quickly in her mind what was going on.

Janie pushed on, "No muffin duty tonight? Where you headed to, Martha?"

Martha quickly weighed her words and replied, "I'm going to a party. Want to come?"

"I love parties!" Janie said ecstatically. "Where is it at?"

"It's down on Hartsons Beach," Martha said as she started to back out and drive toward town.

"A pahty on the beach? Oh my, it sounds wonderful. Who's throwing it, and are any Brigadiers coming?" Janie inquired, kicking into party assessment mode. Martha laughed at the Brigadier reference to fellow workers at the hotel.

"Maybe Jake the pool guy will be coming. It's a party being thrown by our youth group and a couple other youth groups in town … kind of like a mixer."

Janie knew all too well this kind of party. Her parents had toddled her off to church youth activities her whole life.

"Oh no. I'm good, Martha. Just getting a bite in town tonight."

And Martha added slightly facetiously, "And some exercise."

Janie missed the dig and absentmindedly added, "But that lifeguard Jake is tempting."

"Jake will probably be there cuz he is part of a worship band that is expected to jam there tonight," Martha said encouragingly.

Martha knew it was a leap for Janie to come to a church event, but she silently prayed as she drove toward town. As far as she was concerned, this is what her faith was all about: reaching out to the lost and hurting. Martha had never had an opportunity like this, a captive audience on which to try what she had been taught to do all her life: *save the lost.*

"Church gigs ain't my thing anymore, Martha." Janie boldly announced.

"So you used to attend church?" replied Martha.

"Oh yes. I was run out of church for dating a black boy. He was in the worship band, too. Played bass guitar and could lay down a beat like nobody's business. Got people up out of their pews, which was a no-no, too." Janie confessed as she stared far away out the passenger window. She continued softly, "My daddy had him arrested. William Jackson Stone is now a convicted sex offender for kissing a white girl. Praise the Lord!" Janie wiped away a tear and tried to keep her composure with some deep exhalations.

Calmly, Martha pulled the car over into a side street and stopped. "I'm so sorry your boyfriend got treated like that. It's not right. That is devastating!" She was at a loss for words.

"The thing is, it seemed as if everyone in the church was pleased. I was treated like a Jezebel. Do you know who she was in the Bible?"

Martha said, "Yes, I know all about Jezebel."

Now Janie's tears wouldn't stop, and her mascara was bleeding down her face like a charcoal portrait left in the rain. Martha handed her a tissue and stayed quiet. She actually didn't know what to say about an injustice—apparently at the hands of fellow Christians. After a long silence, Martha said, "Janie, won't you please join me at the beach party? Not all Christians behave that way or believe that. Please don't throw the baby out with the bathwater!"

Janie looked at Martha and said, "Say what?"

Martha replied, "It's ... a saying. When done with washing a baby you throw out the dirty water, you don't get real efficient and throw the baby out, too! Well, baby Jesus shouldn't be thrown out, either, even when everything around him is dirty and fouled up, and that's even when it's in church."

Janie gave a hearty laugh over the concept and repeated the phrase. "Martha, I assure you I have not thrown out the baby, but I have flushed the bath water! Can you drop me off at Talbot Square?"

Martha put it into gear and let some time pass before she inquired gently as to the type church and form of worship Janie was raised in to get the feel for her understanding of salvation, heaven, hell ... the basics. "Are you gonna be all right Janie?" she asked as Janie got out in front of the pharmacy.

"Oh yes, Miss Martha, and thank you, sweetie, for letting me emote with you this evening. And oh, and hey, let's keep it between us please?" asked Janie.

"Of course, Janie. We'll pray for you tonight ... without mentioning names."

"Bless you, Martha. Pray for Willie. His faith really took a hit. I'm not sure what he's doing. He stopped playing the guitar. It's too sad to discuss," Janie said as she shut the door and headed toward the pharmacy, avoiding another bout of the messies.

"Man, nothing like dealing with reality to make you want to run from it," Janie mumbled to herself as she pivoted her direction from the pharmacy toward Ship's Pub after Martha's car had disappeared around the corner.

CHAPTER 14

Digger pulled up to the girls' dorm around 9:45 p.m. Margie came bounding down the stairs with a sweater tied around her neck, looking fresh and ready for anything despite having worked breakfast, lunch, and dinner. Digger jumped out to get the door but noticed something was wrong.

"What's up, Marge? Oh I know ... Janie. Janie is up. That's what's up. She is always up. That's what's up ... again. Right?" Digger said with exasperation.

"Digger, she's gone. Her car is here. The music was playing in the room. Her perfume was tipped over and the Jack Daniels is half empty!"

"Is that what I smell?"

"I'm not wearing eau de Jacques Danielles! You're smelling the Jontue perfume. The room reeks, and all my clothes are carrying it."

"Janie is probably with Jerome," Digger said as she helped Margie into the car.

"I hope so. He is actually a nice boy and would never take advantage of her. Where is this beach party again?" Margie asked, changing subjects.

"It's down on Hartsons Beach. Our youth group, which consists of one— you're looking at it—is joining up with several others. Mr. and Mrs. Hartson let us have bonfires there and there will be a battle of the blands ... I mean bands."

"Be nice, Mr. Altar Boy," Margie quipped.

Suddenly the two-way radio in the Jeep squawked to life. "Attention all units. The fire at Hartsons Beach is a permitted and prescribed burn, so please don't issue any citations. And tell any complaining neighbors the papers are on file at Sow Hill and to not call the dispatcher anymore! Be safe. Out."

"Do they know they'll have one of the Port's finest at the fire?" asked Margie.

"Patty, the dispatcher, knows … say, that perfume is actually giving me a headache. You mind if I push the top back and open the windows?" Digger asked, pulling over.

"As long as we get to cuddle at the beach!"

As they pulled off Route 32 and headed down Hartsons Beach Road, they could see the glow of the fire in the distance. Digger stopped the car and unsnapped both seat belts. "Hey, join me up here," he said as he climbed up to sit on the Jeep's roll bar. "Get up here, Margie!"

"I guess we're not in any rush … It's lovely, Digger. What are we doing up here in the middle of the road?" Digger gently put his bare foot on the gear shifter, which was in neutral, and pulled it down to click it into drive. The vehicle started off at idle speed.

"You are not serious?" Margie deadpanned with a hint of delight.

Digger placed both feet on the steering wheel and commandeered the vessel from atop the roll bar. As they drove under a canopy of oak trees toward the ocean, Digger put his arm around Margie and said, "Welcome to the most beautiful road in the world."

"Is driving like this even in the citation book?"

"Nope," said Digger, "therefore, perfectly legal."

CHAPTER 15

In a world away on the other side of town, Chuck Branson was likewise helping a girl he had met onto a machine. It was the infamous mechanical hog at Sledge's Saloon on Route One. He climbed up behind her and gave the signal to start the gyrations. There was nothing for her to grab but two big hog ears and hang on. Chuck scooched up in the saddle and hung on to the waist of his newfound date.

Payday Thursdays followed a trickle-down economic theory. The money trickled down to him through his sales, which on this occasion he was celebrating with … *Mary … Mary? … Mary Margaret. That's it*! He thankfully remembered and noted the idiocy of the double name. "Mary Mah-gret, what's this ride remind you of?" Chuck whiskey-whispered into her ear as they gyrated every which way.

"What pigs men can be, Chuck!" Mary Margaret shouted back over her shoulder to put a chill on his thoughts. Chuck got the message but ignored it. He moved his grasp up to Mary Margaret's chest area during a particularly powerful thrust from the pig much to the delight of Chuck's friends and the regulars at what could only be described as a biker bar. Mary Margaret instantly flailed both elbows out to the sides like a bird about to take flight. This pulled Chuck's hands off her chest, and then she brought her right elbow over in front of her and snapped it back to catch Chuck's jaw and neck, which sent him sprawling into the spongy turf. The crowd erupted with approval. Some had seen Mary Margaret's move. Many hadn't and were just hooting and hollering over the fact that the girl was still on and the guy was in the dust.

Chuck was enraged. From deep in his gut he yelled from the ground, "Why you …!" and as he got up he started to charge her as she sat on the hog that had stopped moving due to the watchful eye of the management. In this case the management was a six foot four inch mountain man wearing only blue jean overalls, tattoos, and a Fu Manchu—Sledge himself. As Chuck charged at the damsel in distress on the mechanical pig, Sledge deftly moved in to intercept as if he had the wings of Tinker Bell. And intercept he did. He grabbed Chuck by the shirt at his throat and by his belt of his pants, lifted him a good four feet off the ground, carried him as he flailed his arms unsuccessfully, and threw him into the gravel parking lot. His landing zone was surrounded by Harley motorcycles.

Sledge bellowed, "Chuck Branson, I've been wanting to do that to you evah since we opened! You're a tresspassah for the rest of the summah. Hit the road, boy!"

Chuck picked himself up slowly, his head still spinning. He looked the direction he was thrown from and saw only beefy tattooed men with their arms crossed over their chests. He yelled as best as he could in their direction, "Sledge, you threw the wrong man out. You'll regret this, I promise you!"

One of the tattooed enforcers stepped forward, but Sledge held him back. Another bouncer replied, "What ya gonna do, Chuck? Cut our lobster supply? We're in Maine, you numbnut!"

Sledge stepped forward. "Move along, Mr. Branson."

Chuck thrust up his fist in an obscene gesture, held it high, pivoted toward the parking lot, and stumbled to his pickup. The bar patrons launched a loud and hearty laugh at Chuck's hand signal, an empty attempt to retain some manly dignity. As Chuck slowly lifted himself into the truck, he heard the crowd return to a normal din with some spiked laughter and shrieks from women.

He seriously thought about pulling his Glock 9mm pistol from under his seat and having the last laugh. He looked toward the bar and saw one of Sledge's henchmen in the shadow of a large pine tree, waiting for Chuck's next move. Chuck again launched the obscene salute in that direction, fumbled for his keys, started his truck, and slowly pulled away. "They're too big and too many," he muttered to himself as he pulled out, pounding his fist on the steering wheel.

CHAPTER 16

At the bonfire on the beach, Digger was indeed cuddling with Margie as guitars played worship tunes. Some sang; some just listened.

Margie looked up at the brilliant stars and said, "This has been the best summer of my life, Digger. And I have you and Janie to thank for it."

He pulled her closer to himself. "Me too, but what does Janie have to do with it?"

Margie pulled away to the side. "Janie was the one who pulled me out of Richmond and brought me up here. It was all her idea!" Digger re-pulled Margie close to his side. "Okay, okay, you're right; I hadn't thought of that." He instinctively knew he had to defuse this stream of thought or the night would head south, so to speak, immediately.

"I'm sorry, did you mention Janie from Richmond?" piped in Martha.

Margie bent over to look past Digger in the firelight, "Oh hey, Martha! It's Margie from the Brigantine."

"Hi, Margie! I wouldn't expect to see you here tonight. I didn't know you were a churchgoer."

"She's in the Secret Service," Digger quipped. Margie elbowed Digger.

"I almost got Janie to come tonight," Martha said.

"You saw Janie tonight?" Margie interrupted.

"Yeah, I gave her a ride into town. She wasn't doing too well. In fact I've been praying for her here tonight."

"What do you mean?" pleaded Margie.

"She shared some things and started cry in my car ..."

Digger's arm was spun off Margie's shoulder as she rushed to Martha's side. He thought, *Not Janie interrupting again ... even when she isn't around.* He rocked his head back in a silent gesture of exasperation.

"Where did you drop her? Margie asked.

"At the pharmacy. She was bumming out over an old boyfriend from her church," Martha said.

Digger rolled his eyes. All too many times had the scandal of Richmond replayed in his summer. He kept his cool, especially in this crowd. This was mission central for compassionate college kids looking for fallen angels to fix. Digger watched as now Margie sidled to within inches from Martha's face and asked, "Was Jerome around? You know Jerome?"

"Yeah, I know Jerome. No, Jerome went home for the night. Something's up with his dad."

Margie spun in the sand, "Digger, please, we have to go get Janie!"

"Aw, Margie! Okay, okay, we'll go shortly. I have friends playing in these bands, and this is important to me. Besides, Janie is resourceful!"

Martha piped in, "She said she wanted to walk to get exercise, but she was reeking of perfume and alcohol." Digger knew that 'bout ruined all chances right there. He stood up and went after Margie, who was headed down toward the water at an angry pace.

"Margie! Margie! I have special plans for us here tonight. I have a bottle of Dom Perignon and some blankets. I thought we could count the stars and hug."

Margie slowed right down. Her body language spoke capitulation. The idea was something she, too, wanted to do more than anything. Time with Digger was so hard to get.

"Okay. She's a big girl. The scrapes she has gotten in and out of ..."

Digger quickly followed. "Yes! Let me go set us a place up on that dune."

Margie asked quietly as she cocked her head to the side demurely, "Are you going to hear the bands all right?"

Digger didn't really get her point but grunted affirmatively as he ran toward the Jeep to get the goods.

Chapter 17

Janie seated herself right in the center of the bar. "Jack and gingeah, sweetie." She saw Rusty blush a redder hue. "I declare, you Mainiacs are such softies."

Rusty remembered previous scenes with this little barfly. "And who's driving Miss Daisy tonight, shugah?" asked Rusty as he began to administer the medication: two parts whiskey, one part ginger ale. He thought to himself, *One good one to deaden the taste buds, then pure soda from here on.*

Chapter 18

Chuck's ego in irons, he sought fortification at each watering hole between Sledge's and the Port itself. There was a small crowd at The Patriot: no band, no girls to make time with, just darts and Musket Shots, which was the establishment's claim to fame: one half-ounce of well whiskey topped with one half-ounce of Bacardi 151 rum—151 proof alcohol, that is. One or two drops of fire shy of grain alcohol.

Chuck's ego started to recover even though his darts started missing the board. He shuffled over to the bar for another Musket Shot and a Labatt chaser. His friend behind the bar, Wet Willy Cummings, said, "Chuck, man, this is the last one. I'd get fired if the owner knew I was still pouring for you after four muskets."

"Thas why theyah call you Wet Willy... I'm outtah heyah aftah this one."

"Okay," said Willy, "but no more darts. You're messin' the tips."

"I pomish," said Chuck.

Chuck was on autopilot. He fired down the Musket Shot, quaffed half the beer, and walked out straight as the crucifer going down a church aisle. Of course, he was doing his absolute best at this show … until he was in the parking lot. Then he spilled left and right, looking for his truck. "Ship's Pub is whar tha booty lay!"

CHAPTER 19

Janie began swaying to the music on her bar stool. Her hair folded over her face as she was lost in the melancholy twang of Neil Young. "I've seen the needle and the damage done, a little part of it everyone, ooh, ooh the damage done!" she crowed loudly—followed in similar timing with, "Rustacious! Another one, please!" The other patrons at the bar who had been watching her in amusement or pity, depending on their own level of depravity, looked quickly to see how the minister of mirth would handle the errant one.

Rusty, believing pure soda would be safer than throwing her out, brought the soda faucet to her glass and filled it with ginger ale and said, "It's on me, Petunia." It pleased the crowd as laughter erupted around the barflies that were watching. Janie sensed at some deeper recess of her pickled brain that this was laughter at her.

In what seemed to be a delay of minutes, Janie shouted, "Hay'ay thayz no Ja'ack in thayat!" Those who had been watching the scene now erupted in laughter over Janie's timing and delivery. This caused the unwary patrons to stop and take notice. When Janie brushed her hair from her face, everyone was looking at her and laughing.

Janie looked at Rusty, who was holding the soda hose, and asked, "What gives?"

Rusty said, "You be a good girl, Janie, and enjoy your ginger. Jack had to go home. He can come back tomorrow night."

The crowd laughed approvingly. Janie twirled around on her stool and saw only red-faced strangers with mouths wide open, knocking their heads back and shaking with laughter. Then the centrifugal force of the stool spin caught up with her inner ear and sent her falling into the arms of a ruddy lobsterman on the stool next to hers. He held her and steadied her as if she were a rag doll and waited for her legs to stop swaying and then set her on them to see if she would stand. She did. The laughter was deafening in her ear, and she became enraged.

She tried to slap the lobsterman. "Get your filthy paws off me!"

He caught her swing and held it in mid-air and looked over at Rusty, who was running out from under the far end of the bar.

"Janie! Time to go." Rusty took over the lock on her body and wrist from the lobsterman who was shaking with laughter but doing so quietly so as not to escalate matters. Rusty started walking and dragging Janie to the door. A girl picked up Janie's purse and followed them. The laughter had ceased. This was becoming too sad to have to ruin a good party night.

The girl with Janie's purse lifted it to her nose and blurted, "Aw gad! Jontue perfume is everywhere! Cheap crap! A southern belle with a middle school smell!" The crowd laughed approvingly.

"Here, Rusty, this is hers."

Rusty grabbed the purse as he steadied Janie. He took her outside but worried about the unattended bar. "Janie, you're not driving, right?" he asked.

She stood on her own and turned toward him, "What d'you care, Yankee?"

Rusty looked in the purse for keys. Everything was drenched in perfume. No keys.

He said, "You don't have your car here do you?"

She said it was at the Brigantine as she started to stumble away, raising her hand and giving Rusty the obscene salute. Rusty slung her purse down the saluting arm and yelled, "Take it slow, Janie!"

CHAPTER 20

Chuck was headed down Ocean Avenue toward Ship's Pub when he spied Janie stumbling on the sidewalk, headed the opposite direction. Chuck muttered, "I believe the little lady needs some assistance." He swung the truck into a U-turn, which it successfully negotiated when you include the curb and sidewalk a few feet behind Janie. She seemed to be confused by the commotion and sweeping beacon of the truck's headlights. Chuck threw it into park and jumped around the front hood. "Miss Janie! Your knight in shining armor has come to your rescue!" he declared.

"Is that you, Chucky? You were laughing at me, too. I hate Rustacious!" she slurred.

"Whoa, whoa! Girl! I was not laughing at you! I haven't even been to Rusty's! I was just coming from that way." He pointed the opposite direction of Ship's Pub.

"Yes suh, and you almost killed me swinging your big rig around here," she replied as she draped both arms around his broad neck and hung on for dear life. Chuck put his arms around her and was stunned, even in his numb state, at her frailty.

"Come on, Janie, I'm taking you to the Brigantine."

Just as he was helping her into the passenger side of his truck, a police cruiser pulled up.

"Charles? Is that you?" asked the officer thru the cruiser's passenger window. Chuck bent down and squinted to see the glowing face of the driver.

"Buzzy-boy! How you doin'?" responded Chuck genuinely. They were locals who abided by the code of courtesy and reserved the busting of chops for the summer folk and tourists.

"I see you have this under control," said Buzz, nodding toward Janie in the passenger seat.

"Oh yes, sir … Some Yankee hospitality, don't cha know. Just gonna give Janie a ride to the Brigantine," Chuck affirmed.

"Wicked good, Chuckles!" Buzz said coyly as he pulled ahead.

Chuck climbed into the driver's seat and said, "That's the way it's done."

Janie, being sensitive to cops, cars, and alcohol retorted, "If this were Richmond, we would've been body searched, breathalyzed, and booked!"

"It's okay, Janie, you're with the Chuckster!" he said as he pulled away from the curb in the direction of the Brigantine and the ocean.

"Say, what is that lovely perfume you are wearing?"

"Everyone is complimenting me tonight on my perfume. I spilled it all over my purse. It's my favorite; it's Jontue." She hitched over toward Chuck on the truck's bench seat. Her foot kicked her purse as she made the less than deft move toward her prey. All the contents of the purse, unbeknownst to anyone, became strewn on the floor of the truck and released a deeper reek of Jontue. Chuck pulled Janie into the clutch of his right armpit. They both felt the night was being redeemed from the dregs.

Chuck's mind was calculating at light speed. *Blanket? Check. Booze? Check. Brigantine Beach? Yes!* Calmly he inquired of Janie, "What do you say we get to know each other a little better down at the BB? I got a little taste of the South in my tool kit in the truck bed."

"What you got, Chuckles? Don't tease me about the South, Yankee."

"I have a little bit of Jack Daniels."

Janie squealed with delight. "If Rusty could see me now," sighed Janie.

"What's he got to do with anything?"

"He cut me off of my Jack and threw me out of Ship's."

"He's a numbnut."

Janie burst into laughter. "A what?"

"A numbnut," Chuck repeated, punching it out.

"I declare, you Yankees talk mighty funny-like."

Chuck pulled into the Brigantine Beach gravel parking lot with his lights off in case there were other lovebirds nesting on the beach. No sign of anything or anyone. Chuck reached down between Janie's legs to grab the four-wheel drive shifter on the floor of the truck, saying "Excuse me."

"Oh, aren't you the gentleman?" she said as she pinned his arm for a moment with her knees.

"Uh ma'am … I'm trying to put the truck in four-wheel drive."

"Don't let me stop you. Wait … stop. Where are we going? Out onto the beach?" She squealed with delight.

"Yes, in just a little bit. Then we're gonna sit in the sea grass on my blanket and ask Jack to join us." Chuck left his arm right where it was—like it was a necessary position for driving in four-wheel drive.

CHAPTER 21

Across the bay, on Hartsons Beach, staring at the same bold stars and listening to the same cadence of waves crashing, Digger and Margie, resembling a large pretzel on a blanket, were discussing the things that they wanted to do and achieve in life. The bands and youth groups were long gone.

"Ever since I brought the body to Government Wharf and helped identify the place of the murder, my adrenaline starts flowing at crime scenes. I want to be involved in the search for truth. I hate it when I hear of wrongfully convicted people wasting years in jail. Our capabilities at forensics and physics are so advanced that false positives should be a thing of the past."

Margie was trying to keep this romantic moment relevant to her and Digger as a couple—possibly forever. He was, after all, a catch extraordinaire in any debutante's book.

"Digger, I love the fact that you aren't squeamish about blood. I can't tell you how many guys in my nursing lab classes turn white and fall right off their stools. With what I'm learning, who knows? I may be treating the victims you're trying to help."

Digger pulled Margie a little closer into the pretzel lock. Exactly the desired affect Margie was milking.

"Digger, do you ever go south during the school year?"

"My dad and I go bonefishing in the Keys for a week after Christmas. Why?"

"I don't know," she lied and dropped it quickly. If he hadn't caught that hook, best to not be too eager. After all, it was only mid-July. She knew how to do some bonefishing herself. *Let the baby run with the hook, feed the line out, let him swallow the bait, hook, line, and sinker. And let it lodge in his lower GI tract and yank!*

Oblivious, Digger continued, "False positives should be eradicated with genetic testing. I'd love to be the prosecutor showing the jury the way through scientific evidence and getting their buy-in for convicting some sicko!"

"I thought you wanted to be a detective."

"I want to be a detective, a lawyer, a legislator, a judge … I want it all!"

Margie was ecstatic. She was warming up to a detective for a husband, but a lawyer or judge … or a senator! She unconsciously clutched Digger harder as if she would never let him go.

Chapter 22

Janie took a pull on the bottle of Jack Daniels. "My dad is the biggest phony I know."

"Why? Just because he didn't want you kissing a black guy?"

"That, yes. And because he raised us in Christian way to love everyone, even our enemies. Then when I followed my heart, I was told it was wrong and terrible things happened."

"My dad would kill me if I dated a bootilicious," Chuck stated matter-of-factly.

"Chuck, what in tarnation is bootilicious?"

"It's what black people call black women. We don't say the N-word up here."

Janie's anger started brewing just south of her heart and quickly headed north to her vocal chords, "What do you mean 'up here?' And how the heck is some derogatory code word better than any other name? Are you implying that southerners use the N-word? We may deserve a bad rap for hanging on to slavery too long, but you northerners are more prejudiced than the South. Look at your ghettos; look at your attitude, ready to criticize the South, taking a holier-than-thou position but being racist yourself. That's worse than the cultural inequities found in the South."

"Janie, Janie, Janie... Here, calm down," he said handing her the bottle, which she could not refuse, almost in an act of anesthetizing her brain against the unfairness.

"Drop it, honey chile," Chuck said as he pulled himself closer to her body on the blanket and leaned over to kiss her. His use of fake southern vernacular was the last straw. Janie attempted to roll to her left to get onto her knees and make her exit from this guy who was just as bad as her father.

"Janie, don't leave me, honey. We ain't done here!" Chuck said as he pinned the right shoulder that was trying to roll left.

"Chuck Branson, you get your cotton pickin' hands off me, you racist meathead Mainiac," referring to his Maine heritage.

That did it for Chuck. These richie riches come into town thinking they are better than the locals … smarter … prettier … richer. Well they ain't stronger!

Chuck scrambled onto Janie's frail body, pinning both shoulders and her torso. "You rich prisses are all alike!"

"Chuck, get off me! I can't breathe," she said in a wheezing whisper.

Janie's mind raced to desperation. She couldn't breathe. "Help! Hel …"

Chuck put his lobster claw of a hand over Janie's mouth and nose and squared his body on her flailing bag of bones underneath him.

"Shut up! Shut up!" He squeezed her mouth and nose and pressed her head into the sand in a jerking cadence, hissing at her to shut up.

Her eyes grew wide in uncontrollable shock, and all of a sudden her body compressed under his weight as if someone had stepped on a pretty crab shell. With her eyes wide open but not moving, a gurgling noise emanated from deep within her chest and resounded out her throat along with foul sputum reeking of alcohol.

Chuck rolled left to avoid what he had seen in the past—another woman who couldn't hold her liquor.

"You're disgusting," Chuck barked, backhanding her with his right hand.

Janie, her eyes still wide open, motionless, and silent was looking to her left in the direction of the Brigantine. Blood trickled down her chin.

Chuck wiped his hand on the blanket, and at the same time he recognized that Janie was not reacting to being slapped. His hand had a dark fluid on the back side. He peered at the blanket and at Janie and saw the same dark fluid flowing at Janie's lips and down her chin.

"Janie?" he asked perplexedly. "Janie?" He jumped over her body, not wanting to touch her but to get into her gaze to her left. "Janie!"

Janie, whose eyes were wide as saucers as if to say: "You did it now, Buster. You are in trouble now, Chuck," didn't say a word.

"Janie?" Chuck sat up in horror. "Janie?" He put his ear next to her nose and mouth, hoping to sense breathing. Nothing but the smell of bile, blood, and booze.

Chuck's mind started racing. *What the heck just happened?* He recalled her body shifting under his weight ... *Have I killed her?* He looked at her and from his angle she was still staring at him saying the same thing with her eyes: *Oh you've done it now. You are in big trouble!*

Chuck began to panic as his mind started racing. He could hear his sister's voice in his ears accusing him of killing the neighbors' cat after it was caught in the Haveahart trap. *Who knew it couldn't hold its breath when the caged cat was dunked under the water of the above-ground pool in their backyard?* He got a lot of unwanted attention for that escapade. *I'm gonna catch it for this, too, oh God!*

Chuck rolled from a kneeling position over Janie to a sitting position and began to moan and groan, rocking back and forth as he sat next to Janie's dead body. *I didn't mean to kill her. She just had to shut up!* What would his father say? Oh, he knew, "Chucky you did it again. Your poor mother is rolling in her grave over this."

Chuck gasped for air he had forgotten to breathe. He began to hyperventilate as he continuously rocked back and forth like someone locked in a mental ward. *The shame on my dad if this gets found out. The shame ... the shame ... the shame,* he repeated in cadence with his rocking rhythm. He began to shake uncontrollably and sob.

He spit out a few words, quietly at first. "Oh God ... why? Why, God?"

With an angry yell, he cursed at God. "You took my mother; now you're after me. You took Janie. *You* did it!"

He cursed again at the top of his lungs. This brought him to an awareness that he did not want to be seen or heard, so he hunched down low to the sand to hide from his own outburst, where he paused and listened.

Slowly he lifted his head and looked furtively around at his surroundings. The magnificent roar of the ocean and the absence of any other activity on the beach made this scene of a lifeless body on the blanket seem small and almost insignificant.

Chuck looked at Janie and began to think about these circumstances and his other flirtations with crime in the past. He had been through some big scrapes, much bigger than drowning the neighbor's cat. He started to breathe more evenly.

He reminded himself how ingenious he had been in the past in deflecting guilt and responsibility for his escapades. Even to this day, the bomb threat during the high school's SAT exams remains at the feet of the weird blind kid who lived up the street from the high school. He reminisced: *An incriminating note on some paper that had the kid's braille pimples on it. Simple. It created a trail to a logical misfit. The freak needed everyone to screw up on SATs. Of course the dummy had to level the battlefield of life and call a bomb threat.* It stuck. The boy was removed from school and ostracized so much that the family moved out of town. *It was brilliant. I am brilliant. I can do this.*

Chuck breathed deeply to pace himself and bring fresh air and fresh thoughts into himself. He had stopped rocking and began rubbing his chin with his fingers as he calculated his next move. He started muttering aloud.

"Janie who did you in? Who brought you here? Who fits? We need a trail."

His mind immediately raced to his meeting on the road with Buzzy, the only one who could place him with Janie. He remembered he had something on Buzz to keep him quiet, but he couldn't rely on it. He needed someone who would take the fall and not recover ... someone vulnerable. He continued to think as he started polishing his fingerprints off the whiskey bottle and taking one big last gulp without touching his lips to the bottle.

Like a lick of a flame shooting up from hell itself, it came to him: Those black boys at the Brigantine ... from the South! Yes! Janie's soft spot, of course! One of them was here tonight. Yes! One of them took liberties with the little white girl from Virgin–i–ay! He immediately thought of the deck at the Brigantine where the black boys all sat waiting for guests. There must be some incriminating articles that would put the police on those boys' trail instead of mine. It wouldn't take much in this county. He smiled inwardly and felt much more in control of his emotions.

He looked into Janie's vacant stare and mustered all the evil within himself that he could to begin his artful deception. "Once you go black you never come back!" he hissed at the corpse.

Chuck got up on his feet to look around but remained crouching. A parked car was still at the far end of the beach but no sign of being occupied. It had been a non-issue all night. *Can't worry about that.*

Before I set the stage, I have to clean it first. He looked around. My blanket, the bottle, her purse? Where's her purse?

He scurried over to the truck, opened the driver's side, and got in quickly so the light would go out. He got a lighter from his pocket and lit it over the passenger's floor area.

"Crap!"

There was everything from shiny wrapped tampons to gum, keys, makeup, and who knows what else. He slithered back toward the driver's side, pushed his seat forward, grabbed his work gloves, and put them on before going back to the female sundries on the floor of the truck, which he then began carefully putting in the purse. Then he exited the truck, still in the crouch position, and brought the purse to Janie's side.

He rolled Janie off his mackinaw blanket and rolled it up. He took the bottle of whiskey and put it in Janie's firm fingers and bent them around the bottle despite their resistance. "You know you like *Jaack*, Janie."

He rotated the bottle several times, pressing her hands onto the glass sides of the square bottle, then slinked away with the blanket and climbed into the truck. He started it up, quietly pulled out of the parking lot with his lights off, and turned up Ocean Avenue, away from the scene. He turned on his lights when he encountered a sharp bend, leaving responsibility far behind.

Chuck became invigorated as he distanced himself from the scene. He took his first left. He needed to double back to the Brigantine to the bellhops' deck. He parked at an apartment complex up the hill from the Brigantine. It was stealth mode from here on out to get to the deck and back. *There has to be something at the deck to help throw the scent off.*

CHAPTER 23

Margie was awakened by a damp ocean chill. Despite Digger's contortions around her body and the blanket, which was now heavy and cold with ocean mist, she couldn't stay warm. She thought twice before waking Digger. *Would his ideal girlfriend, wearing flannel and L. L. Bean fur-lined muck-a-lucks—or whatever they were called—be able to handle this? Probably, but I can't.* Digger snorted and then began a repetition of some guttural snores. *Now's my chance.*

She slammed her elbow into Digger's chest. "Digger, we gotta go! Your snoring is too much. Let's go!" She said nothing about her inability to handle a northern night at the ocean, of course.

"Harrumph! Yeah, of course … sure. Sorry. Man, its freezing! Let's go!"

They grabbed at anything that looked human-made and ran for the Jeep.

"Ugh! The top is down!" groaned Margie.

"Don't worry, I got a trick," he said as he used a shirt to wipe the dew off her seat. "Here, sit here."

He started the engine to get it warming, then took the blanket and tucked half of it behind her back, ran around the front of the Jeep, and loosened some bolts holding down the windshield.

"No, Digger, don't put that down."

"Cool it. You'll like this."

He put an edge of the blanket in the hinge of the windshield, reset the windshield bolts in place, and tightened them down. He got in the driver's seat and pulled the left corner of the blanket tight up around his left shoulder. With his right hand he reached the heat controls and turned them on high. The blanket bulged with the flow of warm air.

"Digger, you're quite the boy scout." She would have leaned to kiss him if it wouldn't jeopardize the heat bubble.

"Home, James!"

Digger pulled a tight U-turn and headed for the Brigantine. He reached for the radio and pushed in a James Taylor cassette.

Margie looked up at the stars and over at Digger. "Thank you, Digger Davenport, for the best night of my life."

"Likewise, my dear—the best!" Digger agreed.

CHAPTER 24

Chuck cut through some light tree covering on the border of the Brigantine and surfaced at the employee parking lot. From the edge of darkness, he took stock of the scene. *No movement. Two lights on in the girls' dorm but shades drawn, dim kitchen lights, fans still droning, good to cover for my footsteps.*

He only had to slip between the girls' dorm and the kitchen undetected and get up to the bellhop's deck, which was just thirty yards beyond the kitchen to the left, away from the girls' dorm. That was his biggest hurdle. He began his approach, crouching and scurrying between the cars and up the stairs, three at a time, toward the kitchen and the girls' dorm. At the top he slid left and was at the loading dock, a familiar spot for him. As he slid left, he was completely in the shadows of the building. He looked up the hill. Dead ahead was the bellhops' deck, completely in darkness. Also ahead and to the right was the circular driveway of the Brigantine. *Zero movement in the driveway.* To his left was the entrance to the dungeon— the dorm for the bellhops, bellboys, cooks, and the laundry chute for all laundry being sent down from the dining room and the kitchen. He had a thought, *Perfect! A blanket for the stage.*

Chuck sidled left into the dungeon door. The hopper for the laundry was right there. In rapid sequence he opened the screened door to the hopper, grabbed the first large tablecloth, rolled it around his arm, backed out the door into the shadows, and hightailed it toward the bellhop deck. When he climbed up on the deck, he found two of the four chairs there still cocked and leaning back against the building. He scoured the area for any artifacts. On one of the chairs was a large red vest. *Yes! Georgie Porgie, you bad boy.*

At the foot of the same chair was a large Styrofoam cup with a lid. Chuck picked it up. It was heavy. He pried the lid off and sniffed. He almost gagged at the smell of saliva and tobacco juice. His eyes rolled into the back of his head. *Perfect!*

Just as he was sealing the lid back on the cup, he heard music coming from out on the street and saw car lights heading up the Brigantine hill and toward the girls' dorm. Chuck carefully put the vest and the cup in the tablecloth and twisted it so it wouldn't tip then put the sack over his shoulder and jumped to the far side of the deck to hide until the car passed. The Jeep, with some James Taylor tune playing way too loud for the hour, didn't pass. It pulled right up to the kitchen loading dock.

Chuck peeked over the deck. It was Digger and Margie. *Not good.* He slipped down slowly and weighed his options. *Best to sit tight until Digger pulls out and reverse steps back to my truck.*

He sat still until he heard the Jeep's reverse gear whining then slipped up and watched Margie go up the stairs and the car back out onto Brigantine road. He skirted the deck with his goods, slunk back to the shadows of the loading dock, and caught his breath.

Margie opened her dorm room door to the stench of the perfume and turned on the light to an empty room. Her heart sank. "Janie, you are gonna kill me with worry! Where are you?"

She walked in and sat on the edge of her bed and thought for a moment. "What can I do about her? I'm not her mother, thank God."

Margie went to see if Janie's car was there. She walked down the hall to the stairs and the exterior landing that overlooked the loading dock and the employee parking and looked over toward where the VW had been parked. It was still there. *Thank God*, she thought. And then she discerned a moving shadow in the parking lot. A shiver bolted through her spine as she squinted at the figure. Someone was running among the cars with a sack over one shoulder. It was like a scene out of Dickens, a waif running with goods packed in a sheet. She peered into the darkness till there was no sign of any movement. She shrugged her shoulders and returned to her room to say a prayer for Janie. "Lord, please watch over Janie and bring her home safely. Amen."

Margie flopped back onto the pillow and fell asleep in her clothes.

CHAPTER 25

Chuck pulled into the Government Wharf parking lot just north of Brigantine Beach. He grabbed the satchel of stage props and slunk to the beach where he first checked the beach parking lot. There were no signs of anyone. The cops didn't usually allow people to park there that long at this hour anyway. Chuck knew he had better set the scene and exit stage left before anything changed.

He stooped over and scurried to where Janie lay. His stomach lurched momentarily over the gravity of the situation. He swore at her. *It's your own fault.*

Keeping his gloves on, he took care to unravel his satchel carefully. He grabbed the cup of tobacco spit first and set it securely in the sand, then took the tablecloth and spread it out next to Janie's lifeless body. He peered over to check her face. Her eyes were still open but not as intense—more comfortable looking. Chuck lifted her body onto the tablecloth. *Whoa! How light and yet stiff.* He grabbed the red vest and placed it under Janie, then took the cup of spittle and brought it to Janie's lips, peeled apart her firm lips, and drizzled a small amount into her gums and clenched teeth. The smell of tobacco emanated from her even in the breeze of the ocean air. *Perfect!*

"Shouldn't be kissing black boys again, Janie. Your daddy's gonna be outraged." Chuck left the remainder of the cup tilted on the sand not far from the tablecloth.

He reached for his lighter to check the scene to be sure nothing was amiss. He patted his pockets but couldn't find it. *Must be in the truck.* He squinted and surveyed the scene.

"Looks like Georgie had a good time here," he said and slunk back to his truck at Government Wharf.

CHAPTER 26

The Brigantine Hotel's claim to fame was lobster—breakfast, lunch, and dinner. Fridays were special. Breakfast at 8:00 a.m., weather permitting, was offered poolside, which sat atop a hill overlooking Brigantine Beach, the Bay of Maine, and the mouth of the Talbot River. The choice seats were down by the high diving board, next to the rail overlooking this vista. The brightly painted lobster boats could be seen and their diesel engines heard growling out to their respective portions of the bay, where their lobster buoys, painted in matching colors, bobbed in a scattered display of colorful dots on the blue-gray ocean surface. From the breakfast tables overlooking it all, one could easily become absorbed in the peaceful activity.

While those seats were choice for breakfast, they were the pits for the wait staff. The high dive section added almost half a football field to the trek with trays of dishes and food.

Margie, having been wakened by a fellow waitress, quickly got into her uniform and white sneakers and headed up to the kitchen through the loading entrance. She looked to her left at the employee parking lot and recalled the creepy shadow of last night darting among the cars and disappearing into the woods. She also had a foreboding in her spirit regarding Janie. She believed that Janie was supposed to be on for breakfast too. She rushed to look at the table assignment chart on the wall by the water station near the swinging doors that opened onto the dining room. One of the waitresses said in a bold voice, "Read it and weep!" as she turned from reading the table assignments.

Would she be inside or, God forbid, get the high dive zone? *Yes!* Margie had the bird cage inside. Then she saw Janie's name next to the high dive. She spun around to look at the freshly painted faces of the other waitresses. "Has anyone seen Janie?"

Martha, the muffin maid, pushed through the throng of girls. "Margie, didn't she come home last night?"

Thinking quickly, Margie spun around to double-check the table assignment and said, "Martha, you're on the deck next to the bird cage. Can you cover my station on the bird cage? I'll cover Janie's station at the high dive. If Claude, the maître d', discovers her missing, she's dead. She has missed one breakfast already!"

Martha replied in an urgent whisper "Man! Margie you *are* a good friend to take the high dive so she can keep a job. God bless you. Yeah, I'll cover the muffins and the bird cage. Go!"

"Yeah I'm a regular saint. If Janie goes, I go too. She's how I get home!"

Margie grabbed a tray and checked her watch. It said 7:55 a.m. *Perfect.* She walked brusquely through the double swinging doors into the dining room. "Showtime!" she affirmed to herself as she plastered her Brigantine smile on.

"Morning, Mr. Claude," she said without skipping a beat and headed right for the porch door that led out to the pool.

Claude Portelier watched Margie walk by without saying a word. He checked her for matching socks, balanced apron bow at the waist, and pressed collar. *This one passes muster,* he thought. *But where did those southern belles ever get the idea you could put Mister or Miss in front of a person's first name? A false sense of propriety, no doubt.*

Margie deeply breathed in the ocean air as she paused to take in the view and reminded herself that doing the high dive station sure beat working even the finest country club in Richmond. If the chilly air would keep the patrons in the dining room, this could be a pretty easy gig this morning. Nonetheless, she'd make Janie pay.

She placed the tray on her shoulder as she approached a single deuce-top at the rail. It was Admiral and Mrs. Prescott, an elderly Connecticut couple who were regulars and would be at the rail no matter what the weather.

"Good morning, Mrs. Prescott, Admiral!' Margie beamed.

"Well, well, good show, Evelyn! We have the other belle ringing this morning," the admiral bellowed between his teeth as they clenched onto a well-seasoned white meerschaum pipe. The admiral had a Greek fisherman's cap on and a pair of small binoculars around his neck.

"Admiral, I trust you have the bridge under control," Margie said, poking the retired naval officer.

Evelyn chimed in, "With an iron fist, dearie."

The girls tittered together. The admiral preened at what he took as a compliment. "Everything is quite shipshape this morning, yes."

"Would you all like some coffee to start?"

"Not for me, dear. The Admiral would like a cup, black as black can be, and we'll put in our order, too, to save you some steps."

"Where's the other southern belle, Angie?" The admiral inquired, half-interested as he scanned the ocean with his glasses and his pipe steaming away.

"Oh, you mean Janie. She isn't here this morning. I'm covering her station."

"We just love listening to you girls speak. We used to live in Newport News and became very fond of the southern charms," said Evelyn.

"I miss home but love the weather and people here. What may I get you?"

As Margie turned with their order for lobster omelets, she saw a four-top become occupied. A short, bald-headed, nebbishy man with a wife and a daughter and son in their teens.

"Good morning! Welcome to the best breakfast spot in the world," said Margie, meaning it dearly.

Margie exchanged the pleasantries including their respective hometowns, her college and major, his profession. She took the order for Dr. Stein (a New York City doctor) and his family: omelets, pancakes, and lobster crepes. After supplying coffees, teas, and juices from the substation at the pool, she informed her guests she would be headed to the kitchen to put in the order. She spun and headed up before anyone else sat down.

The admiral, who had been standing at the rail with the binoculars pressed tightly against his eyes, whispered, "Oh God, no!"

Evelyn looked up. "What George?"

He pulled the glasses down and double-checked where he was looking.

"Evelyn, look there in the grass to the left of the parking lot. Do you see a ... a body?"

Evelyn gasped and stood next to the admiral, who was now pointing.

"Get the management quickly," the admiral barked. "I'm going down there!"

The doctor at the next table inquired, "Is something the matter? I'm a doctor."

"Come with me, Doctor," ordered the admiral.

The doctor's children rushed to the rail and started pointing. Mrs. Stein, the doctor's wife, rushed with Evelyn into the hotel's pool entrance in search of a manager. A dishwasher was restocking glasses in the quiet barroom.

"Where's a phone, young man?" asked Evelyn.

He pointed and grunted to a wall phone by the cash register. *No wonder they kept him the kitchen*, thought Evelyn, pounding zero on the phone's keypad.

"Hello this is Evelyn Prescott at the pool. We believe we have an emergency down on Brigantine Beach. Please call an ambulance and come quickly! There appears to be someone lying in the grass to the left of the parking lot!"

She repeated her name impatiently and then her room number and was put on hold. She looked at Mrs. Stein and held out a dead phone. "Seriously? They put me on hold!"

Just then, squawking started coming out of the phone's receiver.

"Yes, this is Admiral Prescott's wife. I am at the pool. Who is this? Oh yes, Mr. Boynton. The admiral has gone down to check it out. Okay, goodbye."

Evelyn informed the doctor's wife that the manager was coming and calling an ambulance as they hurried back to the rail.

Of course the kids, being kids, had gone from the rail down to the beach itself. In vain, Mrs. Stein yelled, "David, Sarah, get back here!" Only Sarah looked up and waved her mother off. David completely ignored his mom and knelt by his dad to view the twisted body. Sarah stood back a few feet with her hand over her mouth, turning her body away from the grotesque scene.

Dr. Stein looked up at the admiral. "She's been dead for at least five hours."

"I know this girl. She is a waitress at the Brigantine. Janie—she was our waitress two days ago!"

The doctor turned to his right, where his son was also kneeling. "David, go back to your mother right now!"

They all put heads up to listen and heard sirens in the distance.

"David, go!"

David ran up the hill toward the pool. A crowd was gathering at the rail. David rounded the entrance to the pool area as Margie was coming down the ramp from the dining room and kitchen with a full tray of food and dishes with silver plate covers stacked three levels high. Margie was concentrating on her balancing act and didn't notice her tables were bare until she got closer and heard sirens. She looked up to take it all in and saw the teenage boy running by.

"Hey there, young man! What's going on here?"

"There's a dead girl on the beach down there," he said, pointing and proud to be part of an important event.

"My dad is a doctor down there, and said she's been dead for five hours. The admiral guy said it's a waitress named Janie from this hotel," he added excitedly and continuing with details of a true insider.

Margie heard the words and was immediately overcome with nausea and lightheadedness. Her knees buckled, and as she collapsed to the ground, she twisted to the left, sending her tray of plates, metal covers, and food onto the pool deck for one good clanging, smashing, bounce before most of it all rolled into the pool. All the heads at the rail turned around to see a collapsed waitress in an awkward position on the ground. Evelyn and Mrs. Stein rushed to her. David was white with fear having been so close to yet another scary event and sensed his actions might have been part of it.

"David, what happened here?" asked his mom.

"I just told her that the girl down on the beach was dead and that the dead girl was a waitress named Janie."

Evelyn nearly collapsed with the detail. Evelyn was on her knees at Margie's side and could barely hold herself up, let alone cradle Margie's head. She was kneeling in shards of china and puddles of authentic maple syrup. Pancakes and sausage patties were fanning out on the pool's surface in concentric waves from the impact. Half the crowd was at the rail and half gathered around Margie.

Guests came pouring out from the dining room. Claude, recognizing the uniform in a crumpled heap on the pool deck, could see he had an employee down. He ran to the front desk, which was in disarray with telephones to ears and Mr. Boynton on a walkie-talkie to the grounds manager.

"We have an employee *down* at the pool!" he said, emphasizing the word *down* like he was paramilitary.

Boynton looked up at Claude's stressed face, "We're on it, Claude. EMS is headed to the beach now. We believe she's dead."

"Dead? She just collapsed two seconds ago at the pool!"

Boynton hurdled the front desk and ran across the lobby and out the door to the deck that looked over the pool.

"Eddie!" he barked into the walkie-talkie, "Tell EMS down there we have another waitress collapsed at the pool. We need immediate attention. And get all your grounds crew to the pool area. We need crowd control!"

Claude looked in disbelief at the manager. "What do you mean another waitress, and what is at the beach?"

Boynton explained the events as he understood them and ordered the maître d', "Get your dining room under control. Do not allow employees out onto the lawn. Keep them at their stations and politely request the guests to remain inside until matters can be sorted out. Brief the chef to do likewise."

Claude, whose face was streaming with tears, nodded in obedience.

CHAPTER 27

No one in this small village needed a police scanner to detect that something was very wrong. Any vehicle that was red or had a siren or a lighted gumball machine atop it was racing down Ocean Avenue. Digger, who did have a scanner that had been squawking incessantly, jumped into his uniform, even though it was his day off, and hopped on his bicycle to head to Brigantine Beach, where the scanner had informed him that a body had been found, sure that bringing another vehicle to the scene would be an impediment. As he turned the corner of Ocean Avenue, it gave him a full view of the Brigantine Hotel and its beach. He saw about six people up in the dunes to his left and about sixty people up on the deck of the pool overlooking the scene.

He rode to the rocky edge of the beach, ditched his bike, and climbed over the rocks down to the high-water mark. Chief Nickerson had his back to him as Digger approached from the waterside. He saw through the legs of the few people standing around that there was a girl, partially dressed and in a twisted position, on the sand. He surveyed the site and thought about things like wind direction, light angles, and weather patterns as he zoned into what was surely a crime scene. As he approached, the tanned, thin legs poking out at odd angles from a dress he had seen before and the brown hair started to ring up something familiar to his brain.

"Oh God, no!" he whispered. He picked up his pace to come to the chief's side.

"Chief!"

Nickerson spun around in shock at being caught off guard by someone coming from the waterside.

"Chief! I may know the victim!"

"We know the victim. What are you doing here? It's your day off."

"Chief, the scanner was screaming this morning. I'm here to help. Who is it?" He hesitated to have his thoughts confirmed.

"Her name is Jane Dunn. She's from Richmond."

Digger dropped to his knees "Oh God, why?" he cried to the sky.

Nickerson pondered the scene for a moment and softened. "Did you know her?" He quietly crouched down and put a hand on Digger's shoulder.

"Yes, she is my girlfriend's best friend. They came up from Richmond together."

"I'm sorry, Digger. Look … Why don't you take some time off?"

"No, Chief, I want to help catch the murderer!"

"Now hold on, Digger, we got this covered." Then he hesitated and backed off a bit. "But if you're gonna work, I could use your help directing the gawkers and traffic. The county boys are spread thin today."

"Chief, I've studied crime scene preservation and evidence collection."

"Yeah I know, ever since you showed us the crime scene nine years ago. But Digger, I need you over there," pointing to the increasing crowd along Ocean Avenue.

"May I approach the deceased for a positive identification—for myself?"

"Sure, Digger," the chief said as he lit up a cigarette and looked around at the crowd. "I'm just waiting for the DA and MSP to get here."

When he approached Janie's contorted body, he noticed lots of foot dimples in the sand, the whiskey bottle, and the tablecloth with very little sand on it. The foot traffic in the sand all led to the left, away from the Brigantine Hotel, except for the area where the a bald-headed man was standing and talking to a tall man with a black hat. Digger took in the other details of the scene and pretended to be saying his goodbye to a dear old friend when in reality he was observing anything and everything he could.

He carefully backed up to where the chief was pacing and hauling on his cigarette.

"Chief, may I make a suggestion?"

"I'm suggesting you get your CSI buns up onto Ocean Avenue and get the traffic flowing!"

"No problem, Chief. Three things, though: One, your crime scene tape has to be enlarged to cover all of the BB—including the entire parking lot—for tire casts. Two, put out the cigarette and tell Buzzy over there no smoking at the crime scene. Three, tell those civilians over there to back out the way they came in. Oh, and sorry, *four*," he said, looking up at the skies, "get a professional photographer here pronto before the weather changes your scene."

"Okay, Mr. Dick Tracy! Thank you. Get the traffic under control, Officer," the chief erupted as he pointed toward Ocean Avenue.

Digger walked toward the water line then headed left up to Ocean Avenue. Wiping tears from his eyes, he circled back to the crowd at the corner where the pool deck of the Brigantine was twenty feet above the sidewalk and all the ambulances and fire trucks were concentrated.

Digger pulled his whistle out and gave three short bursts to get everyone's attention.

The chief, seeing that Digger was engaged, stepped on his cigarette and ground it into the sand, where high tide would get it, and yelled to Buzzy, "No smoking in the crime scene, you moron! Extend the crime tape around the whole parking lot!"

Next, the chief walked circumspectly over to the admiral and doctor. "Gentlemen! Can you please back up to where the ambulances are? Please try not to make any new tracks." Then he clicked on his radio. "Patty? Ah ... dispatch?" he corrected himself as he knew the radio transmissions would be monitored over this event.

"Go ahead, unit 1" crackled Patty's voice.

"I need a crime photographer down here ASAP before the weather changes."

"That's a 10-4 on the photographer, unit 1. I'll call Richie Cummings. Out."

Richie was part of the volunteer fire department and did a fantastic job on those scenes and even testified at arson trials.

Digger had parted the sea of people and directed all civilians up onto the hill of the Brigantine Hotel. He was now clearing some of the emergency vehicles so as to allow traffic to move. He approached the huge fire truck, which was belching diesel fumes and drowning out coherent thought.

"Hey Spencer!" he shouted up to the driver. "Can you move that rig up Ocean Ave by the parking area on the right?"

"We go where the ambulances go and wherever the dispatcher tells us."

"Gotcha, Spence, no problem." He turned and went over to the ambulance drivers. "Hey Mike!" he said, looking at Mike's name tag. "You got the dispatcher on a radio here?"

Mike pointed to the microphone attached to his shoulder epaulette. "She's right here."

Digger, being rather forward, said, "Perfect, thanks," and leaned into Mike's personal space, "Dispatch, this unit 19."

"Go ahead 19." Patty responded.

"We need instructions to the hook and ladder to move that beast up Ocean Ave about a thousand feet. And park it on the right—in case of nuclear disaster!"

"Roger that, 19. Dispatch out."

"Thanks, Mike, for the shout-out to Patty."

As Digger walked to the back of the ambulance, he overheard the speakers on all the emergency vehicles, "Spencer, move the rig up to the Ocean Ave parking area, a thousand feet south of your position. You Copy?"

"Roger that, Patty." Spencer could be heard in Sensurround sound from all the speakers on the various emergency vehicles.

Digger leaned out to look from the side of the ambulance to see Spencer looking at him with a stone face in his rearview mirror. Spencer revved the engine unnecessarily as if to belch in Digger's face. Digger gave a friendly aye-aye salute and thought to himself, *Man, these yokels can be a real problem.*

Addressing the other ambulance driver, Digger asked, "How many ambulances we need for this event?"

"Not sure, Officer. We're waiting for the chief to let us remove the body. And then we got another waitress up there passed out in shock," he said, pointing up to the pool.

"What? Another waitress? Part of this event?" asked Digger incredulously.

"No, I think that one"—he pointed toward the beach—"has been dead for about five hours, according to that bald-headed guy over there, a doctor from New York City. The girl up there at the pool just collapsed twenty minutes ago, apparently reacting to the hullabaloo down here. Our other unit is up there right now tending to her. Smelling salts was all that was needed ... and some blankets."

With the truck out of the way, Digger started allowing the traffic in both directions to pass at a creep. He stood in the middle of road waving cars on in both lanes because the desire to gawk was overwhelming. In fact, he could tell the visitors had come solely to gawk. Occasionally an Ocean Avenue neighbor would stop things to ask Digger what was going on. He was firm but polite, "We've got a crime scene, Mr. Goodyear; gotta keep moving, please."

A couple of his tennis buddies drove by in a Mustang convertible. "What gives, Diggy-dude?"

Digger leaned over the car and whispered, "Janie, one of the Virginians, was murdered on the beach right over there, but you didn't hear it from me. Gotta scoot, guys."

Skip, the driver, asked, "How's Margie?" as he pulled forward. Digger shrugged but then thought about it. *I better take a break and check on her.* He needed relief. He went back to Mike, the EMT guy.

"Mike, can I shout out again using your radio?"

Mike, sensing the good work this kid was doing, said, "Sure, here." He unbuttoned his shoulder strap and handed the whole gizmo over. "You keep it for a while. We got the truck radio and my partner's. We're all set."

"Thanks, Mike."

"Unit 19 to unit 1," he said twice.

"Go ahead unit 19."

"Can we get another unit on Ocean Ave traffic? I'd like to check on the injured at the pool and see about the deceased's friend. Over?"

"That's a four, 19."

"Buzzy, get over to the highway and keep things moving please," the chief barked.

"Dispatch? Where's my photographer, the DA, and the troopers? This is gettin' old here!" he added with a growl.

Digger saw Buzzy walking right through the crime scene to relieve him. Digger bit his tongue and motioned with his thumb that he was headed up to the hotel. Buzz thumbed up back and took over duty in the middle of Ocean Avenue.

CHAPTER 28

The scene poolside was rather colorful. It seemed as if the far side of the pool already had guests staking out their sunbathing turf and shedding some their clothes for the precious short sun time it looked like the day was going to offer. Getting a tan in Maine would not be thwarted by murder or calamity on the other side of the pool. Two yellow construction ribbons crisscrossed the pool, indicating it was closed. Two seagulls sat in the pool, and two more were up on the edge of the high diving board. They were obviously hoping for more pancakes and sausage.

The crowd gave the policeman space as he walked over toward the rail and the place where the EMTs were hovered over someone on a chaise lounge wrapped in blankets. Digger peered between the EMTs and a couple of guests tending to the waitress, who was wearing an oxygen mask. A wave of concern washed over him.

It's Margie—the poor girl. He approached and the crowd dispersed, which allowed Margie to see Digger in his uniform. She tried to get up with her arms outstretched toward him. Mrs. Stein and Evelyn held her down.

"Hold on, girl!" Evelyn turned toward Digger and stood and extended her hand to shake his. "You must be Digger."

"Yes. Digger Davenport, Ms. ...?" he inquired, shaking her hand warmly.

"Evelyn Prescott, Admiral Prescott's wife," she said, nodding toward the man in the black hat watching with binoculars.

"Your friend has been calling your name and, of course, Janie's name intermittently and incoherently."

"How is she?"

"I think a lot better now that you're here," she said as she directed his hand toward Margie's outstretched arms.

Digger moved in close, displacing one of the EMTs tending the oxygen tank. Margie began talking and moaning emphatically into her mask, making no sense. Digger rolled onto his knees and leaned over Margie and just hugged her without saying a word. Margie's gibberish subsided at Digger's silent gesture, and she began to sob quietly.

After the sobbing subsided, Digger leaned into Margie's ear. "You were a godsend to Janie, the best a friend could ever have!"

Margie interrupted incoherently. "No, no, no, I left her! It's my fault! It's my fault!"

Digger backed off his hug and gently placed his hands on both of her shoulders. "Margie, don't you dare say that! It's not true."

Mrs. Stein thought to protect Margie from this direct confrontation. Evelyn, however, held Mrs. Stein's hand and nodded comfortingly as if to tell her to let the two of them work it out.

Evelyn turned to the hotel guests looking on. "The show is over there, not here, folks!" The people quickly turned their heads back in the direction of the beach.

"Unit 19! Status check?" the radio squawked. Digger stood up and Mrs. Stein stepped into Margie's arms.

"This unit 19. The Brigantine pool area is under control. The deceased's friend is shaken but okay and stabilizing with oxygen and blankets. Over?"

"Roger 19. Photographer, DA, and troopers should be on the scene."

"Roger that."

Why would Patty tell me that information with the chief obviously listening? He pondered that question for a moment.

Evelyn approached him. "Digger, I think Margie has to be moved from this area, but I don't think she should be taken to the dorms. Got any ideas?"

Digger thought what a sad scene it would be in that seedy room with Janie's clothes all around.

"Of course. I have an idea. Can you get her to my house up on Ocean Avenue?" he said, pointing beyond the railing. "I'll call the house and let my mom and dad know what's up. Put her in the bedroom at the top of the stairs on the right. Isabel, our helper, and will be there to get whatever Margie needs."

"Perfect. The admiral and I will see to it. I'll confirm matters with Mr. Boynton, the hotel's manager and try to reach her parents in Richmond."

"Great. Thank you, Mrs. Prescott." Digger closed in on Margie for a hug. "Honey, you're coming home to my house for a little bit, and we are contacting your mom and dad. You do what Evelyn and the admiral say. Okay?"

Margie muttered "Aye, aye," playing on the admiral theme. She motioned to Digger to come closer. He bent down and she whispered distinctly, "Find the monster who did this!"

Digger grasped her hand. "Amen!" he said as if it were a three-way agreement, with God himself included.

CHAPTER 29

Digger headed back to the scene. *I wouldn't want to be the chief today, having to call Janie's parents in Richmond with the news.* He looked up as he approached Ocean Avenue. The traffic was backing up again. Then he saw the cause of the bottleneck. Buzz was having words with Chuck Branson, who was in his big black truck. Digger approached the two of them from the rear of the truck and heard, "Don't you dare threaten me, Chucky!"

Digger was looking at Chuck's face in the truck's side mirror. It was contorted with piercing, beady eyes until Chuck saw Digger approaching in the mirror. Chuck flipped him the bird and peeled out, which caused the bed of the truck to sway slightly into Digger, who raised his arms as if to say "What gives?"

He came up to Buzz and was hit with a familiar smell in the air. Waving his hand in front of his face, he asked "Buzz! New cologne?"

"Got me! It was pouring out of Branson's truck!"

"Chuck Branson had that perfume coming out of his truck?"

Buzz looked a little squeamish and retreated. "It didn't come from me. I don't know where it came from!" Buzz started to walk away quickly while motioning cars to keep moving.

"Hey Buzz, hold up for a sec!"

Buzzy kept walking away from the scene and put up his fist with his index finger pointing toward the sky as if signaling *Hold on, I'll get back to you.*

"Officer, is this the way to Blowing Cave?"

"Yes, Miss, it's up on your right," answered Digger. *That's a good sign, normalcy.*

Suddenly three matching gray Ford LTD sedans pulled up to him.

"Son, where's the crime scene?" asked the driver of the lead car.

"Right here, sir, pointing toward the ocean. If you let your passenger out here and pull it in tight there, you can park it next to the bushes. I can make room for all three cars."

"Good, we need to get at our trunks."

"Yes, sir. Let me tell the cars behind you."

Digger directed the others to pull tightly next to the bushes on Ocean Avenue and radioed their arrival to dispatch.

Six people climbed out of the cars. Two began to suit up in white jumpsuits with hair nets. Two others were in state police uniforms, and two wore crisp dark suits not usually seen in this tourist town in the summer.

Digger quickly introduced himself to get their names and functions before the chief arrived. He met the county district attorney and the state attorney general, two forensic guys from the Maine state troopers in the jumpsuits, the superintendent of the state troopers, and the county sheriff.

He focused on the guys in the jumpsuits. "Female victim, nineteen years old, who had an alcohol problem and eating disorder was sighted at approximately eight thirty this morning by that man up there with the black cap. He and a doctor, also a guest at the hotel, rushed to the scene."

"Hold it! Hold It! One-Adam-twelve," interrupted one of the forensic investigators using a sarcastic reference to the old TV show of the same name. "Hey, Sup! We got a briefing going on here," he said, pointing to Digger, who now wanted to stop briefing because the chief would go ballistic if he saw him briefing the brass.

"I'm sorry, guys, I'm getting a little ahead of myself."

"It's all right, son, bring us up to speed," the attorney general encouraged.

Digger looked over his shoulder to see the chief coming and extricated himself. "Chief! Over here!"

Precisely at that moment, the attorney general looked over Digger's shoulder, saw the satellite truck of the press corps lumbering in, and said, "Excuse me a second, let's make sure the fourth estate is settled in here."

Digger heard the oblique comment and turned back to see the satellite truck starting to park in the wrong place and put down its leveling bars.

"Chief, this is Superintendent …"

"Thanks, Digger," Chief Nickerson said dismissively.

"How are ya, Brad?" the two shook hands cordially.

"What do we have here?" asked the superintendent.

Digger drifted out of this conversation to deal with the satellite truck. As he approached, the attorney general, with the DA and county sheriff flanked on each side, were already being interviewed live. Digger shifted right to stay out of the camera's view. *This is not a good spot for interviews,* he thought. *And how in the world can they comment on something they hadn't been briefed on?*

"We are confident that with resources we are making available to Sheriff McGeary and the watchful eye of this county's district attorney, Jack Butterworth, the responsible party or parties will be swiftly brought to the fullest measure of justice," the attorney general boldly declared.

"Sheriff McGeary, can you tell us what happened here this morning?" asked the attractive news reporter.

"Tracy, as you know, when we have a criminal investigation underway, our ability to share information with the public is limited. Confidentiality is key at this stage of an investigation. More importantly, however, out of courtesy and in deference to the victim's family, we, at this point, are constrained to discuss the details."

"Thank you Sheriff McGeary, DA Butterworth, and Attorney General Bill Knight. This is Tracy Thomas for First Responder News 8 at the Brigantine Beach in Port Talbot, Maine. We will have all the coverage of this tragedy as it unfolds." She froze in a smile for a few seconds. Camera lights off, everyone exhaled, and the smiles returned to the interviewees.

Digger knew the names of the leaders interviewed. Most everyone recognized their names this summer. They were up for reelection, and their names were on signs everywhere.

He marveled at how amazing it was that politicians could blabber on and on in such an earnest manner and yet say nothing at all ... and without knowing any facts.

The candidates turned and passed by with expectant smiles as if the next person they met would want to congratulate them and shake their hands, perhaps even ask for an autograph. Digger looked beyond them and returned to police mode. He delayed a few moments to allow the Princes of PR to get some distance from the sat truck.

He held the walkie-talkie speaker to his ear and cocked his head to the side as if trying to hear instructions. "What's that Chief?" he feigned. Tracy Thomas looked at the handsome young police officer.

"Yes, sir. Immediately!" he barked to the imaginary caller.

"Ms. Thomas, I'm a tremendous fan of your work, so I'm sorry I have to tell you this, but the chief of police said this rig has got to move and move now." He served the words in an aw shucks manner with a side of lite syrup.

"You can call me Tracy, Officer. Thank you for your kind words. I'll have Walter pull chocks immediately. Tell me, Officer, off the record, what do we have going here?"

Digger knew better than to say anything but also knew to build allies. The relationship could come in handy. Plus she was gorgeous. To play this up, Digger conspicuously looked over his shoulder as if he were going to spill the beans and leaned over and said, "What do you know so far?"

Tracy said, "We've been told there is a young girl dead on the other side of those bushes and they believe it is murder. That's it!"

Digger grabbed at his speaker, "Hold it a sec, I'm getting buzzed." He twisted away from Tracy, cocking his head again toward the imaginary caller and walking a few steps away, "Yes, sir. ... Yes, sir, I did! Yes, sir, right away!" Turning back toward the reporter, he said, "I'm sorry, Tracy. I gotta run. Chief needs that rig moved ASAP."

"No ... no ... Officer. I understand completely; go!"

"There is a parking spot a thousand feet up on the right." He doubled back a couple of steps. "I'm sorry, I got to run. Do you have a card? Maybe we can talk again."

Tracy smiled and said, "Of course!" and pressed one into his palm and held it for a second too long.

CHAPTER 30

The traffic was moving smoothly. A deputy sheriff had arrived and was helping on Ocean Avenue. Digger had Patty patch him into his house telephone to talk to his mom about Margie convalescing at their home and to say that she would be delivered by Admiral and Mrs. Prescott. It was not surprising that his mother knew the Prescotts. Digger approached the chief, who was conversing with the sheriff and the DA.

"What is it, Digger?"

"Chief," he whispered, "You know I'm studying forensics. Do you mind if I observe these guys in white suits from a safe distance and make sure no civilians interrupt the scene?"

The chief looked heavenward. *Why am I plagued with such difficult things?* Loud enough for the other brass to hear, he said, "Mr. Davenport, please observe the forensic team, and be sure no civilians disrupt the scene." He gently pushed Digger back toward their activity.

Digger heard the chief say to his guests, "He's a regular Eliot Ness!"

They chuckled, and Butterworth, the DA, said, "How old is that kid? He did a great job getting us situated and briefed. Is that David Davenport's kid from up the road?" The chief gave the inquirers the details of his young hire.

Digger watched as the boys in white photographed every angle and seemingly unimportant areas surrounding the body. They outlined the body in tape, showing her exact position. They examined her hands, feet, face, lips, and sunken eyes. Something about her lips interested them. They took a swab of her mouth and placed it into a plastic container. They lifted her dress, and even Digger could see everything seemed intact underneath.

They said that she wasn't sexually assaulted but would wait for the autopsy to confirm their findings in the field.

They picked up every foreign object in the vicinity after photographing its location with a location marker. They placed the items in evidence bags.

One of the men backed out carefully and went over to the DA, sheriff, and superintendent. Digger shifted over to be within earshot.

"We're ready to lift her out. Let's have the ambulance folks come in from the south. All ingress and egress from the scene looks like it occurred from west toward the parking lot or east toward the hotel, even accounting for the witnesses who discovered her. After she is gone, we will examine the site and parking lot more carefully. We'll take some castings of tire tracks in the parking lot over there. But we need her autopsied as soon as possible. What do we know about this girl and her next of kin?"

Chief raised his hand to summon Digger over. "Digger, tell our team what you know about this girl, and let's get Patty on tracking down her parents."

"Yes sir, Chief. Her name is Jane Dunn, and she's from Richmond, Virginia. Her father is Adam Dunn, a prominent attorney in Richmond."

The chief turned to the side. "Dispatch, this unit 1. I need a 10-20 for one Dunn, D-U-N-N comma Adam. Copy that?"

"That's a roger unit 1. I have the info here at base when you need it. Anything further, unit 1?"

"Stand by, dispatch. Yes. Send over Mike with the stretcher tell them to come in from the beach to the south. Out for now."

"Copy on the approach from the south. Out."

"Janie worked right there," Digger continued, pointing at the monstrosity overshadowing their position.

"She was a waitress and lived in the dorm behind the hotel."

"Did she have a vehicle?" asked the man in white.

"Yes, a yellow 1968 VW convertible."

"Why you are a wealth of information?" asked Butterworth.

"I'm dating her girlfriend, who came up from Richmond with the deceased. So we spent a fair amount of time together."

The superintendent said, "Chief, under the interagency protocols, you're the lead, if the FBI is not involved, and I don't see any reason for the feds at this point. So I imagine you want her room cordoned off and the car impounded."

"I sent Officer Buzz Edwards up to the dorm to guard her room. We'll take the car to be impounded." The chief paused. "I got to make a call to the parents … but can you tell me what am I saying happened here?"

The man in white said, "We can't be sure of the exact cause of death, but we are absolutely sure of battery. The facial bruising and abrasion with blood is clearly consistent with physical violence by a second party. I doubt more than one person. Still, the tracks in the sand could lead one to conclude more than two people were here last night."

"Okay, we have a homicide investigation but exact cause of death unknown until autopsy results. Fair enough?" All officers nodded in agreement.

Chapter 31

By this time the ambulance crew was tiptoeing into the scene with a hand-carried stretcher. Wearing gloves, the two men easily lifted Janie's body onto the stretcher and tiptoed backward out of the scene.

The state forensic man bent over and picked up a red garment. "Super?" he called out to the superintendent of the state police. All the officers focused on the large red vest. The forensics man walked over, displaying it as he walked.

"I don't think this is hers."

"Hold it!" Digger interrupted. Using a pen, he opened the flap to reveal a Larry's Laundry tag stapled on the inside. "This belongs to one of the bellhops." He bent over to read the laundry label. "A bellhop by the name of George. He's a black male, approximately twenty-five years old, approximately two hundred pounds and five foot ten."

One of the forensic men asked, "Does he chew tobacco?"

"You know, I believe he does, but I cannot be sure," Digger replied. "I know all the bellhops live together in one dorm room. They're all African American, and I believe all of them are from Florida, but I can't be sure on the tobacco."

The chief looked at Butterworth. "We got enough to arrest?"

The DA interrupted, "Let me ask, what's the significance of chewing tobacco?"

The forensics man replied, "I'm reasonably certain that we got a Styrofoam cup half full of relatively fresh spittle within one foot of the deceased's body."

"I tell you what," said the DA after pondering it all. "We got probable cause to believe that a transient black bellhop from Florida better be taken in for his own good and possibly the good of the community as I believe we may have this poor girl's murderer. Let me get ahold of Judge Rehfuss for an arrest warrant for him and a search warrant for his living quarters and vehicle, if he has one. Chief, you have enough right now to pick up and detain. Radio me with his full name and addresses for the paperwork."

"You got it, Jack." To Sheriff McGeary, Chief asked, "Sean, you want to assist on detaining a person of interest?"

"Absolutely. I'll bring my boys as backup."

The siren of the ambulance carrying Janie away began to wail.

To Digger the chief said, "You stay with forensics and keep the scene clean."

"Yes, sir."

"Sean?" Looking at his watch, the chief said, "Ten thirty. Let's meet at the bellhops' dorm at eleven, okay?" The sheriff agreed.

To his forensic guys, the superintendent said, "When you're done here, come up to the Brigantine dorms. We'll sweep the girl's room first and wait for the warrant for the bellhop's room." To the investigation's point person he added, "Does that sound okay, Chief?"

"Absolutely. I'll tell Buzzy to keep it under wraps until they get there. And hey, guys ..." the chief added, getting everyone's attention, "Let's coordinate all comments to the press through my office. I'm not saying that I have to do the speaking, but let's speak with one voice. They'll be coming thick and fast." He nodded in the direction of the satellite trucks parking up on Ocean Avenue. There were now two more of them and some other press vehicles. From the beach they saw several tripods bearing cameras with long-range lenses.

Everyone nodded in agreement.

The DA suggested, "Why don't we schedule a press conference for four thirty today at Sow Hill? I believe we will have some answers then."

"Good idea, Jack," responded the attorney general. "That way we can say no comment until four thirty at Sow Hill. You okay with that, Chief?"

"Ten-four, gentlemen." He looked at his watch. "I gotta go call some folks in Virginia."

The powwow on the beach split up, and the camera crews on the ridge started to go mobile to intercept them.

CHAPTER 32

Digger was able to draw a little closer to the forensic guys as they made their tire molds and sifted sand and took pictures with identification cards. They folded the tablecloth and put it in a bag that they were able to seal, initial, and date. Likewise with Janie's purse, which still yielded a sweet aroma.

Digger spoke up. "Did the tablecloth look as if an altercation had occurred on it?"

The forensic guys looked at each other, and one of them said, "Hard to tell, Poindexter. What, are you studying criminology in school?"

"Yes, sir." Digger figured he better play up the soaking sponge of knowledge.

"You are onto something, son, and that's why we're photographing the sand under the tablecloth, which shows impressions not seen in the way the tablecloth was found and photographed. We're putting string around impressions so they show up in the photos. But frankly, this seems like an open-and-closed case."

"Oh, I see," Digger responded evenly.

With the casts retrieved of what appeared to be two sets of tire tracks and several shoe impressions, the forensic men indicated they were done and the tape could come down.

"I'll get the tape," said Digger. "I'm gonna head up to the dorm soon. Am I okay sitting here for a minute?"

"Suit yourself, Officer." They muttered something about the Zen of crime solving.

Digger sat right to the right of Janie's impression in the sand, looked out to sea, closed his eyes, and envisioned it was 3:00 a.m. He remembered how cold and damp it was. He tried to summon up some sort of understanding, some insight into the tragedy. He got nothing. He opened his eyes and saw more press moving to intercept the detectives. Then he noticed Chuck Branson's unmistakable truck parked in and among the press vehicles. When Digger squinted, it appeared almost as if Chuck was watching him with binoculars.

He knew Chuck had wanted this job, but surely the lobster delivery man had better things to do.

CHAPTER 33

Digger was walking through the hotel lobby on his way to the girls' dorm when he was approached by Mr. Boynton, who also went to Digger's church out on the point.

"Digger, what can we do to get back to normal here? I have the beach wrapped in yellow tape. I got the press camping out by the shuffleboard. This is gonna kill business."

Digger thought better than to speaking mind. "I understand, Mr. B. I have removed the tape at the beach. Let me see how the chief wants to handle the press. I guess the hotel is private property ..."

Suddenly there was a commotion out front. Cameramen and women in tight skirts and high heels were rushing toward the kitchen wing and the dungeon dorms.

Mr. Boynton and Digger rushed out the front door to see two beefy deputies strong-arming George out the dorms and into a waiting cruiser. A hotel towel was draped over his head to shield his identity. Reporters started shouting questions at him. "George Williams, did you do it?" "How are you going to plead?" "Who is your lawyer?"

Chief Nickerson waved Digger over. "Give me the whistle!" he said.

The chief started blowing it and telling the press to get back. Digger and Buzz joined the process of pushing back the press.

"Unless you're a guest of the Brigantine, you are a tresspassah!" yelled Chief Nickerson.

"Chief, is George Williams being arrested for the murder of Janie Dunn?" asked Tracy Thomas.

"Come to Sow Hill at four thirty for a full briefing. In the meantime, move out! Now! Or we will start issuing trespass and obstruction citations."

Tears were streaming down George's cheeks as the cruiser pulled away, which also drew the press corps away.

Chief asked aloud, "How did they know to come over to this spot, at this particular time? And how the heck did they know George's last name within five minutes of me learning it? What the heck is going on here?" he asked rhetorically.

Mr. Boynton spoke up. "Chief, if you don't know and you're the lead on this matter, that's not particularly encouraging."

The chief turned beet red and whispered toward Mr. Boynton, "This is the second murder at the Brigantine involving its employees that I have had to triage, and frankly, if you were more careful in your hiring practices, we wouldn't have to ruin your lovely spot in paradise!" Boynton waved him off, pivoted, and headed back to the breezeway and lobby.

Digger headed up to Janie and Margie's dorm room. The boys in white were dusting tables and bagging all sorts of articles. Digger stood at the tape line across the door's threshold.

"There's that smell again," Digger observed.

"Here's the source, we figure." The man held up an empty bottle of Jontue. "It looks like it spilled here and must have soaked her purse."

"Anything important here?" asked Digger.

"The perfume is important, but no, nothing much else other than hidden bottles of Jack Daniels and 151 rum. These girls are lushes."

"That was a fault of Janie's, not Margie's," said Digger in her defense.

"You're sweet on Margie, I believe," one of the detectives said as he held up a lacy pink brassiere from Margie's drawer.

Digger had heard about enough of these guys and their chippy comments but held his tongue.

"I expect Margie will need some of her clothes. When can she get them?"

"In case you haven't noticed, this is a crime scene, Officer," said the detective.

"Actually, the way you're parading through her underwear drawer, it slipped my mind that you guys are doing a homicide investigation," retorted Digger.

The other detective intervened before it escalated. "Digger ... It's Digger, correct?"

"Yeah," Digger said.

"We can sign off on some of Margie's clothing and personal effects going with you. Frank, hand me that suitcase. Is that Margie's?" he asked Digger.

"I believe so. It has a tag."

"Margie George, 8 Loudon Rd, Richmond, VA. Frank, you got any problem with Digger packing her articles on that side of the room if I give him some gloves?"

"Whatever it takes to move him along."

Digger brought the suitcase to the lobby entrance and passed by the bellhop stand where Reggie and Ethelred were sitting, both with their heads hung low. He intended to pass without a word, but his police uniform invited comment from Reggie.

"You done hauled off the wrong man, yessuh. I was *wiff* dat boy most all night. It's a shame! Dat's what it is ... a cryin' shame. No better than what we get down south. No diffent at all."

Digger intended to keep moving, but the red vest in plastic on a hanger draped over one of the chairs next to Reggie caught his eye. Without thinking, he blurted, "Whose vest is that?"

"That be George's clean vest. Every Friday and Wednesday mornings Larry the laundryman takes the dirty one from here and replaces it with the pressed one."

"So last night George's other vest would've been where?"

"Right there where's that clean vest is at."

Digger moved closer to the deck and offered his hand to Reggie. He said, "Listen—We want nothing but the truth on this matter, and I appreciate your honesty. I'm Digger Davenport. What's your name?"

Reggie looked toward Red, who continued to hang his head low. Then Reggie looked back at Digger, got up out his chair, and shook Digger's hand. "I'm Reggie. And you got the wrong man in jail today."

Red started to make a grrring noise as if to say, "Reggie don't get involved."

"Reggie, you don't have to say anything to me, but let me ask you, have you ever seen George and that Janie girl together?"

"Never, suh!"

"Did George chew tobacco?"

"Yes, suh, but he did not spit around here." He gestured at the deck. "He used a cup." He pointed toward the base of the chair where the vest hung. "He used a Styrofoam cup that used to be there." He continued pointing.

Digger had probably ten more questions but realized this was not his job and he could get in serious hot water with the chief and the DA if he somehow queered the case with a key witness. So he decided to keep moving.

"Keep the faith, Reggie. Let the process work!"

"Bullshee ... That's bullshee, man!" grunted Ethelred without even lifting his head.

Digger walked back up Ocean Avenue after dropping Margie's suitcase at the front desk and having a few words with Mr. Boynton about Margie and keeping her job. His bike was right where he ditched it. He rode home, calling it a day. The satellite trucks were gone. Chuck's truck was gone. *What's with Chuck?* he wondered.

CHAPTER 34

Margie was downstairs in the solarium, staring out to sea, when Digger walked in. She stood up and gave him a hug. "Thank you for letting me stay here with your family."

"I'd die if I had to stay in that dorm room."

Margie started to tear up. She started waving her hand at her face as if to dry the tears before they came out. It appeared to work or distract her.

"I've done enough crying for now."

"Would you like some wine or something stronger?" asked Digger. "Dad is a true Episcopalian."

"No thanks. Your mom fixed me some sweet tea, and it's just like I am home."

"Where are they?"

"I believe they are running the dogs at the long beach."

Digger looked at his watch. "There's a press conference on Janie in ten minutes. I'll get changed and be right back."

"Is it something I want to see?"

"I think so. I believe they're announcing an arrest."

"What? Who?" Janie gasped.

"George the bellhop."

"George the black guy? Oh God. I hope he gets what he deserves. Mr. Dunn is gonna flip out. They better protect George till they hang him proper."

Digger understood her emotional response but couldn't help but have doubts.

"Margie, you know Chuck Branson, the lobster guy, right?"

"Yeah, the cute lobster pot guy. Why?"

"What do you mean the lobster pot guy? He really is a delivery guy. He doesn't pull pots."

"No, ninny! Chuck is known at the Brigantine to deliver lobsters and pot!" It's underneath the lobsters! That's what Jerome told us."

Digger let this fact pass without reaction and asked, "Did Janie and Chuck ever date this summer?"

"No. Janie would talk about Chuck as if she would like to date him, but the opportunity never came up. Why?"

"I can't figure out why Chuck seems to be watching this investigation so closely."

He continued to think about it and shuddered at the recall of the sweet smell coming from Chuck's truck this afternoon. It was very much like Janie's perfume. But he kept his thoughts to himself and excused himself to change.

After changing out of his blues, he returned to the solarium where he could hear the drone of the TV. His parents had arrived and were glued to the TV, as was Margie.

"Digger, you're all over the screen!" David Davenport said. "They must've been using telephoto lenses."

Mrs. Meredith Davenport held open her arms for a hug from her only baby.

"I don't like you chasing criminals, dear. It's dangerous."

He replied dutifully if not half facetiously, "Yes, Mom."

"Enough of that." Turning to Margie, Meredith said, "Have you spoken with your mother and father yet?"

"Yes, ma'am, they're grateful of course that I am alive and wished me to express their gratitude to you directly for letting me stay here … temporarily."

"Here it is!" Dr. Davenport said, referring to the start of the press conference.

Chief was flanked on right and left by taller law enforcement people who wore Gruff McGruff mugs for the cameras.

He introduced the attorney general, sheriff, and DA.

"Ladies and gentlemen, I'm sorry to report that our peaceful community has been shattered by the murder of a young seasonal worker from one of our hotels. The collective hearts of our community go out to the family of Jane Dunn of Richmond, Virginia. Jane, known as Janie to her friends, was only nineteen years old, and was discovered dead on the Brigantine Beach early this morning. While the Port Talbot Police Department is taking lead on the investigation, every level of law enforcement in this state has come together to produce some significant results.

First, our state attorney general will comment on the forensics in the field to the extent appropriate for an ongoing investigation. Next, our county sheriff and district attorney will inform you of their actions in seeking justice for the Dunn family. Then we will take some questions. Mr. Attorney General?"

"Thank you Chief Nickerson. At nine thirty this morning our state's CSI unit arrived here from Augusta to collect evidence and piece details together. It did not take long to conclude that Ms. Dunn had died as a result of assault and battery. While we are waiting for a more complete explanation of these findings from an autopsy, foul play was determined at the scene. Thru some expert criminology, details of which will have to wait until a court hearing, a person of interest was determined. At this point I would like to have District Attorney Butterworth address the next developments."

Dr. Davenport piped in, "These guys are pretty darn sharp for little ol' State of Maine."

Digger added cynically, "Chief is letting those who are candidates grandstand this thing. The attorney general shouldn't be there at all."

"Thank you, Attorney General Knight. Based on the strong forensics at the scene of the crime, I petitioned Judge Phillip Rehfuss for a warrant to search the residence of the person of interest and also because of the transient nature of the individual and weight of available evidence, I petitioned for a warrant to arrest one George Williams of Hialeah, Florida. I commend Judge Rehfuss for his important rulings. I will present the evidence in open court in the next forty-eight hours unless Mr. Williams waives his right to a preliminary hearing as is afforded to him under Maine's law."

Butterworth backed from the microphone, nodding toward the next candidate. "Sheriff?"

Sheriff McGeary stepped up to the mic and, after birthing a pregnant pause, said with a seemingly genuine sigh, "Arresting someone is the toughest part of my job. At eleven o'clock this morning, I apprehended Mr. Williams on the grounds of the Brigantine Hotel. Pursuant to the authority of the warrant, I conducted a search of the suspect's quarters. Mr. Williams is in custody, and the justice system may now take over."

Chief stepped up, looking ever-so-slightly perturbed at the grandstanding. "Now we will take a few questions."

A crush of voices could be heard from off camera.

"Tracy?"

"Chief, what specifically was the cause of death?

The attorney general stepped in. "We are waiting for a complete autopsy before commenting more." Then he stepped back.

Chief stepped forward, "Dwayne?"

"What kind of criminal record does Mr. Williams have?"

The sheriff stepped forward. "No previous record is present in NCIS." He stepped back.

Dwayne followed. "What specifically led you to Mr. Williams? His red vest at the scene?"

The attorney general stepped forward. "The forensics include other details we are not liberty to discuss."

The give and take continued with the press and law enforcement until the chief stepped up to the microphone, held his hand up, and said thank you. The camera followed the officers' retreat into the station house. Dr. Davenport stood up and turned off the TV. "What do you think?" he asked Digger.

"I don't know, Dad. I don't feel right about the conclusions drawn so fast and so definitely."

Margie piped up, "You don't think George Williams killed Janie?"

"I am uncomfortable with such a quick conclusion. That's all."

Dr. Davenport said, "There is a lot of fact-finding yet. An autopsy and presumably a good attorney for George to test the evidence and challenge what we have heard tonight."

Looking down, Margie shook her head. "Poor Janie. I miss her. She lifted me out of my boring moods, out of my boring life. She lived life way fast, too fast." Margie was on the verge of breaking down.

Mrs. Davenport went over to Margie and rubbed her back. "I'm sure Janie is with the Lord where there is no more of the pain this life brings us."

"I believe that, Mrs. Davenport," whispered Margie. She stood into the hugging arms of Digger's mother.

Then out of the fog of Margie's emotional turmoil she offered, "There was someone running through the parking lot last night with a bundle on their back. I just remembered that weird scene." She continued looking at Digger. "You had dropped me at the girls' dorm, and when I saw that Janie wasn't in the room, I went to the outdoor landing to see if her car was in the employee parking lot. As I peered to find the VW, I noticed movement between the cars and saw what appeared to be a man with a satchel on his back scurrying between the cars and then disappearing into the woods on the far side of the parking lot."

"What kind of satchel?"

"The kind you think of a hobo having, like a blanket all pulled together at the corners ..."

"Or like a tablecloth?" asked Digger, thinking out loud.

"I suppose," agreed Margie.

"Was the person white or black?"

"He was white with dark hair. I'm quite sure. I watched him scurry under those pathetic parking lot lights. I saw his profile a couple of times. It kinda creeped me out, especially with Janie not home."

Digger rubbed his chin and cheeks as he mulled this piece of information.

"That had to be around 3:00 a.m., right?" he asked.

"At least," Janie agreed—sheepishly in front of Digger's parents.

The Davenports looked at each other in an acknowledgment of significance but didn't say anything on such an emotionally charged subject, nor wanting to correct their son in front of Margie for having such a nice young lady out at such an hour.

After some pensive silence, Mrs. Davenport said in a hushed tone, "Isabel has made a fine dinner for us. Let's freshen up and meet in the dining room in ten minutes. Okay?" Everyone agreed.

Dinner was held in the stunning dining room, which had views to the ocean in every direction through large picture windows that were streaked with salt lines from the sea spray billowing on the rocks below. To the left and right of the picture windows were smaller windows on side hinges that opened like small doors. The conversation couldn't be quiet as the Davenports always dined with several of these windows open, weather permitting. The thunk and splash of waves below caused everyone to speak up over the constant drama of the sea.

After a good hot meal, the sea air and ocean action had a hypnotic effect. Mrs. Davenport said, "I hope you'll excuse us, Digger ... Margie, but this day has been a tough one, and we are ready to put it behind us. Right, David?"

"Absolutely, love." Dr. Davenport got up and approached Margie. "Miss Margie you are welcome in this house just as long as you need to figure things out." He bent over and kissed the crown of her head like a father would. Mrs. Davenport hugged Digger and crossed to kiss Margie goodnight.

"Thank you Dr. and Mrs. Davenport. I'm feeling so much better because of your love and hospitality."

"Good night, kids. Don't be too late. Emotional stability requires rest," Mrs. Davenport gently cautioned as they rounded the corner to head to their upstairs wing.

Digger kept quiet and just looked toward the ocean, but the reflection of the room's lighting allowed only the light of the bell buoy and Boon Island Lighthouse to pierce through the paned glass on this moonless night.

Margie spoke first. "I can barely keep my eyes open. This oceanfront living knocks the tar out of you!"

"Let me walk you to your room, Margie. I'm not ready for bed. I want to sort the day's events out before crashing."

They walked upstairs together. At her oceanfront room with double twin beds, he made sure she had towels and extra blankets. Her suitcase had been picked up at the Brigantine and was on an antique wooden luggage rack with silk straps. He walked over to the widows and began to lift them. "You'll want this," he said as the noise of crashing surf filled the room.

"Really? Won't I freeze?" He walked to the bedside table between the twin beds and pushed a button on a little white box that started to glow orange.

"That's what the electric blanket is for and these extra blankets." They hugged and parted. Margie sensed that clearly something was on Digger's mind.

CHAPTER 35

Digger went to his father's study and started mapping out his observations of the day on his dad's legal pad. He appreciated learning at the feet of the state's forensic guys. The vest was an easy connection. The spit cup was also easy. The Brigantine tablecloth … easy. He couldn't help but see someone running through the parking lot with all three items … just as Margie had seen.

But that still didn't explain how Janie got on the beach. Digger said out loud to only himself, "We need to reconstruct Janie's night!"

He thought: *Martha had her at the Pharmacy earlier and believed she was headed to Ship's.* Again, speaking to himself as if it were a committee reviewing evidence, "We need to scope out the barflies at Ship's to see what we can learn about her movements."

Digger changed his clothes again to get into a local grunge look. Blue jeans and a black Rolling Stones T-shirt with the tongue logo would set the tone nicely. A Patriots ball cap backward on his head completed the image that said "Where's the pahty dude?"

Some Allman Brothers tune was wailing from the speakers as he entered Ship's. He was so out of character that he was proofed by the bouncer who normally recognized him.

"You're good, Digger," the bouncer said without making any fuss.

Digger ducked left to the big room, where the dance floor was. He wanted to avoid Rusty off the bat so as to avoid calling attention to himself. He wanted to be a barfly himself.

It was Friday night, and there was an acoustical player on stage. The atmosphere was acoustical: light, somber, clear … depressing. It seemed as if the tragedy of the day had infected even Ship's. As he stood like a wallflower, watching the guitarist, he heard a girl at the table in front of him say, "I hope he fries. Too bad Maine got rid of the death penalty."

The boy at the table said, "What do you expect? She was bombed and alone. Rusty had to kick her out." The words punched Digger. He knew such words would slay Margie.

He pretended to be engrossed in the performer to stay and glean more information. The topic changed, and Digger moved on to a new perch in the big room. He scanned the room and saw a familiar face sitting alone in a corner, Buzz Edwards.

"Hey, Buzz," Digger said as he pulled out a chair to sit. "Mind if I join you?"

Buzz quickly and unsteadily rose to his feet and slurred, "It's your sheet, I mean seat, I was just leaving."

Digger put a heavy hand on Buzz's shoulder. "Don't make me drink alone. I'm buying." Buzz plopped down into the chair, not able to muster the will to fight nor the desire to pass up free booze.

"I thought you had graveyard shift," commented Digger and then turned to a passing waitress. "Another for him and a beer for me, please."

"I worked graveyard last night, and Chief called me to work at eight thirty this morning. I couldn't work tonight. It's against union rules." Buzz was slurring his words slightly but certainly making sense. Digger so wanted to cut to the chase about Buzz's verbal altercation with Chuck today but decided to be circumspect.

"What you think of Chief's press conference?" he asked.

"You mean the campaign rally for the incumbents? It was hogwash!"

"Exactly what I thought," Digger chipped in, building commonality.

"What's with the attorney general commenting on forensics?" asked Digger rhetorically.

"This murder and a black culprit behind bars couldn't be a better godsend to those guys politically," opined Buzz.

"I'm not sure the chief likes being used for their campaign ads."

"What goes around comes around," said Buzz. "You watch. Something good is gonna come Chief's way."

The drinks arrived, and Digger threw a twenty on her and told her to keep the change. He didn't want her coming back for a while.

"I'm not sure that black guy did it," ventured Digger.

"Digger, stop it. He held up his drink, a Coke concoction, and put his hand on Digger's shoulder, drawing him toward his drink. "Drink the

Kool-Aid, unit 19! You're a team player, aren't you?" Digger wanted to throw off Buzz's grasp but played along.

"Digger, you're part of the prosecution's team, like it or not, and you must tow the party line, or this will be your last law enforcement job."

"What if I am aware of some evidence that implicates someone else?" Digger said, fishing.

"Like what? Like who? You better be very careful."

"You agree with me that if there was other evidence out there that we knew about we'd have to come forward, right? Isn't that what it means to be in law enforcement?"

Buzz took a long haul on his mixed drink as if he were about to make his getaway. Digger put his arm on Buzz's. "That perfume coming from Chuck's truck today was the same as the decedent's perfume in her purse and dorm room. That was bizarre wasn't it?"

Buzz stood up looking wild-eyed and guilty about something. "I got to go, 19."

"Why did you tell Chuck not to threaten you?"

Buzz shook off Digger's hold and started for the door.

"Brian!" Digger said loudly calling Buzz's real name. "Give me some hints. Drop some bread crumbs and it needn't be traced back to you. Dude!" He implored, "We wear the white hats! Okay?"

Buzz looked around to see who might have heard these comments and saw only a faceless crowd as he made his hasty exit.

Out in the parking lot, Buzz swore loudly as he fumbled for his car keys. Inside his vehicle he slumped over the steering wheel as his mind raced. He was a good guy! He always wore the white hat, he never stole ... He began to breathe deeply. He never hurt anyone. He never lied ... except—he paused as he reached for the pot pipe in the ash tray—for this! Buzz looked around furtively, struck the lighter and inhaled deeply as if it could transport him out of his predicament. He did it again and again.

This is Chuck's fault ... threatening me ... This is my fault! Why can't I quit this crap? Ooh, it's too late anyway! If Chuck tells on me that I use pot, I'm toast at the force, I'm toast in this town.

Another puff and pause. "I'm toasted!" He giggled inexplicably. "Buzz is toast; toast is Buzz. Far out! That could be a song." He paused in silence. Then he turned the rearview mirror to reflect his face. He looked into his own eyes, which were illuminated by the ambient light in the parking lot. He got closer to the mirror and stared.

Finally he quietly hissed to himself in a voice he rarely heard, "You are bad, you are a liar, you'll never be good, you love marijuana, you are a druggy, and you'll cheat for it. You wear a *black* hat, Buzz." He started the car and peeled out of the gravel parking lot.

CHAPTER 36

Digger rounded the corner to where the bar was and caught Rusty's eye. Rusty held up his index finger to say "Hold on, I want to speak with you." He moved down to the corner of the bar closest to the front door and yelled, "Seamus! You're on!" motioning for him to come behind the bar.

Seamus jumped off the bar stool. "Cool!"

Rusty ducked under to get out from the bar area and said to Seamus, "I'm bouncing for a while. Don't give away the store."

"Yes, sir!"

The barflies hollered and hooted as Seamus crawled under the bar to take the helm. Someone yelled, "I'll take a shandygaff!" Another yelled, "I want a pink squirrel!"

Seamus said to the crowd. "It's gonna be drafts, folks!"

Rusty put his arm around Digger as they walked out of the bar and stood outside by the front door to talk. "I'm very sorry to learn about Janie, Digger. That girl was burning the candle at both ends and the middle."

"What happened here last night, Rusty?"

"Ah … Digger, you on Port time right now? Or are we speaking as sailing buddies from years gone by?"

"Strictly as buds. I'm trying to piece things together. And frankly, I'm not sure we have the right guy … between you and me, okay?" Digger paused and looked into Rusty's eyes and held the look.

"Sure, Digger. We're tight. Janie came in about 8:00 p.m., ordered Jack and ginger, and pretty much parked herself front and center, next to big Mike, and rapidly got soused. I titrated down the Jack early on. Then about midnight, she saw me pour one without any Jack."

"Who was she with?"

"No one that I could see. I mean she left the bar a couple of times to go to the bathroom or check out the big room, but it was a quiet Thursday night."

"When did she leave?"

"Around midnight or a little later she saw me pour a ginger ale and she made a stink about it, and the folks to her left and right laughed at her, which upset her even more. She got up and fell into Big Mike's arms. He steadied her. I came out from the bar and walked her to the door. She assured me she wasn't driving and seemed relatively stable for walking purposes. Oh, as she left, Sandra came out with her purse, which stank of cheap perfume, and I draped it on her arm and shoulder. That is the last I saw of her." Rusty quietly looked at the ground.

Digger put his arm on Rusty's shoulder. "There is a criminal out there who shoulders the blame, my friend."

Rusty shrugged his shoulders, not buying Digger's attempt at solace.

Digger was about to ask his most important question when a tall, thin girl emerged from the shadows of the parking lot where she had just parked a little sports car.

Rusty commented under his breath as she approached the front door, "I guess I will definitely have to ID this young lovely." Digger snickered and then recognized her.

Speaking loudly, Digger said, "Rusty, surely you know Ms. Thomas, First Responder News. She's on your side," referring to the news channel's motto.

Rusty put out his hand to shake hers and added, "Not sure you want to be on my side. It's a little wild. Rusty's the name."

"The wilder the better, Mr. Rusty. The world is dying to be entertained," Tracy retorted. She extended her hand to Digger. "Officer?"

"Please call me Digger." Again she held it a second too long or too short depending on one's intentions.

"Shift change," announced Rusty as he held the door for Tracy.

"Hold a sec, Rusty," asked Digger.

"I'll be alright boys. You come along anytime," Tracy said coyly over her shoulder as she headed for the bar.

Digger didn't waste any time. "Rusty, did you see Chuck Branson with Janie last night? Or for that matter at any time this summer?"

Rusty raised his eyebrows and asked, "You think he's got something to do with this?"

Digger spoke with his facial expression only to say maybe.

"No, didn't see Chuck at all last night and have never really seen them together. But my birdies tell me that Chuck was physically thrown out of Sledge's last night for roughing up a young lady on the hog. He grabbed more than the ears. My vast network then reported that he stumbled out of the Patriot an hour later and headed toward town in his shiny black truck. How's that for intel, inspector?"

"Terrific, man. That would place him over here around midnight. Rusty, what can you tell me about Chuck's moonlighting in drug sales?"

"Put it this way, he has such a brisk business out of that truck that if it caught fire, the firemen would walk away stoned trying to put it out. I'm sure he has done business in our parking lot, and of course at all the hotels where he delivers lobster. Lobster for the tourists. Pot for the service workers. And he is untouchable!"

"Why is that?"

"No one wants to cross the princeling of the lobster lobby. Besides, he is probably packing a Glock under his seat. He is the Lobstah Mobstah. You remember Chuck growing up? He is twisted! You weren't here one winter in eighth grade when he darn near killed two bullies from tenth grade. He picked up two bricks and came from behind the guys and clapped the bricks together on each side of their heads. He somehow was the hero. Said it was self-defense. The boy is wicked bad. Be careful with that one, brother."

They turned to walk in together.

Tracy was standing up on the foot rail and bending over toward Seamus, who had a silver shaker in his hands and was blushing.

"No, silly, not schnapps. Vodka and then the tequila then the splash of Coke."

"I told her we didn't have iced tea," Seamus explained to Rusty.

The bar erupted in laughter. Rusty crawled under to rescue the kid.

"Is it a Long Island iced tea we're after Ms. Thomas?" asked Rusty.

"Aw, Rusty, he was doing so well!" she yelled across the bar.

Seamus was happy to get out from the pressure cooker and back to his post.

As he passed Tracy, she thrust a ten-dollar bill at him. "You were getting it, young man. Keep it up!"

"Thanks so much," he said without stopping. Her beauty was more than he could engage.

Digger sidled up next to her and signaled to Rusty and using his fingers in the shape of an N and then an A.

Rusty knew the code. It meant an NA beer in a mug. Nonalcoholic beer had just hit the markets and was perfect timing for the increased enforcement of drunk driving.

He clinked his mug with Tracy's and nodded his head toward the big room where acoustic tunes were picking along. They found an available table away from a speaker.

"You from Long Island?" Digger asked lamely.

I went to school in New York, Newhouse School of Communication. But I grew up in Winchester, a suburb of Boston."

"Sure. I have some friends at college from Winchester. I'm a big fan of your college, though. I grew up in Lake Placid; Syracuse's Orangemen were our heroes on the basketball court."

"You still in college? How did you get a police job?" she asked incredulously.

"Port Talbot hires young cops for summer jobs at dirt pay."

"You wear the uniform well. You looked like you knew what you were doing out there today. You were the one that got out the pen and opened the vest to see the name, right? Very professional."

"How do you know all that?"

"We had you all in living color on our monitors using our telephoto lenses. If we had a lip reader we could have figured out what you were saying."

"How did you know George's full name and where and when he was being arrested? That was freaky. It really rattled the chief."

"It was freaky on our end too. We got a call from our news director at the station saying someone had made an anonymous call that a raid would be made at the dorms at the backside of the Brigantine, and the caller predicted a man named George Williams would be arrested. This was well before the police started leaving the beach."

"Was it before you saw me examine the vest with the pen?"

"Absolutely. We had already sent a cameraman up to hang out by the shuffleboard area, but the rest of us weren't moving until you guys broke up the huddle on the beach."

Digger rocked back in his chair "Oh, wow, that makes no sense! We didn't know the culprit until the vest ..." His voice trailed off into silence as he remembered his present company was the dreaded media.

"Digger! That means someone knows the steps of the police before they do!"

"How can that be?"

They looked at each other and leaned in and said it slowly and quietly together, "Unless it's the killer himself!" Tracy rocked back and covered her mouth with her hand.

"Someone wanted the world to see George, a black man, get put in the police cruiser for the murder of a white girl. It's as if the killer wants to churn up the court of public opinion, not trusting the court of justice," Digger theorized.

"Your wisdom is beyond your years, Mr. Digger," Tracy said in compliment.

Ignoring the nice words, Digger looked down to think and closed his eyes to concentrate. Tracy gave him space. Finally, he looked up. "Tracy, I'm in trouble if I reveal that we didn't know the name until the vest was discovered."

"Mum's the word. Don't worry about it. Discretion is the coin of my realm."

"Fair enough, but now I need to go a level deeper. I need to disclose to the chief that an anonymous call came into the station before we knew the identity of the perpetrator."

Now it was Tracy who looked down and concentrated. Digger understood the technique of tuning out the clatter.

"Our station wasn't the only one tipped off. I'm sure channel ten logged a call too, and the *Journal*. They were all hanging by the shuffleboard waiting for you guys to catch up! I think we agree here and now that these facts that are sensitive to our respective organizations and can be established without us throwing each other in. You know what I mean?"

"Sort of," said Digger. "How can I establish that a tip came in before we IDed the culprit without saying a newsperson admitted such? Subpoenaing logs of phone calls to the media will get quashed or fought till kingdom come. I need a way to convincingly tell Chief that a tip came before we knew the name."

"Wait a minute," interrupted Tracy. "We are the dauntless defenders of the truth. It is in our companies' best interests and those of a wrongly accused person to get at this disturbing fact. All I have to do is ask whether the chief first learned the name of the culprit at the time it was seen on the name tag of the vest while we rolled tape from Ocean Avenue. That doesn't implicate you. Then I show him the date and time log on the camera we used to watch you figure out the name. Then I willingly, excitedly, *proudly* disclose we got an anonymous tip approximately thirty minutes earlier. And ask him how can he account for it. That's good journalism right there."

Digger thought about it. His boss would be on the spot, but it would also help his boss understand what took place at the Brigantine dorms today and possibly open up the investigation beyond fingering George Williams.

"Your log will become exculpatory evidence, but if it fits within your raison d'être or mission for truth, then you would willingly disclose it. Sure … makes sense," Digger reasoned out loud.

"Digger, it makes *dollars* and cents too! Listening to our station manager, I get our mission mixed up. But this will pull in viewers, a wrongfully charged black man killing a white girl from the South? Oh please, this is gonna be lead story news on a nonstop cycle; never mind the above-the-fold in print media"

"When would you explore this with the chief?" asked Digger.

"Probably tomorrow after the director approves this approach."

"Saturday," Digger said, thinking of schedules. "I'm on downtown. Chief is in and out, but the sooner the better because if this is of any value, it is to catch the real murderer, and the further we get away from the event, the harder it will become."

Tracy switched gears. "I wonder who the real murderer is? I'm sure it's a 'he' because it was a male voice giving the tip."

Digger just looked silently at Tracy and then looked away when she stared back into his eyes. Tracy bent her head and body around to get into the direction of his deflected gaze.

"Do you wonder who it is? Digger? Are you holding back on me?"

Digger threw back the last of the NA beer and responded as he stood, "Threads, Tracy, mere threads."

Tracy shot up and squarely pressed into him. "You see what I do with threads? I make quilts. I'm an investigative journalist, and our mission is the same: the truth. Let's collaborate," she said encouragingly as she put her hand on his shoulder.

He backed a half step. "I have your card, Trace. I'll call you if I need help. Good luck." And he put his hand out to shake hers for one of those long grasps.

Chapter 37

Back at his house, sitting on a bench that sat atop a rocky bluff, Digger thought through the evening's discoveries.

Chuck Branson was a person of interest in his book. Janie's perfume wafting out of his truck was not enough, though. Without more detail, Chuck threatening Buzz was insignificant. After all, what else was new for a meathead like Chuck? A white man running in the shadows of the Brigantine parking lot with a nondescript bundle on his back. It proves nothing. Chuck selling pot, while provocative, doesn't solve the murder.

If Chuck could be placed in the presence of Janie at any time that evening, that would help. And if he could somehow be placed at the scene on the beach, it would blow the investigation wide open.

Digger envisioned what it might look like: Janie stumbles along Ocean Avenue. Chuck, always on the prowl, picks up Janie and takes her to the beach. Of course! The tire casts! And how about forensics inside the truck?

He continued to think matters through. If only there was a way to go over the truck with a fine-tooth comb. It would be impossible to convince anyone in Lincoln County to haul Chuck and his truck off for examination regarding a murder where a suspect has already been apprehended.

Chuck's truck could be impounded for other reasons. Presence of contraband perhaps? Digger smiled. He remembered that instruments used in the distribution of drugs didn't just get impounded, they got forfeited under a federal law. Increasing the length of time the truck was held could be important if the lobster lobby started to weigh in.

Digger formulated his plan as he gazed out to sea.

***

Saturday morning Isabel went up to Digger's room. "Digger? Digger? Wake up, sugar. There's an important call for you—a Miss Thomas?"

He shot up and reached over to the black Princess phone on his nightstand. He thanked Isabel with a thumbs-up while saying, "Hello, this is Digger."

"Digger, this is Tracy. I just thought you might be interested in an upcoming press conference. Mr. Dunn, Janie's dad, is scheduled to have one out at Brigantine Beach at 11:00 a.m. today. We also got a press release from the Black American Defense Counsel. Reverend Justice is representing George and is planning a news conference at 5:00 p.m. today. You know about Reverend Justice, the lawyer from New York, don't you Digger?"

"Who doesn't? He be *bad*," he said in ghetto talk, referring to Reverend Justice's motto for his organization. "Anything else?"

"No, that's about it. But it's only 8:00 a.m."

"Shoot! I gotta run. Thanks for the tip."

"Sure. I'm just weaving threads here. See you on the streets."

He hung up. He got washed up and into his blues and went down the hall to check on Margie. There was no response to his knock. He gently opened the door. She was racked. He closed it and slipped out of the house and headed to Sow Hill to get his bike.

Patty was in the dispatcher's cage and looked up as Digger came in the door. She reached over to grab the *Journal* and pressed it against the Plexiglas. The headline read "Port Murder Pulls in Maine's Best Cops." The huge picture showed Janie being carried off the beach in the foreground with a white sheet covering the stretcher. The rest of the picture was Digger opening the vest with a pen like he was demonstrating something to the team of police. Patty gave a thumbs-up as she was handling a call.

He ducked into her cage to grab the paper. No question, it was a full frontal of him showing the label on the vest to all the cops. He was embarrassed to be at the center of attention. He wasn't sure how the chief would take it. The candidates would rather see *their* mugs there.

Page three had plenty of pics to make them happy: the news conference, some beach shots, and there was a nice inset of Janie, with her date of birth and date of death—such a beautiful girl.

He didn't have time to read the paper. He had to punch in, get his radio, and get downtown. At the time-clock he looked down and saw something that to his recollection he'd never seen, the night log. He opened it and started to read.

He soon deduced that it was each officer's notes of their activities that occurred during the graveyard shift. He thumbed to the last entries and saw Buzz's entries for late Thursday night through early Friday morning.

11:30 p.m.—Waited for locksmith to assist Charles Scarborough gain access to white Pontiac Bonneville (Me. Plate #MWB 621) in the 100 block of Shore Road.

12:15 a.m.—Responded to noise complaint at Sledge's Saloon. Issued Sledge third warning since July 4.

12:45 a.m.—Assisted driver and passenger of black Dodge Ram pickup truck stopped on Ocean Avenue.

Digger looked closely at the last entry. There had been alterations. White-out had been used under the words *driver* and *passenger* and under *pickup truck*. Digger held it up to the light to see if it would reveal the hidden words. Patty walked in with a coffee cup in her hand.

"What the devil are you doing, Digger?"

Not lowering the book but just squinting harder, he said, "I'm trying to figure out Buzz's entry here."

"Good luck. The night log might as well be a creative writing manual. The chief requires the graveyard guys to write something—anything to help justify the shift in case the town selectmen want to pull the budget for the shift."

"I see," he said, continuing to tilt the book in the light and nonplussed by the explanation.

He asked, "Can you figure the entry at 12:45 a.m.?" He handed the book over and picked up his radio from the charger and strapped the radio pieces to his waist and shoulder.

Patty read it aloud. "At 12:45 a.m.—Assisted driver and passenger of black Dodge Ram pickup truck stopped on Ocean Avenue."

"As I said," Patty said, "it's creative writing. It doesn't matter. No one looks at these!"

"Sure, but then why meticulously white out two entries and carefully print over the correction fluid? That takes some time and skill. I know. I do it at college all the time. It doesn't makes sense." He backed out of the area and took the log with him to the copy machine, placed it face down, copied two pages, folded the sheets, and put them in his breast pocket as Patty watched in stunned silence.

"You mind telling me what's going on here, Digger Davenport?"

"I'm not sure, Patty. It may be that the less you know, the better."

"What did Branson do now?" she asked impatiently.

"Branson? Who said anything about Branson?"

"Who else has a black Dodge Ram pickup truck in this town at that hour, Numby?"

Patty grabbed the book and reread the entry. "It looks like he whited out the identities and the plate number. Now why would he do that?" Patty's eyes widened "Was Chuck with the Dunn girl the night of the murder?" she said, gasping.

"Careful, Patty. That dialogue doesn't fit into the current campaign themes. Look, I gotta get downtown. Don't lose that book. It may be important."

"Sure, 19. Be safe out there," she said in a vacant, stunned voice.

He went to the shed to unlock his bike. A dead squirrel was pinned to the bike seat with a knife plunged through the animal's stomach and its appendages reaching heavenward. The tires were sliced as well.

He went back into the headquarters. "Hey Patty, do we have a camera around here?"

"Yeah, right here." She reached under the cabinet in the cage. "Here." She picked up a call.

Digger photoed the bike, brought the camera back, and motioned to Patty that he was driving a car into town. Patty gave the thumbs-up.

CHAPTER 38

The demeanor of the locals on the street was clearly affected by the murder. Tourists weren't really plugged into what had happened under their nose yesterday. Digger walked the beat. Those in the know treated him like a hero.

"Good job, Digger!" "Great nab, Officer!" "That was fast work, Digger!"

He would invariably reply, "Thank you. The investigation is ongoing."

He stepped into the pharmacy's phone booth muttering, "I'll say it's ongoing." He picked up the receiver and punched 411. "Boston Massachusetts, please ... Department of Justice, please ... Yes, the Drug Enforcement Agency ... Is there a tip line? ... That's it ... perfect." There was a pause. "Hello? Hello?" He pulled out a scrap of paper from his shirt and read it carefully.

"Yes, I would like to report major drug activity going on in and out of Port Talbot, Maine, and the selling of the drugs across state lines. A shipment is expected to be distributed by the principal, Charles Branson Jr. All distributions are made from his 1977 Black Dodge Ram pickup truck, Maine plate number L-O-B-S-T-A-H. His transactions will occur at hotels in Maine in the morning, and New Hampshire and Mass in the late afternoon under the guise of selling lobsters. The drugs are located under the lobsters. Caution is urged as he is believed to be armed with a Glock 9mm pistol and may have local law enforcement on his payroll. Please help us in New England fight this scourge. Thank you."

When Digger emerged from the phone booth, he waved at Alex Ruge the pharmacist and helped himself to a root beer in the cooler. He toasted Alex in thanks.

He took to the street muttering again. "The investigation is indeed ongoing." By his calculations, the FBI from the Portland office would be down here in an hour, if not sooner, with a federal APB for Chuck's truck.

CHAPTER 39

Adam Dunn, a prominent trial attorney in Virginia, came to Maine to identify his daughter and bring her home to her final resting place. He wouldn't do so without letting the community know that Janie's life was not for naught and that he would use every resource in his power, which was considerable, to bring this monster to justice. The buzz in town about the press conference out at Brigantine Beach had circulated far and wide. It had made the papers, and Mr. Dunn had invited the general public.

Chief had Patty instruct Digger to direct traffic on the exact same bend in Ocean Avenue. When he arrived, the parking lot was full. Thankfully, the satellite trucks had parked on the ridge up Ocean Avenue. Digger got out his whistle and kept the cars moving. He watched over the parking lot where he saw Tracy with her cameraman. The chief and the other brass stood next to Mr. Dunn, a very tall gentleman.

Digger wished the traffic would go away so he could listen, but the gawkers were endless. He looked up Ocean Avenue and saw Margie and his mom walking toward the press conference. Digger waved.

Then he looked the other way to direct traffic coming from town and saw the jet black pickup truck heading right for him. He looked the other way and saw a steady stream of vehicles also coming. He had no place to go. Surely Chuck was not thinking he could simply plow into him. Digger turned and faced Chuck, put one hand on his hip and stuck out his other, palm out, issuing the stop signal, and blowing the whistle for all it was worth. Chuck swerved away from hitting Digger at the last second and was laughing loudly as he went by. Digger breathed easy and spun around to watch where he went. Chuck pulled over in the same spot up on the ridge overlooking the beach. Digger checked his watch: 10:55. It had been two hours since his call to Boston.

"Digger, you almost got killed by that maniac!" his mother said when she was about to cross to enter the parking lot of the beach. Digger gave two short bursts on the whistle, which seemed permanently affixed to his mouth. He had learned to talk through it without making it whistle. He held up his hands to stop the traffic in both directions and motioned his mom and Margie to cross along with a handful of guests coming down from the hotel. Bringing up the rear was Mr. Boynton. Digger said to his mom as she passed, "All in a day's work."

"Yes, well I pray for a desk job," Mrs. Davenport replied. Margie simply patted his back as she walked by.

"Hold it, Digger, I'm coming!" shouted Mr. Boynton. "I wish my grandfather never deeded the beach to the town," he grumbled as he passed.

"Taxes and liabilities, Mr. B!" called out Digger.

"Right you are lad, right you are!" he yelled back.

Digger turned to the line of cars to his north to point at the driver and wave them on. He found himself waving at a chestnut brown Crown Victoria with tinted windows, fancy wire antennas on the back of the roof, and a spotlight mounted outside by the driver's window. The driver was in a suit and didn't bother to wave. The next two cars were identical. They pulled up only a hundred feet past Digger and pulled to the side. They all had Massachusetts plates. Traffic was flowing easily. Digger pretended to ignore the Crown Vics but stole glances at every opportunity. Surely these were his federal friends.

"Ladies and gentlemen," began Mr. Dunn, "not twenty feet behind me, my daughter was murdered by George Abernathy Williams of Florida. For those quoting me, add the word *allegedly* please … to confound the Black American Defense Counsel who would love to sue me for defamation.

"I'd like to thank the attorney general, Bill Knight, DA Jack Butterworth, and Sheriff McGeary for their quick action in apprehending the suspect. Their unwavering determination to see swift justice meted out should be an example to law enforcement throughout the rest of the country." He bowed to the brass standing beside him. Chief had said he'd rather stay in the crowd.

"I plan on bringing Janie home to her mother tomorrow for a Christian burial in Richmond. Then I am coming back to Maine for as long as it takes to ensure Mr. Williams gets what he deserves."

The crowd murmured approvingly.

"Any time a crime is committed," Mr. Dunn continued, "there are at least two victims. One of course, is the person directly acted upon. The other victim is the community in which it occurred. It is why the case is called the People of the State of Maine versus George Abernathy Williams. This is *your* case, too!" The amens started to rise from the crowd.

"This is *your* beach, *your* quiet town. Are you going to let strangers have their way with *your* daughters, employees or children?"

The crowd answered in unison with a resounding no.

As he listened from the road, Digger concluded this guy was good, and he was getting the crowd whipped up. He looked over at the Crown Vics. The trunk lids were up, and men in Kevlar vests were pulling weapons out of the trunk and getting back into the vehicles. They showed zero interest in the press conference. Digger saw the driver of the lead car on a walkie-talkie at first and then looking through binoculars, first toward Chuck's truck, but then he kept looking to the south over the Bay of Maine.

"We are all victims! One in three people has been the victim of a serious crime in America. Look to your right or your left. One of you has been attacked. Is Port Talbot going to stand idly by while crime comes to take your child?"

The resounding no was muffled then completely drowned out by the building wap-wap-wap crescendo of two Blackhawk helicopters that swooped over the crowd and then moved south toward the ridge of Ocean Avenue. The assault copters briefly showered the press conference attendees in swirling sand and engine noise that shuddered through everyone's body.

From Digger's vantage, he saw the Feds move out in their cars with gumball light-strobes flashing blue and red and move in on Chuck and his truck up on the ridge of Ocean Avenue.

Turning to the attorney general, Mr. Dunn ad-libbed, half yelling in order to be heard, "Thank you for sending a show of strength!"

The attorney general shrugged and yelled back, "Not ours!"

Some in the crowd thought it had something to do with Senator Whitten on the point until both gunships stopped and hovered over the media vans and the black truck on the ridge.

Then someone yelled, "They're busting the media vans!"

Everyone could see from the beach that unmarked cars had ascended to the site and that their drivers were outside their cars in battle position.

A loudspeaker from one of the Blackhawks bellowed, "Charles Branson Jr.—Your vehicle is subject to a federal warrant for search and impound. Remain in the vehicle. To all occupants of cars, vans, and trucks, please evacuate north to the hotel."

Immediately bodies fled from press vehicles. Some headed over the rocks and down to the beach. One cameraman back at the press conference on the beach said to his talent girl, "We're off. I lost the satellite feed," and put the camera down.

"Roll tape, Eddie, this is better," the well-dressed newscaster urged.

"Wrong camera, Stephanie ... we got nothing!" he said in a facetious tone.

At this point the press conference had been completely commandeered by the helicopters and echoing voice of doom. People had run down on the beach and were taking pictures of the SWAT operation. The brass were on their two-way radios, trying to figure out what was happening.

"Patty, can you tell me what is going on out here? We got the army or the air force trying to arrest Chuck Branson. Over?"

"Chief, I got nothing here. The telex is silent. No cross jurisdiction protocol invoked. Nothing. Over?"

"Call the FBI in Portland and see what is going on here. Out."

"Roger, unit 1. Out."

On the ridge the doors of vans and trucks were wide open and swaying from the wind caused by the helos. The only sign of life was someone sitting in a black pickup truck.

"Charles Branson Jr. exit the vehicle with your hands in the air. Exit the vehicle now!"

Movement could be discerned in the truck's cabin. Slowly the door of the truck opened and Chuck stepped out, hands held high and waving in a circular pattern as if to say, "Really? Are you kidding?" Two SWAT men approached with pistols locked in an aimed position. "Branson, put your hands on the hood."

"Whatever you say," he yelled back.

The SWAT team member pressed his neck microphone. "All clear, air support, thank you muchly."

On a three count, the choppers faded left in formation and buzzed the beach letting the taxpayers know the power of their tax dollars at work.

On the ridge, four officers were congregating around the truck with a German shepherd sniffing and barking excitedly. Two agents stood next to Chuck; one handed him the search warrant. At the back of the truck, one of the men pulled the tailgate down. The dog leapt into the bed and started barking at the tool trunk built into the bed as if the there was a squirrel hiding there.

"Keys, Mr. Branson?"

"In the ignition."

An officer reached in, grabbed them, and tossed them to the dog handler. They opened the tool trunk and dog started burying its nose in the four-foot-wide box that was about two feet deep. The dog shifted to the right corner and escalated his barking.

"Zeus! Zeus back! Good cop! Good cop! C'mere Zeus!"

The dog was drawn back, and another officer started pawing through the right side of the toolbox and lifted out a five-gallon drum marked Lobster Meat, opened the lid, and gave the other team members a thumbs-up. Chuck dropped his head and nodded at the ground.

Shortly thereafter, handcuffs were placed on him and ankle chains were attached. He was read his rights and was motioned toward a waiting car. Chuck took short, shuffling steps toward the car. Zeus was brought to the cabin of the truck, and he began to sniff for something as if his life depended upon it. "Good Zeus!" And he was pulled back and officers began rummaging through the jump seat. Zeus was rewarded with some hunks of cheese from the handler's pocket. *What a deal for the taxpayers*, thought Digger. *Mere cheese.*

By this time, Digger had moved up Ocean Avenue to the area of the ridge to hold the southbound traffic from passing through and to make sure there was a lane of travel for northbound. He saw Chief and the brass walking across the beach in his direction. This would be a scene watching these guys in street shoes climbing the rocks to get up onto Ocean Avenue.

The first Crown Vic pulled out with Chuck in the back seat and slowly approached where Digger was standing in the middle of the road as if he was part of the operation. He noticed the Crown Vic approaching and blew the whistle a few short bursts to give people a heads up to make way. He leaned over to look down the north lane of travel and blew the whistle at some people walking in the road and gave them a hand signal to make way. They moved up onto the sidewalk. The car pulled slowly up to where

Digger was waving it through and it slowed to a stop. The window came down.

"Thanks, Officer, for your assistance. Tell the chief sorry for the lack of notice. Good job on the traffic."

"Thank you, sir." Bending down to look Chuck in the eyes, Digger added, "It has been *my* pleasure to assist you." He stood up and said to the driver, "Agent sir, be careful with that one," nodding toward Chuck. "You may have more than a pot dealer on your hands." The agent reached over to a metal clipboard on the passenger seat and loosened a business card from its grasp.

"Call me"—he bent forward to read Digger's name tag—"Davenport."

Digger looked quickly at the card and held his hand out to shake the driver's.

"Agent Barnes, I'm Digger."

"Johnny," the agent said as they shook.

Chuck bellowed from the back, "Enough of the lovefest! I got a lawyer who has to be called to sue your sorry carcasses."

"Uh-oh, he can get squirrely, Johnny," Digger said, making a veiled reference to the dead squirrel Digger found pinned on his bike this morning.

Digger double-tapped the roof, a sign the police used to mean "all clear to go." Johnny pulled out slowly. The next Crown Vic pulled up and just cracked the window to say thanks. Digger gave a thumbs-up.

CHAPTER 40

Chief emerged from the beach huffing and puffing from the climb up the rocks. "Diggah, can you brief me on what is happenin' heyah?"

"I'm not sure, Chief. For some reason Chuck Branson has been watching this murder investigation. This is the second day he parked here to watch the goings on."

"I'm talking about the air force, Rin Tin Tin the dog, and Branson in ankle chains for gosh sakes! What do you know?"

"I'm sorry, I'm not sure, Chief. I think Chuck was busted for drugs or something, but why here at the murder scene I can't figure." Digger was linking Chuck to the murder scene in as many ways as he could.

As the chief left him and walked toward the vans and the remaining officers with Zeus still examining Chuck's truck, Digger reflected on the developments.

With Chuck's truck in custody, at least his connection with Janie's death could be examined. As much as he did not like Chuck, he recognized Chuck, too, was innocent of murder until proven guilty. Just because Chuck had some power over Buzz shouldn't give him a free pass out of a murder investigation. The fact that Chuck's drug dealing was being used as the lever to undo Chuck's power over Buzzy and create a level investigative field was, in Digger's mind, totally legitimate, if not a blessing to the community.

Chief and the sheriff approached the DEA agents at the truck.

"Hey, boys!" yelled Chief over the incessant barking of the dog. "What do we have heyah?"

The agent not responsible for Zeus came over to Chief and McGeary. "Agent Jason Smythe, DEA." The local fellows introduced themselves and shook hands.

Smythe began, "I'm sorry we couldn't invoke the interagency protocol. We had to move quickly." He neglected to let on that the tip-off about Chuck may have come from a dirty cop.

Chief pressed him. "We can move quickly, too. Why was the protocol neglected, Agent Smythe?"

"Ah … Chief, Sheriff, all I can say is that secrecy was invoked in accordance with federal drug enforcement regulations."

"I know those regulations. I been in this business for thirty years. You're saying our department is dirty. That's what you're saying, pal!" The chief was starting to get huffy.

The stress of the moment was interrupted by Zeus escalating his barking and hopping at the rear of the truck.

McGeary asked, "What's with that dog? He's having a fit."

"Excuse me. It usually means one thing," Smythe said, waving them to follow him to see what the dog was emphasizing. The dog seemed to be barking at the license plate. The handler said, "Where is the spare tire on this rig?"

Chief spoke up. "It's underneath there. You need the jack wrench to crank it down."

Agent Smythe was already rummaging through the tool trunk and held up a rod-like item. "Is this it?"

"Yeah," Chief acknowledged. "Let me see it." He held out his hand. Agent Smythe, recognizing the importance of getting local agency buy-in, handed the chief some latex gloves from his back pocket and handed a pair to McGeary to send a message to both of them that they were all in this together.

Chief took the wrench, inserted it in a slot in the tailgate next to the license plate, and started rotating it. Zeus kept bouncing and pouncing at the rear of the truck and caught the movement of the spare tire lowering. The dog got down on his haunches as if he was stalking prey and attempted to do the doggy version of a military crawl toward the underside of the truck.

"Zeus! Na-Kimba!" the handler barked. Zeus froze and just watched as the prey, a big black tire, kept slowly lowering toward the ground.

Digger had allowed traffic to start moving in both directions. This signaled to the media folks to start approaching their abandoned vehicles. Digger ran ahead to get instructions.

"Chief! You want me to keep the people back from their vehicles or can they return?"

Chief inquired of the DEA agents. "What do you say we allow drivers only to retrieve their vehicles and disperse the rest? Unless you're ready for an impromptu press conference on your activities. What do you want to do?"

The agents conferred briefly. "Have your officer allow drivers only to secure or remove their vehicles and keep the rest at bay. Before we go, we'll give you some briefing points on today's event."

Chief looked at McGeary and half-rolled his eyes.

"Digger, allow drivers only. Keep all pedestrians at bay. We'll have a brief statement at the conclusion of our investigation." He put his fingers in the air to symbolize the putting of quotation marks around the words *our investigation*.

"Roger that, Chief." Digger ran back to the approaching crowd.

He blew his whistle a couple of bursts with his hands high in the air. "Listen up, folks! We got three groups here, and we got to figure which is which! The first group is the drivers, *drivers only* of those vehicles."

He stood in the middle of the road and talked to the folks crowding the sidewalk. And he issued stop signals to the north- and southbound traffic. "Drivers only! Front and center! Please cross the road to retake your vehicles."

Amidst some rumbling in the crowd, twelve people filtered onto the sidewalk and crossed in front of the standing traffic. After they had safely crossed, he got out of the road and motioned the traffic to continue, then turned to the crowded group on the sidewalk. "The next group ... listen up! The next group consists of the folks taking a lovely walk along Ocean Avenue—like my mother back there. Raise your hand if you're just trying to pass to walk the walk!" Half the group raised their hands.

"The rest of you take one giant step to your right." Digger showed them what to do by demonstrating as if we was doing the hokey pokey. The crowd laughed and did exactly what he said and the other half of the crowd doing the walk started to file by Digger saying things like "Good job, Digger" and "Thank you, Officer." He gently encouraged them to stay on the sidewalk and stay away from the ongoing investigation. He turned to the remaining group.

"The third group consists of people who belong in those vans and trucks. Am I right?"

Most everyone nodded their heads in agreement. Mr. Dunn and Boynton were in the remaining group. Digger added, "Or you want to know what is going on here?" Everyone vigorously shook their heads in agreement.

"Okay, listen up! There will be a brief briefing after they're done, but I want to keep this sidewalk open, so we are going to muster on the other side of the street until the briefing occurs. If your drivers need to leave and pick you up as they go, we can handle that as needed. We'll cross on the count of three!" Digger stepped into Ocean Avenue and signaled for both lanes of travel to stop. When it was clear, he loudly counted, "One … two … three," and the crowd slowly ambled across the road to a grassy area just north of where the agents were still working.

As Mr. Boynton crossed, Digger shook his hand. "Mr. B, you want to do some PR with this crowd? I'll introduce you."

"You bet, Digger. Thanks." Boynton beamed.

As Mr. Dunn crossed, Digger reached his hand out. "Mr. Dunn, Digger Davenport. Janie was a very good friend of mine. Please accept my sincere condolences."

"Sure, Davenport, thank you. You are the officer dating Margie, right?"

"That's correct, sir." Digger looked at the burgeoning traffic. "Can you come to the house this evening about five thirty? It's up on the right just past the church." He pointed down east. "I know Margie would love to be with you," he added quickly.

"It's a date. Thank you for your hospitality."

Digger stood in front of the mustered crowd and was about to introduce Mr. Boynton and offer Mr. Dunn for some Q and A, but Tracy emerged from the small crowd of reporters. "Officer Digger, is this police action here any part of the murder investigation?"

"No comment," Digger said with an ever-so-slight smile. "Let's wait for the briefing. In the meantime, perhaps you would like to talk with the manager of the Brigantine, Mr. Boynton." Digger raised his hand to wave at Mr. Boynton, who raised his hand to wave in return. "Also, I assume Mr. Dunn is willing to take your questions. Would that be alright, sir?" Adam Dunn nodded in agreement. "Please wait here. I'll check on timing."

As Digger left the little feeding frenzy that he created, he heard comments like "This guy is great." "How old is that kid?" "My daughter should meet him."

At the back of Chuck's truck, the spare tire had been dragged out and a black bag that was pressed into the wheel cavity had been partly ripped open to reveal dry green and gold vegetation. Poor Zeus was subdued about three feet away, having been given some bizarre command, but he wanted nothing more than to roll in the contraband and celebrate his discovery.

The DEA agent said, "We have about sixty pounds of pot, about a hundred thousand dollars' worth of street sales, in one truck. That was a great tip!"

"This bust was based on a tip?" asked the chief.

The agent said, "Between us chickens, Chief, we have been following the flow of marijuana into Maine through its ports and its movement southwestward. We had been narrowing the activity down to north of Portland and south of Penobscot Bay. And then, yes, we got a tip early this morning—a very informed tip. Based on that and how it corroborated our findings from the field, we got a warrant signed by Judge Ambrewster for this truck."

Digger had come upon the group as they were mentioning the tip. His gut tightened. The chief asked him, "How we doing? Crowd under control?"

"Yes, sir. I have them corralled right over there, awaiting some sort of briefing."

"Agents? Who wants the honors?" asked the chief.

The agent in turn posed his own question. "Chief, can you secure this vehicle? Under federal forfeiture laws, this truck fits squarely within the 'use and aid' provision of the law. We would want it secured until the underlying criminal charges are disposed of."

McGeary spoke up. "We can take care of it at the county garage."

"We'll figure it out," Chief said to Sean, not conceding the issue. "I'll have Patty get the wrecker here and tow it to the Sow Hill lot for the time being."

"Who is gonna brief the flock of seagulls over there?" he asked again, nodding toward the press.

"We're pretty much a no-comment agency until after conviction," said the agent. "So if we lead the briefing, it'll be over in seconds."

The sheriff volunteered. "I'll lead it, but what are you comfortable with me saying? Can I say that as a result of multi-agency efforts, a major drug bust has been effected and that any other comment will have to wait?"

"Sure, that's good. It's multi-agency now," the agent agreed.

"Can we mention the poundage estimated and the name of the person arrested?" Digger asked.

The agent commented, "This guy is Johnny-on-the-spot. Yeah, those facts are okay to provide. Say the weight is just an estimate."

"Listen," he said to the chief and the sheriff, "We're gonna seal this stuff up. Let Johnny here witness us packing up the contraband, and you and chief brief the seagulls."

To Digger he added, "Johnny, you are over eighteen, right?" They all laughed, including Digger, who considered it an honor to be so young and at the heart of such important law enforcement activity.

"Yes, sir. You can call me Digger … or Johnny…whatever works for you."

The sheriff approached the crowd and spoke up. "Ladies and gentlemen … Hello, folks!" he said louder. "Let's gather around." Mr. Dunn was still in the crowd.

"First I want to recognize Mr. Dunn by saying we are sorry the message you were so eloquently conveying was cut short by yet more criminal activity on our streets. Nothing can be more important to us in the law enforcement community than bringing justice for the Dunn family at this time."

Adam Dunn gave a thank-you salute to the sheriff and the crowd, but he clearly looked deflated and exhausted.

The sheriff continued. "Due to the sensitive nature of this particular investigation, we are going to have a short briefing here. What I can tell you is that you all witnessed the arrest of one Charles Branson Jr. for the possession of the largest amount of Cannabis sativa we've seen in our town. In intercepting this material, we have prevented approximately one hundred thousand dollars of marijuana from being dealt on the streets of our community and affecting the minds of our children." The sheriff obviously had a silver tongue and couldn't have hoped for a better two days of campaigning.

Digger asked for some gloves. "Did you find a Glock?"

The agents looked at each other. "Who said anything about a Glock?"

Digger smiled slightly. "I think Branson has been known among the locals to be packing a 9mm Glock."

"Yeah, we got the Glock and no concealed weapons permit either, so that's another charge. No permit, no right to bear this arm. What else do you know about this defendant?" asked the agent coyly.

Digger thought he'd play along the edge with the agents. "I'll tell you one thing, hotel employees up and down the coast are gonna be upset by your actions today."

The agent added, "You mean the ones in Maine in the morning and New Hampshire and Massachusetts in the late afternoon," almost parroting the language of the tip.

"Exactly. How'd you know?" asked Digger.

"A birdie flew in the window of our Boston office and sang a sweet tune."

"A birdie that would be protected like an endangered species if it were discovered?" asked Digger coyly.

"That's the way we fly, right Mike?" the agent said to Zeus's boss.

"Like birds of a feather," Mike affirmed.

Changing the subject, Digger warned, "He'll post bail no matter the amount because he is the princeling of the lobster lobby around here."

'Say … given the tip we got this morning, is this truck gonna be safe at Sow Mountain?" asked the agent.

"I don't think the truck would go up and missing, but I couldn't vouch for the contents. Just this morning someone went in the police shed on Sow Hill and stabbed a squirrel, pinning it to my police bike seat, and slashed my tires."

The agents stared at each other in silence.

"Do you mind if I double-check the cabin for evidence of something else?" he said as he put on the gloves.

Again the agents looked at each other, wondering who is this guy?

Mike said, "Sure, Digger, what are you looking for? We'll help you."

"I'm the only one on the force who presently thinks this vehicle and the defendant were involved in a murder two nights ago, and I want to secure any incriminating evidence before it is lost. By the way, the chief would have my head for venturing out this far, but until now the lobster princeling has been invincible."

"Let's see what we can find here," said Mike, handing Digger a small, powerful flashlight.

He looked under the passenger seat, and immediately a shiny cylinder reflected the light.

"Mike?' Digger called.

"Yeah, what do you have?"

"Not sure. Need some corroboration here. What is that under there that looks like a lipstick case?"

Mike took the flashlight and reached under and pulled out a lipstick. Digger handed him a plastic bag. "That could be key. What do you say we keep this and run the prints from Portland?"

"Sure," said Digger.

"What else we got?" They pushed the passenger seat forward to get access to the jumbled back jump seat filled with junk and started pulling stuff out slowly.

Digger asked the other officer, "You smell anything?"

"Yeah, cheap perfume. What is this guy, a cross dresser?"

"No, that's Jontue perfume. The decedent spilled it the night she was murdered."

"We can't really bag that up, so hopefully what we find physically will be of assistance."

***

"We can take a few questions now finally," said the sheriff.

"Tracy? I guess you're always the first responder," he said with a kindly smile.

"Thank you, Sheriff. May I quote you?" everyone laughed.

"You may, indeed."

"My questions are for Chief Nickerson, if I may?"

"Absolutely," the chief retorted, stepping forward.

"Chief, is it safe to say the identity of the suspect in Miss Dunn's murder was revealed when the vest with his name on it was positively identified?"

Sensing a trap, the chief chose his words carefully. "There are many items of evidence that support our arrest yesterday. What specifically are you getting at?"

"Chief, do you remember at the time of the arrest at the dorms you were surprised by our presence and our knowledge of the suspect's last name?"

"Yes! Uncanny, you investigative journalists! I should put you on my payroll." A little rumble of laughter came from the crowd.

She continued. "Assuming your identification of the suspect was at the time of discovery of the vest, we filmed that event at 11:00 a.m. However, approximately thirty minutes *earlier* our station got a tip over the telephone that a raid was going to occur at the bellhops' dorm of the Brigantine by mid-morning. Can you tell us how the identity of the murderer or his place of arrest could be predicted and revealed to us before you fully realized who it was or where you would apprehend him? Who could make that call?"

The chief looked at the sheriff. They both started to stammer, but the chief prevailed. "Tracy, I'd say your call logs are some sort of evidence at this point. Please don't destroy them."

From the rear of the crowd, Mr. Dunn spoke up. "It sounds as if Mr. Williams may have more than one enemy. Perhaps one of his co-workers is seeking to make sure he is apprehended."

The law enforcement people began nodding their heads in agreement.

Tracy spoke up. "Or could it not mean that the true murderer was trying to make sure there was extensive media coverage of the African American that he was framing for the crime?"

The members of the media started writing furiously on their pads, and the cameras were filming in every direction according to who spoke up.

Dwayne, from a competing station, asked Tracy pointedly, "Are you insinuating that George Williams is innocent and is sitting behind bars wrongfully?"

Tracy answered quickly. "Dwayne, being a first responder requires us to ask the tough questions. The answers are with law enforcement."

Everyone looked to the officers for guidance.

The sheriff stepped forward. "Mr. Williams is innocent until proven guilty in a court of law by proof that is beyond a reasonable doubt. Thus far, based on all available evidence, there was sufficient evidence to allow a judge and arresting officers to conclude that there was probable cause to believe that George Williams committed the crime. When there is that degree of evidence, it is simply enough to detain him, to take his freedom away until bond is posted, or if bail is denied, until a trial is had where a greater degree of proof would be required to convict. So based on the evidence before us, Mr. Williams is right where he should be."

Digger signed some evidence slips attached to the now-sealed bags of marijuana, the Glock, and the lipstick case. The agents bagged up some innocuous items, including sunglasses, matches, and the contents of the ash tray.

"Digger, if your suspicions have any merit, you need to be able to place the defendant at the murder scene."

"Well, now that we have the truck, I plan on having the tire track casts compared to these to see if we have a match."

Mike looked at the tires. "They don't look new, so you might be in luck."

"I think we're done here. I got to feed Zeus some steak. He did a great job."

Zeus understood perfectly and bounced up for action. Mike walked to the back seat of the third Crown Vic, led him into it, and turned on the car for its air conditioning. Just then the tow truck pulled up. The agent said, "You got this?"

Digger said, "Yeah, thanks for your help."

"We got your back son. Good work." Mike pointed to the surroundings. "The best location I've ever busted anyone in my entire career, Digger. Oh, and thank the brass for us," he said, nodding toward the impromptu news conference, "We're outta here."

"Will do, and I'll get with you regarding the prints on the lipstick," Digger said. They gave thumbs up as they pulled out and headed south on Ocean Avenue.

The tow guy pointed at the truck. "Do I have the honor of towing the lobster king's truck?"

"Ten-four."

"What? Did Chuck break down? Is he here? He'd have my head if I just took his truck."

"No it's been impounded by the DEA. Let me double-check where Chief wants it."

Digger walked down to the press briefing in time to hear Tracy talking about what it means to be a first responder. *Whoa* he thought, *this is delicate.* As the sheriff offered his long-winded legal reason as to why Williams belonged in jail, Digger whispered in the chief's ear, "Do you want Branson's truck towed to Sow Hill?"

Chief looked back up the hill and saw the lift being put under the truck. The sheriff had come to the end of the explanation, so Chief put up his hand and pronounced an end to the questioning. "Thank you!" He then put his arm on the sheriff to turn him and bring him away from what had started as a feeding frenzy by a flock of seagulls but had devolved into a school of piranhas. All three lawmen turned and walked briskly from the chummed waters.

Mr. Dunn's voice rose above the crowd. "What the sheriff has underscored is that jail is the right place for George Abernathy Williams …"

As they walked, Chief said to McGeary, "Let me hold the truck. I think Senior will feel slightly better knowing it's close at hand."

"Sure, Chief. Last thing I need is to have the lobster lobby working against me this campaign."

Chief barked to Digger, "Tell 'em Sow Hill and leave the keys in the ignition. I'll secure shortly."

Digger lingered. "What was that briefing about? It sounded more like a class in Con Crim Pro … I'm sorry … a course in Constitutional Criminal Procedure."

"Well, tricky Tracy, the newscaster has a theory there is another killer out there and threw some gas on the fire. We'll have to follow up the leads," responded Chief Nickerson.

Sean McGeary mopped his brow. "I don't need another killer out there; thank you very much."

Digger left that comment hanging and ran ahead to the tow guy to tell him, "Sow Hill it is!"

Not wanting to mix it up with the chief and the sheriff, he yelled back at them, "Chief, I'm headed home this way, okay?" The chief just waved for him to go on. When he got some distance, he looked back. The two men were climbing in the tow truck to get a ride back toward Brigantine Beach. They were avoiding the rocks and also avoiding walking through the gauntlet of the press. Either could be treacherous.

CHAPTER 41

Digger realized he had a lot to be grateful for as he walked home along Ocean Avenue. He punched a fist in the air upon recalling the high drama of Chuck getting hauled off for peddling dope. It's not that he didn't have friends who smoked pot, nor did he escape the peer pressure at his day school in Lake Placid. In fact, from a law enforcement perspective, it seemed there was much less carnage from pot than from alcohol: the domestic violence, the drunk driving, and the broken families. It seemed that the socially acceptable drug was more socially disruptive. But it wasn't his call.

The drug laws were to be enforced, and he would do his best to not be a phony about it. Besides, Chuck deserved every bit of what lay ahead including booking, parent telephone call, arraignment, jail cell, bail hearing, press inquiries, trial, conviction, sentence, and jail time.

Digger started to delight in Chuck's apparent downfall. *After all*, he thought, *he has been gunning for me ever since I can remember.*

He reminded himself that the goal was to bring to light Chuck's involvement in Janie's death. He knew in his gut that they had been together that evening. Between the weird behavior of Buzzy when the subject of Chuck came up, Buzz's "corrected" entry in the night log, and the unmistakable odor of Janie's perfume in Chuck's truck the next morning, it all coalesced in Digger's mind to implicate Chuck.

This walk home was helping him. He needed to get Chuck's tires checked against the casts taken at the beach.

It's not like I could just go to the chief and say I smelled Janie's perfume in Chuck's truck—let's check his tires. Also by the way, Buzzy, your full-time officer of two years, is covering for him. No ... that could seriously backfire. It's best if Chuck's involvement comes out without his pushing it.

The log book? A casual request by the state forensic guys to check the cast against the tire of trucks in the impound lots? A confession by Buzzy identifying Chuck in the center of things? Maybe that would work given Chuck's new predicament. How would the chief take a call from the FBI that an item in Chuck's truck was linked to Janie?

Digger assumed the Branson kid being named in a murder charge would blow the town apart and would be resisted unless evidence was compelling. He thought about the nature of circumstantial evidence, how someone's life can be changed dramatically just by the presence of granules of sand on a shoe, lipstick on a collar, or zigzags of a tire track. He loved this stuff.

CHAPTER 42

Chuck's trip in the back of the Crown Vic with Agent Johnny Barnes was a regular game of cat and rat.

"Tell me about yourself, Charles."

"Why? Anything I say can and will be used against me. Why don't you tell me about yourself, like where do you live? Are you married? Got any children? Where do they go to school? You know, the regular things people chat about. You go first."

Johnny thought he had a real piece of work on his hands. "To begin with, I am single, and my favorite thing to do is hunt. I like to use firearms but much prefer the knife and stalking the prey up close and at night, if in season. And you, Charlie?"

Chuck, sensing the game, didn't want to play. "Up yours!"

The car pulled into the county's jail at the Batson River facility, where all arrestees were processed and held for court proceedings. Agent Barnes pulled through the wire fence, which opened upon hand signal to the gatekeeper. County sheriffs emerged from a metal door and held it open to process the new detainee.

Chuck emerged from the back seat and saw the first deputy. Chuck greeted him, "Good day, Billy! Fancy seeing you here."

Billy looked a little scared. "Hu ... hullo, Chuck!"

"Don't worry, Billy, we're tight," Chuck muttered.

Agent Barnes, grabbing Chuck's arm, pushed past Billy saying only, "Friends?"

Barnes's job was to process the arrestee, arrange for some phone calls, and see that Chuck got placed in a holding cell.

"We going to find these prints on anything else in town that needs solving?" agent Barnes asked as he pressed and rolled Chuck's fingers on the ink pad.

"Not unless you're trying to solve where to get the best lobster in town."

Johnny pressed an intercom button. "We're done here. Mr. Branson is ready for a nap. You got a cell mate that can sing softly?"

The plastic box on the wall squawked back, "First we got to get him in his fresh orange jammies and slippers. Then yes, we got someone who will sing some gospel spirituals to soothe his drug-dealing soul. We'll take him from here."

"Hey, I get to make some calls, don't I?" asked Chuck.

Johnny pressed the intercom. "He wants to call someone before his nap. Can we accommodate that?"

"That's a four. We'll take care of that."

The heavy metal green door opened. "Mr. Branson?" a large guy with a shiny bald head and wearing a gray uniform inquired.

Johnny nodded. "I'll need my shackles. We're winning the war on drugs."

The bald jailer said, "We got him from here. It's pure sport if they try to run from this point on. Thanks for what you do, Agent Barnes. It keeps us employed. Be safe out there."

"It's my pleasure," Johnny said seriously as he headed toward the door on the opposite side of the room.

"Door two clear," said the jailer into his radio set.

"Okay, Mr. Lobstah, head to the left. There are some phones on the wall and some phone books on the tables. You got ten minutes."

Chuck dialed his father's office. "Marty, is dad in? It's Chuck."

"Chuck! Are you okay? Where are you? Your dad went to Sow Hill. He's furious. It's all over the news channels. Helicopters? What the heck?"

"Marty! Marty! whoa there, girl. I'm in the Batson River facility. Can you call over to Sow Hill and see if you can get Dad?"

"Sure, Chuck. Hold, please. Let me see about patching you two together."

The line went silent. Chuck started thumbing through the yellow pages of criminal attorneys. The pages were dog-eared and some torn out.

"Chucky?" the gravelly voice inquired.

"Pops?" Chuck answered in a humble tone.

"What the heck is this all about, son? I can't believe the newsreels. Helicopters? What in the devil's name is this about?"

"Dad, they're trying to bring us down. It's a setup. Someone planted some pot on the truck and called in a tip. It's crazy."

"Who is 'us?' Are you saying someone is after me? For what? I'm a businessman. Whadya talkin' about, Chucky?"

"The fellas at Cape Harbor don't like our lock on prices and figure they can break us with this."

"What are you talking about, Chucky? The harbor master is with us. He would've alerted me to something. I got nothing, Chuck. Nothing! No. I'll tell you what, this is your crap. The harbor boys aren't gonna put 100k worth of nothing in anyone's truck for a betta price on lobstah. No. Chucky, you made some enemies and they're calling you on it. This is a different day, Chuck. The drug war is serious. Your mother is spinning in her grave over this."

"Aw Pops, please!" Chuck urged in a harsh whisper.

"Seriously, Chucky, this is bad. Bad for you, bad for me, bad for the company. Gordy already called telling me that forfeiture laws could reach into the company property. Is there any of that crap at the warehouse?"

"Dad! Stop! One, these phones are not secure. Two, I told you this is a setup! Now I need an attorney and quick! I need to be bailed outta here. I know we can beat this rap, but I gotta do the battle on the outside. I'm looking in the book and see Charlie Tremaine. Didn't he help us with that unlicensed charge outta Augusta?"

"Forget him. He's administrative law. You need Peter Coffey. He's the best. He's in Boston but admitted in Maine and New Hampshire. Marty? Marty? You on the patch?"

"Hello? Mr. Branson? Yes, this is Marty."

"Marty, check the Rolodex for Peter Coffey on Comm Ave."

"Yes, I got it. How do you want it?"

"Can you tie in a fourth line?" asked Charles.

"Yes, I believe I can. Please hold." Everyone was momentarily cut off from one another. Chuck loudly whispered yes to the wall.

"Go ahead, Mr. Branson; Mr. Coffey is on the line."

"Peter!"

"Charles? Where's my lobster on that hockey game?"

"I got your lobstahs up heyah and I have a feeling you're comin' up. Chucky, you on?"

"Yeah, Dad, I'm here."

"Chucky, tell Mr. Coffey your predicament."

"Hold it, guys. Chuck, are you in a law enforcement facility?"

"Yup. Batson River facility."

"Okay, don't tell me nothing. I'll ask questions—simple questions. I want simple answers. Ready?"

"Ready."

"What are you charged with?"

"Possession with intent to sell, and possession of a concealed firearm without a permit."

"What time were you arrested?"

"About noon."

"Warrant?"

"Yes to search. Not to arrest."

"Search only?"

"Yup. Search only."

"It's a tip. You got some enemies, Chucky. Then they arrested based on discovering stuff?"

"Yup."

"How much?"

"I don't know. It was planted."

"Peter, can you help us?" the father pleaded.

"Of course. I'll get a bail application going right away and be up there by 4:00 p.m."

"Thank God. Chucky, sit tight," Charles said.

"Charles, can I reach you through Marty?" inquired the Boston attorney.

"Yes, sir, and thank you for jumping on this."

Everyone hung up.

The guard stepped forward toward Chuck.

"Nap time! Put these on, Tinkerbelle," the guard said as he handed the orange prison pajamas to Chuck.

Chuck was ushered down a bone-colored hallway with grimy bone-colored bars on individual cells with two and three people in them. Someone mentioned Chuck's name, but he didn't react. His mind was on the next part of the experience, his cell mate.

The guard used a strangely shaped brass key to unlock the last cell on the left. Chuck breathed a sigh of relief, *No one else was in the dark cell.*

Then he discerned movement on the bottom bunk. Chuck squinted and still couldn't see anyone but an orange jumpsuit.

"Chuck Branson, meet George Williams. Mr. Williams? Meet Chuck Branson. I'm sure you'll get along famously."

CHAPTER 43

Digger walked home from the eventful morning on Ocean Avenue and had lunch with his mom and Margie. His mom commented on how she had never seen so much crime in the Port as this particular summer. Margie agreed. It was keeping Digger away from home. Digger mentioned that Mr. Dunn was coming over at 5:30.

Mrs. Davenport said, "Digger, I wish you would coordinate with me. Pastor Brad and Tina are coming over at 5:30, too, for dinner. We were going to discuss the sea wall renovation at the church."

"I'm sorry, Mom, it just seemed like the right thing to do at the moment."

"And it was," his mom agreed. "We can make the swordfish go around a little leaner."

"I should get back to work. The Chuck Branson arrest could make things busy at Sow Hill."

Both ladies commented on the drama they witnessed on Ocean Avenue and how it sucked the life out of Mr. Dunn's press conference. Digger gave each woman a hug. Margie held him longer and caught his attention as Mrs. Davenport left the room on cue. "I'm going back to the Brigantine tomorrow. If I don't like the dorms or work, I'm headed back to Richmond."

"Are you sure you're ready for that? There's no rush. You can relax here."

"I know, thank you. You are so busy with work, and your mom and dad are really busy. And I am ready to be busy, too. When it goes slow, I get depressed thinking of Janie and her final hours. I think getting back to work will be good. Who knows—having an ear on the inside of the Brigantine may prove very useful."

"Hadn't thought about that. That's a good point. Let's enjoy our last night at the house together and have a bonfire down on the rocks. You want anyone to come over?"

"No thanks, I'm gonna be fine with your parents' guests and Mr. Dunn. Then maybe some cuddle time with you alone will be what the doctor ordered."

"Deal," Digger said. "See you after work."

CHAPTER 44

Digger rode down Ocean Avenue on his own bike to where his Jeep was parked, loaded his bike on the rack, and drove back to Sow Hill. There he saw Chuck's truck in the so-called impound lot. The lot was created when the town constructed a huge water tower on top of the hill and wanted to keep kids from climbing the 120-foot metal structure by encircling its perimeter in a ten-foot chain link fence. The tower was a sore subject in town during its siting and building twenty years ago, but when it was completed and the lobstermen and other boaters could see the tower from the ocean and its red light became a navigational aid even though it was two miles inland, it became a beloved item. The town then painted its logo, a lighthouse with five flags behind it, each flag representing the jurisdiction that controlled the town since the time of the Indians.

The town parked the harbor master's boat there in the winter and various other law enforcement toys like the DARE trailer and the chief's snowmobile.

He saw the chief's car in his parking spot and then saw Mr. Branson pulling out in his Mercedes with a grim look to his profile. Digger was glad he had missed that moment at the station.

He walked in to a somber setting. Chief was at his desk with his arms propped at the elbows, resting his head in his hands and rubbing his temples. He didn't even look up when Digger entered the foyer of the station. Digger looked over at Patty, who picked up a magazine and buried her face in it, which meant don't come over here.

He went back to the punch clock and radio charging station area where he immediately noticed the night log was missing. He put the radio on the charger, returned to the foyer, and walked into the chief's office.

"Hey, Chief, how are you doing?" he asked softly.

Not good, Digger. I had to fire Buzz Edwards today."

"What? Why?"

"He has been caught falsifying police records."

Chief had the night log on his desk with a bookmark poking out. Digger's stomach tightened. "I'm sorry to hear it, Chief. Anything I can do to help?"

"Well, until I can replace him, I may need longer hours from you."

"Sure, Chief, whatever you need."

"This summer, Digger, is the bummer summer of '78. I'm telling you ... a murder? A DEA bust on Ocean Ave? Helicopters? Are they serious? Charlie Branson's boy carted off in ankle chains? A Port Talbot policeman altering potential evidence?"

Digger thought better than to inquire for details and just let the chief continue.

"The press is telling me facts about my case! What is up with that? It's the bummer summer of '78, I'm telling you! And what is going on with the dead squirrel stuck to your bike? Who has the guts to come on police property to pull a stunt like that? You issue a ticket to some irate Canadian? Who did that, Digger?"

Digger confessed, "Chief, the only person that's openly hostile to me is Chuck Branson. We've never been friends, but this summer he has anger toward me that's on steroids." He didn't know exactly where his transparency would take the conversation.

"He got his today and is gonna be madder than a wet hen," Chief said.

"Maybe he can mellow out in jail on those drug charges ... I would think."

"His dad was just in my office talking with some hotshot attorney from Boston who expects to bail him out at 4:00 p.m."

"Which attorney?"

"Coffey?"

"Peter Coffey?"

"Yeah, you know him?"

"I go to school with his son. His dad came and spoke to our Con Crim Pro class."

Chief's brow furrowed.

"Sorry ... constitutional criminal procedure. You think they'll let him out on bail?"

"Absolutely! The federal magistrate in Portland is a former civil rights attorney. It's certain."

Digger looked at his watch. Chief picked up the signal and concern on Digger's face.

"Digger, what do you know about Buzzy and Chuck the other night?"

Digger wasn't sure whether Patty had thrown him in regarding the night log or whether sharing his concerns would hurt or help.

"All I can tell you, Chief, is that when Buzz was directing traffic at the murder scene, Chuck pulled up and stopped traffic to talk to Buzz. I was approaching from the rear of the truck, and I heard Buzz say, 'Don't you dare threaten me.' Chuck looked at me in the rearview as I was approaching the driver's door and where Buzzy was standing. Chuck punched the gas pedal and peeled out, almost hitting me as the car spun out and slid my way. I asked Buzz what it was all about, but he hasn't wanted to talk about it."

The chief didn't let Digger know what he was thinking, but said, "Charles and I have been friends for forty years. This business with Chucky … I hope it doesn't get worse before it gets better." His voice trailed off as he grabbed his hat and walked toward the door. "I can be reached at home," he said with a sigh as he walked out, leaving Digger standing at the front of the desk. Chief gave the home sign to Patty as he walked out the front door.

Digger went over to Patty, who was removing her headset and getting up out of her dispatch cage.

Patty put her finger to her lips, mouthed the word *shh*, cranked her head toward the chief's office, and starting walking that way.

She reached across the desk, grabbed the night log, turned to the bookmarked page, and began to speak in an official monotone as if reading from a manual. "It is the dispatcher's duty to monitor and maintain the integrity and security of the night log."

Digger looked down and squinted at the entry. The white out had been removed to reveal the names Chuck Branson and Jane Dunn.

"I knew it! That's proof right there! How did the white out come off?"

Patty again put her finger to her lips and whispered, "Ancient Chinese secret."

Digger put his nose to the page and sniffed. "Acetone!"

Patty buffed her nails on her blouse then looked at their shine, "There's a hundred and one uses for nail polish remover!"

She shut the book and pulled Digger by the sleeve. "Let's get out of Chief's office."

Patty explained how she had taken it upon herself to "maintain the integrity of the log." And when Chief came back from eating lunch and locking the truck in the tower lot, she showed him the before and after of the log.

"He stood up from his desk, his face a whiter shade of pale, and told me to get Buzzy to the office immediately. I reminded him it was Buzz's day off. He yelled like I haven't heard in five years. 'I don't care if he is on his death-bed! I want him here now!'"

"I reached Buzzy by phone. He sounded out of it. He agreed to come over, and when he did, his eyes were bloodshot and he had a very subdued demeanor … like he was on something. Chief took him into his office. I couldn't hear everything, but I did hear the chief say something about altering evidence. Buzzy came flying out of the office like a shot out of a cannon and just kept going out the door! Chief fired him on the spot."

Digger remained quiet, rubbed his chin, and mumbled, "Poor Buzzy."

"Did you say poor Buzzy? Digger Davenport! Don't you start feeling sorry for a pot-addicted cop! Who, by the way, is covering a potential lead in a murder case. Poor nothing! How bout poor George Williams?"

Chapter 45

"What they get you for, Mr. Chuck? Possession?" George Williams inquired of his new cellmate after a long, awkward silence of the two in the cell. Chuck didn't answer and surveyed his surroundings nervously as if he hoped for an exit.

"Don't worry," said George. "I'm a friend of Reggie's at the Brigantine," referring to Chuck's middleman for dope dealing at the hotel, one of the other bellhops. His eyes widened. He put his finger to his lip to say, "Shh," and motioned to the walls as if they had ears.

Finally, Chuck spoke up after thinking things through. "What are you here for?" he asked, feigning ignorance.

"Shoot, man! Haven't you heard? I'm the Brigantine murderer! I'm the sorry black-'n'-shellacked bellboy who raped and killed the pretty white southern belle!"

"Rape? You're charged with rape?" interrupted Chuck in disbelief.

"Oh, they're gonna try to solve a few rapes and murders with my sorry carcass in here. But what they don't know is that I got justice on my side. Reverend Justice from New York has agreed to be my lawyer."

Chuck quickly responded, "You're not talking about the guy with the Afro that represented the guy that played for the Celtics, are you?"

"One and the same," George assured his newfound friend. "He is a Harvard Divinity graduate and a Yale Law School graduate, yes sir! He started a not-for-profit ministry called Black American Defense Counsel. They're BAD … really bad, man."

Chuck knew that this attorney made a circus out of every case and usually won.

"The reverend spoke with me yesterday afternoon and already figured that the cops are pursuing multiple leads."

"That should be good for you," Chuck said in the most encouraging tone he could muster.

"You bet. They took tire casts in the beach parking lot, and I don't even have wheels up here! BAD is organizing a rally for me today, trying to build some public pressure to get me out of here."

"Great," Chuck responded. He lied.

Chapter 46

Digger and Patty talked about the importance of the log on Chief's desk as evidence and its need to be secured. They discussed the squirrel stabbed onto the bike and tried to think who was holding a grudge against the department or Digger. They agreed on the need to have forensics conducted on the truck to see if anything was related to Jane Dunn.

Digger went out to the bike and pulled the knife out of the squirrel and pulled the tires off and put them in his Jeep and whipped the squirrel into the woods. Then he brought the knife in a plastic bag into the station house and figured he would dust it for prints himself in due time.

Patty signaled him to come over. Covering the receiver of her headset, she said, "Do we have a hold on Charles Branson Jr.? Batson Creek wants to know."

"I wish we did," said Digger. "Better call Chief to be sure."

A few moments later, after confirming with the chief on another line, Patty informed the Batson Creek facility, "No, Port Talbot has no hold on Mr. Branson at this time."

"Chuck's out; God help us," Patty said, sighing as she disconnected the call.

Digger went out to the tower lot to double-check the lock on the parking area fence and came back in. "It looks tight to me. Of course anyone can climb a fence."

Patty said, "I can't believe this is Port Talbot. It's like we are under siege!"

Digger said, "I'm going to head home after I drop the bike tires off at Joan's service center. I'll see you in the morning, Patty. Hey, awesome work with the acetone. You're a regular forensic aficionado!"

"You're the sleuth, Digger. I just figured Chief would take it better from me than you. After all, maintaining the log book is in my job description. Have a good night, Digger."

CHAPTER 47

Mr. Dunn's rental car was parked in the driveway. Pastor Brad and Mary probably walked. Digger decided to enter through the kitchen door.

Isabel was wearing a white apron over a black service uniform type dress.

"Well, aren't we spiffed up?" asked Digger as he entered the kitchen.

"Yes we are, Officer, and you're late. Everyone is in the solarium."

"Okay, I'll be right down." Digger went up the back stairs to his room to get into regular clothes.

When Digger entered the solarium, the voices rose, announcing his arrival.

"There he is! Digger, join us," his father said. "You know Mr. Dunn …"

"Sir, again, I am so sorry for your loss. As you know, Janie was a personal friend, and I am deeply disturbed by her death."

"Thank you, son. She was a free spirit and lived more of life in twenty-one years than most people see in a lifetime. I miss her deeply and can only focus on bringing her captor to justice."

"Absolutely, Mr. Dunn. I know the local, county, and state officials are working hard to get the killer."

"Looking for the killer? You found him. For gosh sakes, what are you talking about?"

Digger realized he was coming up against some emotional power and needed to tread lightly. "Of course, Mr. Dunn. I mean that until there is a conviction, law enforcement must remain alert for all possibilities."

"Are you saying there is another suspect?"

"Mr. Dunn, I'm not in any position to comment on that; I'm sorry. I just know we need to be ever observant until conviction."

"I agree about that, but …."

Dr. Davenport turned up the TV. "Hold it, folks. This is live from the jail."

In the foreground, a tall black man with an even taller Afro, wearing a white clerical collar and a black suit was speaking to some other minorities in suits against a backdrop of an untold number of mostly African Americans holding various signs. The camera panned to the right, where Tracy Thomas commenced speaking in a hushed and urgent tone. "We are here at the Batson correctional facility, where a veritable civil rights movement has erupted overnight over the arrest and incarceration of George Williams, an African American from Hialeah, Florida, for his implication in the death of Jane Dunn of Richmond, Virginia. From the looks of it, we have community leaders from Portland and their constituencies bussed in, and we have Sheriff McGeary's opponent in the upcoming primary, the only Caucasian near the microphone, Eric Marquis." Tracy looked to her right and added, "It looks as if Mr. Williams's attorney, Reverend Jack Justice from New York, will start things here."

The camera widened to show the full scene. The crowd of at least a hundred people was standing to the left of the entrance of the jail, presumably so as not to block the entrance. Several correctional officers and sheriff's deputies held that invisible line of demarcation. A bank of microphones was in front of the speaker. The camera focused on some moving signs, including one that said Justice for George! Not Politics for Mick! (a reference to Sheriff McGeary) before zeroing in on Reverend Justice.

"The days of lynching the black man closest to the crime scene are supposed to be long over! Except apparently in Port Talbot! George Williams, a hardworking young bellhop, originally from the projects in South Florida, was summarily rounded up yesterday and hauled off to jail, accused of killing a white girl before her cause of death was even known!" The reverend paused to allow the crowd to respond, which it did as if on cue, with moans and boos.

He continued, "George is locked behind me on the flimsiest of evidence that a crime even occurred or that he did it, and he should be released immediately!"

The amens were heard throughout Reverend Justice's oratory. Upon his mentioning the *release* word, the crowd seamlessly joined in a chant of "Release George Williams, Release George Williams!" During the chorus, the reverend looked at some notes and held up his hands to hush the crowd. "Citizens of Maine! Do not rest easy this day because you feel the murderer is in jail. If the Dunn girl's death was foul play, the murderer is still amongst you. This will be clearly revealed to you when we secure George Williams's release, as I intend to do in the coming weeks. Thank you!"

The crowd erupted with applause as the reverend stepped back and the only white person sidled up to the microphone. "Ladies and gentleman, knee-jerk justice can no longer be tolerated in our community! I am Eric Marquis, and I plan to remove the knee-jerk incumbent sheriff in this summer's primary! It is exactly this type of case that has inspired me to run against Sean 'Knee-jerk' McGeary. It has got to stop!"

At that moment the crowd, seemingly unprompted, erupted into a chant, "Knee-jerk Sean is Gone! Knee-jerk Sean is Gone!"

A voice-over from Tracy piped in, "Howard, the looks of the event is changing from a civil rights gathering to a pep rally for Sheriff Sean McGeary's opponent."

The TV screen split, showing Howard the news anchor at the station and Tracy on the scene at the jail.

"Tracy, I notice a number of deputies in the background. Is there any sign of Sheriff McGeary?"

The picture switched to Tracy full screen at that moment. "Howard, we will endeavor in fairness to reach Sheriff McGeary for his comments on this case. Some interesting statements from Mr. Williams's attorney bear repeating."

In the Davenports' solarium, Mr. Dunn was the first to speak. "Civil rights movement? pure hogwash. Happens every time they empty the projects by offering a free bucket of fried chicken on the bus transporting them!"

The room went silent over such an inflammatory comment from one whose daughter had just been killed. The pastor was slow to respond. "Adam, I think it is unfortunate that politics seems to be injected into the search for truth. Having the sheriff's opponent speak was unwise."

"The search for truth is over! This ni … ni … Negro better not get off with these shenanigans or I will personally dispense with justice. Hey, who is that in the background?" Mr. Dunn interrupted himself and pointed at the TV.

Everyone stepped closer and bent in to look at the activity over Tracy's left shoulder. As Tracy was recapping Reverend Justice's talking points,

Chuck Branson and his attorney and his father could be clearly seen walking out of the entrance of the correctional facility.

Mr. Dunn exclaimed, "That's the guy that hijacked my press conference today!"

The news anchor recognized the party as well and interrupted Tracy's recap. "Excuse me, Tracy … Tracy? Tracy?"

"Yes, Howard?" Tracy paused, holding her earpiece more firmly to her head so as to filter out the ongoing chanting of the Williams rally.

"Tracy, the other big story out of Port Talbot today is the arrest of a prominent member of the community. I believe the Bransons are exiting the facility behind you."

Tracy spun to her left to see then looked back at the camera. "Yes, Howard, I believe you are correct. Let me see if we can get a comment."

The TV screen split into two pictures. One showed, with jiggling camera, Tracy running in high heels toward the Branson party. The other side of the screen showed Howard at the news desk and speaking. "Channel 8 First Response Team member Tracy Thomas will try to get a comment from Charles Branson regarding his arrest earlier today on alleged drug possession charges. Hopefully we will have this for you after this brief station break."

Digger spoke first to the dinner guests hovered around the TV in their home on Ocean Avenue. "It looks as if Chuck Branson is out on the street. That was quick. His attorney, Peter Coffey, is the dad of a friend of mine at UNYQ. He is pretty well regarded."

Mrs. Davenport spoke up, sensing the commercial was a good break. "Can we adjourn to the dining room to eat?"

Mr. Dunn responded, "I've seen enough," and started moving away from the TV.

Digger hung back, waiting to see whether Tracy got an interview.

"Howard, we are here with attorney Peter Coffey and his client Chuck Branson, who has just been released from the Batson facility."

Turning to the attorney she asked, "Mr. Coffey, do you find it ironic that a rally for a black suspect who is not released is occurring a hundred feet to my right at the same time as your client, a young white man from a prominent family in the community, is being quickly and quietly released?"

The attorney, without skipping a beat nor being concerned about the subject matter of the question itself, launched into making his case for his client.

"This afternoon we have been able to take the first step in correcting a travesty of justice by releasing on bail an innocent man, Charles Branson Jr. Our thanks goes to Judge Simon Weist, who signed the bond release this afternoon in Portland. Never in my thirty years of practicing law have I seen such a presumption of guilt been so unfairly played out by federal law enforcement. It is no wonder the local forces have had nothing to do with this charade. I have instructed Mr. Branson and his extended family to refrain from any comment until the charges have been dismissed. Please do not take their silence as an admission of guilt or wrongdoing. In accordance with our professional rules, I, too, must restrict my comments. Thank you."

The whole time his attorney was speaking, Chuck could be seen unmistakably looking over at the Williams rally as if it were more important to him than his own impromptu press conference.

Tracy brought his thoughts back instantly. "Mr. Branson, how many pounds of drugs were seized from your truck?"

Mr. Coffey put up his hand like a stop signal and started to move, signaling to both his client and the inquisitor that this would not be answered and that it was time to go.

Tracy moved, too, and pressed on. "We have videotape of a firearm and bags of marijuana being taken from the truck. Are you saying it was planted?"

Mr. Coffey turned back to Tracy. "We look forward to answering those questions before a jury of Mr. Branson's peers of this community. Thank you."

Digger saw Mr. Branson, the father, standing to the side with a stern face and grimacing at his son. The three got into a black limousine and sped off as the newscaster was speaking in the foreground and another box on the screen showed the footage of helicopters and Zeus sniffing in the truck bed.

Mrs. Smith, who had stayed back with Digger to watch the newscast, stood at Digger's shoulder and said, "Those Bransons are pulling out the stops. A limo? You think that will affect the prosecutors?"

"I hope not." But then Digger thought he better check on the prints on the lipstick case and get the tire tread casts checked tomorrow. Digger and Mrs. Smith left the solarium and headed for the dining room.

"Adam, may I freshen your libation?"

"That would be great, Davenport, thanks," Mr. Dunn said as the dinner guests were seating themselves.

Pastor Brad changed subjects deftly. "Please let us know whether we can be of any assistance with getting Janie home. We have good relations with the funeral homes that would be making arrangements. And if you just need someone to be with you as you're dealing with matters here in Maine, please consider me available to assist."

"Thank you, Pastor. We are supposed to get the autopsy results on Monday at the county morgue at 11:00 a.m. Sheriff McGeary has asked me to come there. It might be nice to have a friend with me, actually.

"Consider it done," Pastor Brad confirmed. "The morgue is located within the Reilly funeral home across the river."

CHAPTER 48

"Hello, this is Jack Butterworth."

"Mr. Butterworth, this is Pete Coffey, Chuck Branson's attorney. I am so sorry to contact you on a Saturday night at home, but I thought it important enough."

"Sure, Pete, go ahead, and please call me Jack."

"Okay, sure Jack, thanks. Chuck Branson informed me of something that occurred while he was in the jail cell with George Williams that would make your life considerably easier. They had a conversation, and according to Chuck, George made some highly incriminating admissions."

"I'm all ears, Pete. Lord knows we are not accustomed to civil rights rallies in Maine, and the community is on edge," the DA responded.

"Is there a way we could meet this evening to discuss Mr. Branson's cooperation in return for some leniency on his current possession charges?"

"Peter, I thought you had a defense of entrapment or a search and seizure screw-up. Why do you need a deal with me? Isn't this a federal case?"

"That's what I want to talk to you about. I need insurance—layers of protection, you know."

"Sure, Pete, I understand. Come on over. I'll be happy to see if there is a way to resolve these cases. In fact, bring your client. We will prepare a statement for him, and I'll call the US attorney, Ken Sussman, to get his buy-in."

"Sounds like a good beginning. Let Sussman know we will withdraw our plans to countersue for civil rights violations on improper search and seizure. It may help sweeten the deal. See you at your place at 8:00 p.m.?"

"I doubt that will help. Let me package the concepts here. Okay?"

"Good deal, Jack. You drive the bus. I'll see you at 8:00 p.m."

Chapter 49

Chuck was pacing in his room at his house on Benson's Creek. He was cooking up a scheme along with some methadone. His anger was climbing as fast as his high on crystal meth. "Who did me in? Who do they think they're messin' with? I'm a Branson! We're the lobster mobsters for gad sakes! No possession charges and no murder charges for me … untouchable! You jerks … get over it!" he yelled to no one as he danced and swayed under the influence.

His meeting with the DA that evening had gone reasonably well. It was a compelling lie. Why wouldn't poor George Williams be scared to death and make admissions to him, a fellow ruffian? It seemed as if the DA was quite pleased to believe him. Between his attorney's slick pitch and the DA's desire to win reelection among the locals, Chuck's story about George's jail cell confession fit everyone's needs for resolution … except George's, of course.

Chuck thought to himself that he could be free of everything if he took the stand and just kept to the story. He had purposefully kept George's confession short and simple. *I can do this,* he affirmed to himself.

He thought about his areas of exposure on Janie's death: Buzzy saw them. The truck may have her prints somewhere. The truck treads at the beach. The truck, the truck, the truck. His mind was racing. *The truck is impounded. That's a problem!* he thought.

His father had already been served with a forfeiture notice on the truck as it was registered in Senior's name. The notice was crumpled and rolled in a tight ball on the floor of Chuck's bedroom. He muttered to himself, "They're dancin' with a Branson, and they're not gonna like it!" He kicked the wadded-up forfeiture notice like a soccer penalty kick.

"That's *my* truck. Ain't no one getting it or anything in it," he hissed with a Charles Manson look in his eyes. He had a scheme and there was no turning back.

He put on a dark hooded sweatshirt, cleaned up his drug paraphernalia, and crept silently out of his room, down the stairs, out the back door, and went down to the creek. He was relieved to see that it was high tide. Otherwise he'd have to drive, and he didn't want his father to hear him leaving the house and borrowing his car—not at 2:00 a.m.

Benson's Creek turned completely to mud at low tide. He had to hurry. He dragged the skiff that normally lay on the sea grass in their back yard down to the creek and silently put in and started rowing for his father's dockside warehouse. He rowed the third quarter of a mile through the twists and turns of Benson's Creek to finally reach the harbor, which he had to cross to get to the warehouse. This was the worst part of the whole trip. He couldn't be spotted.

He rowed between the moored lobster boats, silently leapfrogging his way across the harbor by staying in the shadows of the moored boats. Some light came from the pier, and if he could just stay on the other side of the boats, he could make it to within fifty feet of the pylons of his Dad's warehouse. No one knew that you could row between the pylons at the warehouse and get under the building where there was a trapdoor you could climb through that right into the warehouse.

As Chuck rowed quietly by the moored boats, the quiet slapping of the oars echoed off the hulls of the lobster boats. He stayed away from the moored sailboats because they might have a recreational boater sleeping aboard. He successfully crossed the harbor and rowed under the warehouse between the pylons. The water discharge from the lobster tanks let go with a torrent of pouring water every eight minutes. The lobsters in the tanks above him were getting fresh seawater flowing in and out like clockwork. Each cycle the pump turned on to pull in the fresh saltwater, and the relief valve opened to release the stale water.

Chuck knew the operations like the back of his hand. He rowed to the area where the intake was in pitch blackness. When he heard the pump kick on, he reached out for where the pipe had to be. "Gotcha, you slimy sucker." While keeping his hold on the pipe, he walked himself to the bow of the boat, grabbed the bowline, and tied it to the pipe. He felt to the left of the pipe and felt the rungs on the ladder. How many times had his father made him climb down this ladder and get in the water to clean the pump's intake screen from seaweed? He shuddered to think.

He climbed the ladder until his head hit the trapdoor, then bowed his head down completely so his shoulders hit the trapdoor and lifted using his shoulders and bent neck. The door lifted right out of place.

Chuck climbed in and, using the ambient light from the pier, walked effortlessly around the floor of the warehouse, which contained mainly large, green fiberglass tanks gurgling and burbling with gently flushing water and crustaceans prancing in slow motion below the surface. Some were huge and some measured just over the legal limit. Some had one claw. Some, having barely survived a battle in the tank, had no claws. Most had two claws. Most lobsters had their claws banded shut to reduce the tank battles.

Chuck got to work quickly. He went to the back right side of the tool closet and flicked the lighter briefly. There he saw the object of his journey, "Redneck fish sticks!" he hissed in a husky voice. The Bransons had made a pretty penny selling bait fish to the lobstermen in the years past. There was no profit in bait fish if you had to catch with a hook or trawl the seas with nets and use fuel. Enter the redneck fish stick. A red stick of dynamite thrown twenty feet from a boat would kill hundreds of fish and bring them to the top for easy skimming.

It was strictly an off-season operation and had to be done off the remote isles, but it worked in the good ole days.

Chuck had a better use this evening. He grabbed four sticks and a green coil of fuse and started to back out of the closet. But he paused and said, "No, they can't have any part of that truck," and reached for two more sticks. He grabbed a pair of gloves and wire clippers, put everything in a burlap oyster sack, slung it over his shoulder, and headed for the trapdoor.

Suddenly car lights swept the room as a vehicle pulled down to the pier area and paused. Chuck dropped to the ground, scrambled to the trapdoor, and paused to listen. He heard only his breathing until the car door opened. He wrapped the neck of the burlap bag around his fist and wrist and used his other hand and arm to hold onto the ladder as he lowered himself down. The car lights were still illuminating the warehouse as Chuck dragged the trapdoor over his head and jiggled it into position. He heard the car door shut and looked out through the pylons while lowering himself down the ladder. His skiff had pulled to the left of the ladder, a reminder that the tide was moving out and he'd better get back or he'd be stuck in the middle of Benson's Creek. He quietly got situated in the boat and waited. A flashlight beam hit the sides of the lobster boats moored in the harbor. They were all required to have reflective license numbers that lit up when hit with a beam of light.

Chuck untied the boat and moved pole by pole toward the edge of the harbor. The person above was now walking on the dock and Chuck saw the glowing trajectory of a cigarette butt being flicked into the harbor twelve feet away. The person walked on the dock back toward the car. The door opened and closed, and the headlights swept the harbor as it backed up and pulled away. Chuck secured the bag high and dry and started rowing back to his house.

He beached the skiff on the lawn where it had been and went in the house to see if all was still quiet. After smuggling the bag up to his room, he started to construct his fireworks display. First he got the canister of gunpowder that he used for packing his own shotgun shells for duck season. He wrapped six sticks of dynamite together with masking tape and then braided the six-inch fuses together and put a small band of tape to hold the braid still, then took one end of the extra fuse coil and weaved it among the fuses of the braid. He undid the coil and pulled it across the room so it wouldn't recoil after lighting and shorten the burn time. Considering the length of the fuse across the room, he smiled and thought, *I'll be in bed asleep before this fires up.* After all, Benson Creek was just down the hill from Sow Hill, maybe a quarter mile at the most.

Chuck next got a piece of masking tape, laid it with its sticky side up, and poured a liberal dose of black powder onto the tape. He muttered to himself, "Thank you, Uncle Bob," referring to his pyrotechnics mentor each Fourth of July.

He carefully laid the braid of fuses and the intertwined long fuse onto the bed of gunpowder on the tape and carefully wrapped the tape around the fuses, which packed gunpowder between the sinews of the braids. "A little boostah for success." Chuck added another wrap of tape to keep the gunpowder from sifting out. Finally, he carefully packed the dynamite into the sack and snuck out of the house after verifying he heard his dad snoring at the end of the hall.

Chuck climbed Sow Hill from the back side, which was steep and rocky. He had to cross through a neighbor's backyard and up and over granite boulders and ridges and through brush. He could tell his proximity by looking up and seeing his position relative to the water tower. Finally he reached flat land and started crawling toward the police station, which was illuminated by the office light reflecting through the bushes.

He came to the fence, the same fence he had climbed as a younger kid to get to the tower, and felt a pang of regret for the days of his innocent youth. He swore, got out the clippers, clipped five strategic places, and pulled up the fence, then army-crawled toward his vehicle, past a snowmobile and a skiff on a trailer. He couldn't help but look up at the huge water tower over him. It caused him to shudder; it was like an alien ship on its launch pad. He got up under his truck and even thought about trying to get the pot out of the spare tire. *Forget it. Plenty where that came from.*

He opened the bag and lifted the package out, then wedged the bundle up by the fuel line, where the transmission tapered down from the engine. Dynamite needs tight areas to be most effective, so he started sliding out, feeding the long fuse out as he backed toward the fence opening. When he got about eighteen feet from the truck, he crouched by the skiff's trailer and looked around. There were no signs of a night shift at the station. *All quiet.*

He lit the fuse, scurried through the hole in the fence and down the rocks, and walked quickly to his house. Once he was safely back in his bedroom, he peeled his clothes off, down to his boxers, and climbed into bed.

As soon as his head hit the pillow, his room lit up with a flash. A second later an explosive shudder knocked paintings off the wall and caused glass to crash in the kitchen. His father came running down the hall in his underwear to Chuck's room. Chuck purposely stayed in bed playing stupid.

"What in God's name was that? Did you hear that, Chuck?"

"Yeah, I heard something. What was it, Pop?" Chuck sat up scratching his head like he had been in a deep sleep.

"Oh my God, Sow Hill is on fire!" They both went out onto the front porch where they saw their neighbors outside their homes, too, pointing up the hill.

Someone yelled, "The water tower exploded!" and pointed at rivers of water streaming down the road and gushing from yards that backed up to Sow Hill. A loud rushing of water could be heard in the distance.

Chuck's heart sank when he heard about the water tower. His father said, "Chuck you stay here. I'm going up there."

"Okay, Pop." Chuck was happy to obey this command.

CHAPTER 50

When Mr. Branson arrived with his neighbors, the station was still standing, but in the dark, a column of water was arcing out of the tower through a four-foot hole torn in its side underbelly. A boat was hung up on the fence and on fire, and there was a crater on the ground where Chuck's truck had been. It was twenty feet around and its depth was unknown because it was filling with water and had a geyser shooting up in the middle of the crater.

Sirens started to wail. Charles ran into the station. It was locked up, with no sign of anyone there. He tried to walk around back, but the force of the water coming out of the tower was too heavy to get near the back of the building, which was being ravaged by a torrent of water falling from the tower. Even in the dark, one could see the roof shingles flying off the police station roof like oak leaves blowing in the fall. The aluminum siding was torn away from the corner that was also getting a direct hit.

Chief Nickerson showed up at the same time as the fire chief. Chief ran into the building with a flashlight and pulled things from his office. The fire chief went in, too, and was trying to pull the chief out. They were yelling at each other over the din of the falling water, which stopped on its own accord, allowing everyone present to hear the two chiefs yelling obscenities at each other. The police chief stopped yelling, shook Fire Chief Burrow's hands off of himself, and walked back into his office, where he looked straight up through the missing roof and saw the gaping gash in the water tower. It had run dry. He looked over at the crater. It was a bona fide pond that still had a bubbling geyser percolating in it.

"I believe we are watching the last of the town's water come up through the hole over there. What happened here do you suppose?" he asked, turning to Fire Chief Burrows.

"Ed, unless you're storing dynamite in your impound lot, it looks like sabotage."

By now, volunteer firemen were hosing down the boat smoldering on the fence.

"Wait a minute here … Chuck Branson's truck used to be right there," Chief said, pointing at the pond. "It's been taken." He was looking around as if it might be parked somewhere.

Fire Chief Burrows looked up at the hole in the water tank. "Ed, I'm gonna guess the engine block of that truck is in that tank," he said pointing through the missing roof over the chief's office. The looming water tower looked like it had been through a war.

Chief Nickerson looked for a place to sit down, ankle deep in water and papers in his office. The fire chief pulled in a dry chair from the foyer and steadied his friend into the chair. "Sit tight. I'll take care of this out here."

Chapter 51

In the morning, the entire town was a rattled by the explosion of the water tower, not just because their quiet town was being subjected to a crime spree of epic proportions, but more so because they had no water to flush toilets and drink on this Sunday morning. The water tower had replaced the pumps used twenty years ago and fed the entire town by gravity pressure.

The selectmen convened an emergency meeting at the school and concluded that the plan was to repair the tower and to truck non-potable water to three sites in town until the repairs had been made. The explosion had not just punctured the tank but also blown the main trunk line feeding the tank. This line had been directly under the truck.

The Bransons were holed up in their house at Benson's Creek, and the press were camped outside, wanting to know why their truck was blown up and their opinion on the security at Sow Hill. The chief, who had gone home for a while after the explosion to get some sleep, was back at the helm, cleaning his office as roofers were battening down new plywood and shingles. Fans were blowing in his office. The town's maintenance men were ripping out the rugs and cheap office furniture made of composite wood, which had become bloated and burst its compressed shape.

Digger was out front doing what he was hired to do: directing traffic. Gawkers from miles away were driving by to see the devastation. The water tower's supports were blackened by the explosion, and the hole in the underside was about two feet by three feet in size and had brown edges as if had been hit by a flaming missile. Several camera crews had been allowed to set up in part of the parking lot to ply their trade to the masses via satellite.

After Digger cordoned off the area in yellow tape, he got permission to take the rest of the day off. He headed home to change for church and join his parents at the eleven o'clock service. The church was usually packed at the 10:00 a.m. service because the children were able to get in the act by being the ushers. It had become tradition. The kids did everything ministerial: rang the bell, received the offering, and handed out the order of service.

At the eleven o'clock service, it was the serious and older parishioners. The Davenports had morphed into this service time after Digger outgrew the kid's service. As in many Episcopal churches, they had their own pew. None of them were marked, but the family pews were known to the attendees of the eleven o'clock service. Occasionally a tourist visitor would unwittingly occupy a family pew. This was a perfect opportunity for the maven or patriarch to show grace by not skipping a beat and sitting as close to that pew as possible, perhaps stepping over the interloper and joining them in the same pew as if nothing was wrong or amiss. But every regular knew it was amiss and would comment on the new person in the Pepperrells' pew, for example.

This Sunday Margie was in the pew with the Davenports. She appeared to be crying at different parts of the service. After church, on the short walk up Ocean Avenue to Digger's cottage, Margie blurted, "I'm going home, Digger! I can't take it here. I don't want to go back to the Brigantine.

"I don't want to go out with you anymore, either. I'm afraid I might fall in love with you, and you are just way too driven by things other than me. I think you could go a whole day without even thinking of me. Even when we are together, you're more interested in developments at work or which fish are biting. I like you too much to change any of it for me; but I also like myself enough and know myself enough to say that I don't want to fall in love with someone who isn't head over heels in love with me. So no hard feelings. I'm leaving when we get home. I can make Richmond by midnight."

Digger looked at his watch. "Honey, I'm sorry you see it that way, and I'm sorry that work has been so crazy. I can't really argue with you about your feelings ..."

"Digger, don't say anything. Let's leave it this way. We had a great beginning, a devastating event occurred that interrupted things, and maybe the good Lord will unite us in the future, if it is His will, okay?"

Digger was relieved at the way Margie tied a bow on it because, truth be known, he was too busy for an emotional relationship and had felt guilty about ignoring her. She was convenient—not compelling. That was a feeling that he could not share with her. Thankfully, Margie spared him from the platitudes and apologies.

They hugged and kissed in an obligatory manner at her car and parted with half-sincere promises of staying in touch through the school year and road tripping to one another.

As Margie's car pulled out, Digger checked his watch again. The high tide was about to start falling—feeding time for bluefish.

After church, it was Digger's custom to take the family boat out and go fishing. This Sunday was no different—blown-up water towers and failed summer romances or not. He headed to the club where their boat was docked. Sundays were active at the docks.

Digger motored the twin 150-horsepower engines on the twenty-two-foot Robalo fishing boat out to the mouth of the Port Talbot River and then pushed the double throttles all the way down. The boat responded like an angry beast, lurching up on the water, roaring a loud growling, moaning noise before settling down into a speeding rocket skimming across the water with a finely tuned humming noise.

Digger arced the trajectory down east to the best fishing spot off Lands' End. As he pulled up, he saw Butterworth's boat already there. There were also seagulls circling overhead. He brought it down to idle speed as he pulled in closer. Butterworth waved him over as he was frantically fighting something on his pole. Digger glided closer and cut the engine, allowing the silence to speak loudly.

"Plenty of room and plenty of fish, Digger! Hurry on this flurry of blues!"

"Yes sir, Mr. Butterworth! Thank you," he called back as he baited his hook.

"Call me Jack, copper! We're on the same team now that you're the Port's Bike cop!"

"Thanks, Jack. It's quite the summer to be on this team. I would have thought you'd be over at Sow Hill," he said, nodding his head in the direction of the water tower, which could be clearly seen from their boats.

Jack looked for a moment at the tower to see if the hole could be seen and then commented, "Yeah, quite the summer so far. I was at the tower early this morning with the chief. What a scene. It makes no sense."

"I think it makes sense," Digger stated boldly, with a little adrenaline flowing in his veins as he was about to share his theories with the one man who could do something legally about those theories.

"Oh really? Nickerson let you off the bike to do some CSI?" the DA asked in a joking tone.

"Actually, Chief Nickerson has allowed me to do things I never imagined I would get to handle."

"So what's your theory on the water tower?" pressed Butterworth.

"It's more my theory on the Jane Dunn case that matters," Digger said as he cast in the opposite direction of Butterworth's line.

"Hold on, son. The Dunn case is solved. I'm not at liberty to speak about it. But new corroborating evidence came in last night, confirming the physical evidence collected at the scene."

Digger knew better than to inquire but simply added, "I think there may be some other physical evidence that may become relevant."

The DA stopped winding in his line and held a pregnant pause just looking at Digger before he said, "Digger, I got the murderer, plain and simple. And you'll hear in my press conference tomorrow, so I might as well tell you now that I'm requesting a Harnish hearing to forestall bail and expedite the prosecution of George Williams. Having said that, I don't want to hear any cockamamie contrary theories that would obligate me to share supposed exculpatory material with that showboater, Reverend Justice. Do you know what I mean when I say exculpatory material?"

"Yes, I understand. Any evidence that tends to show that the defendant didn't do it must be shared with the defendant."

Jack added, "I don't need half-baked concepts that trigger the reporting requirement. But let me say this, Digger, if you have slam dunk evidence, I want to be the first to know. You got that? Can you remember this number, 285-8585? That's my personal line. You call me … you cross-body-block me in the hall … you do what it takes to get to me first in any case when you have ironclad evidence. You understand? I need to know before the enemy knows."

"I hear you loud and clear, Jack," Digger responded with a concluding tone, realizing that his theory shouldn't be shared at this time.

Chapter 52

Monday morning on the other side of the county, at the Reilly funeral home, the medical examiner, Dr. Beebe, and a biochemist from Portland Hospital were meeting with the DA and the county sheriff. The sheriff spoke. "Chief Nickerson asked me to lead this meeting and to liaise with the Dunn family on these results while the chief deals with the explosion at his station. What do we have, Doctor?"

"Jane Dunn died at approximately 2:00 a.m. on Friday morning from crushed lungs, or suffocation. Her rib cage was completely collapsed, much like one would expect from coming into contact with a steering wheel. Except that there was no sign of blunt trauma to the rib cage. It is as if ..." He hesitated. "Excuse the non-medical terminology ... It was as if she was squashed to death. I noted in my report that her bone structure was very frail. I believe that Ms. Dunn was anorexic, and this may have contributed to the cause of her demise."

The DA spoke up. "That is of no legal significance. The perpetrator takes his victim as he finds her, as they say in law school."

"I'll leave that to you to sort out, counselor," the doctor replied.

"Her blood alcohol content was through the roof for a girl of her size, measured at 2.4 parts per million. A normal person would be unable to function at such levels. The only evidence of trauma was to her right cheek and lip which had split open and bled significantly. This trauma was consistent with being punched, most likely with a fist or backhand, but clearly not any instrument.

"Besides the crushed rib cage, bruised cheek, low body weight, and BAC level, nothing else was out of the ordinary. Her sexual organs seemed to be ordinary, with no signs of molestation. In fact, it appears that the decedent's hymen was completely intact."

The doctor addressed the biochemist. "Sandy, you want to brief them on what your findings were?"

"Sure, Rick. My name is Sanford Reims. I'm a doctor of biochemistry working at the University of Portland and the hospital there. Dr. Beebe ask me to consult on the substance found in her mouth." The law enforcement people looked at each other with puzzled faces.

Miss Dunn's mouth was full of tobacco saliva from Mr. Williams, the defendant. We tested the substance found in the cup at the scene and the substance in her mouth with cheek swabs of the defendant. They were identical. Somewhat odd was the lack of her own saliva. It was 99 percent saliva of Mr. Williams. Further, there was no residue of lipstick on the cup lid but a slight lipstick residue on the side of the cup's rim."

"So they were kissing then," the DA chimed in.

"Perhaps ..."

"Good then. Anything else?" the DA said, urging them to conclude. "I have to brief Mr. Dunn and prepare for Mr. Williams's hearing this afternoon. I think this seals it. Thanks, guys."

The medical professionals glanced at each other as if to recognize they were being given the boot.

Sheriff McGeary stepped forward and shook their hands. "Thanks for this excellent work. Is this the report?" he asked, holding his hand out to take the folder from Dr. Beebe.

"Yes. It's all in there. It's certified as an official governmental record, so it goes into evidence at your hearing. But let me know if I need to testify to provide further information."

The DA and sheriff stayed behind in the little conference room in the funeral home. McGeary shut the door. "This looks pretty good, right?"

The DA responded, "A cakewalk! Did you see how heavy Williams is? He suffocated her, the fat jerk."

"Okay, I *hope* it's a cakewalk because our election is riding on this. We are looking very good because of this fat wad. If you can get a conviction, we are reelected, and I can probably close on that beach house."

The two candidates high-fived each other just as there was a knock at the door. The funeral home's receptionist ducked her head in just in time to observe the sportsmanship. "Mr. Dunn and Pastor Brad Smith are here."

"What's the minister here for?" The DA asked snidely.

"Maybe moral support?" the assistant retorted quickly and slightly sarcastically.

CHAPTER 53

After informing Mr. Dunn and Pastor Brad about the coroner's and biochemist's findings, and after taking Mr. Dunn to view his daughter and officially identify the body, the DA informed them that he was also in possession of a sworn statement of a witness who heard George Williams admit to killing Jane Dunn. Mr. Dunn expressed his encouragement with that development and the wealth of other corroborating evidence.

"The Dunn family can put Janie to rest knowing justice has been served. Thank you so much, Mr. Butterworth and Sheriff McGeary," Mr. Dunn said with little shelves of water building on his lower eyelids.

"Mr. Dunn, would you be willing to stand with us at our press conference in a few minutes over at the courthouse a few blocks away when I explain the Harnish hearing that we will be holding on Wednesday in this matter? Having your confidence alongside of our explanation will go a long way in returning our community to the peaceful resort town it always has been."

"It would be my honor, Mr. Butterworth. I think having the reverend here alongside me would be good as well. After all, they have their Reverend Justice, we have our Reverend Smith."

McGeary couldn't hold back his delight. "Oh yes, Mr. Dunn, a very good idea. Brad, you okay with it?"

"I … believe so," he said haltingly. Can you brief me quickly on the sum and substance of the press release?"

CHAPTER 54

Digger walked into the station house to report for duty Monday morning. Patty was in her dispatch booth, handling multiple lines ringing. The chief was removing items from his wall that had gotten drenched from yesterday's water tower explosion.

Digger went into the conference room, which could double as an interrogation room. The table was covered in plastic, and the chief's papers were drying there. A fan was on low, and a heater was gently blowing. The windows were completely fogged up, and the smell of wet paper was overwhelming. Digger walked around the conference table looking at the various documents drying. The emergency mobilization plan for Port Talbot, the handouts on the domestic violence conference, and the remains of the night log. Digger moved closer to check it out. The pages had disintegrated. So much for the paper evidence tying Chuck to Janie. But others had seen it, and of course Buzzy could be compelled to testify.

Digger looked out the window toward the crater and thought about the tire tread analysis and about going through the truck with a fine-tooth comb. That, too, was now history. Like the perfume fading, so were the other items of evidence.

"Guys!" Patty yelled while tapping on the glass booth that surrounded her. She pointed to the TV that had been on mute in the conference room. Digger turned up the volume while Sheriff McGeary was speaking at a podium in the county office building.

"… deserves to know in an open society what its law enforcement personnel are doing to insure safety of the inhabitants. Today we are pleased to report further confirmation on our actions to detain and charge George Williams for the murder of Jane Dunn. I am joined here by Jane's father, Adam Dunn, a respected legal scholar from Richmond, Virginia, also by the family's local spiritual leader, Reverend Bradley Smith, a Harvard Divinity graduate and pastor to our community at his parish on Ocean Avenue.

"We are cognizant of members of distant communities traveling to our town to complain of our legal process. It is a free country, and we respect their freedom of speech. But it can put a community on edge. We believe that through the swift and detailed work of your district attorney, Jack Butterworth, we will be able to silence those unfamiliar voices and restore peace in our community. Without further ado, Jack, can you explain what legal process is going to occur next and how our community will be served by it?"

"Yes, thank you, Sheriff McGeary. But first I want to publicly thank you for placing your team at our office's disposal to get to the bottom of this tragedy. Both you and the Port's Chief Nickerson have been invaluable in moving this matter along."

The chief had slipped into the conference room to listen alongside Digger and Patty, who had put the phones on hold.

"Leave me out of this!" yelled Chief Nickerson at the droning TV box.

"Maine, unlike many other states, allows the prosecutor to bring on a Harnish hearing against the defendant to prove that (a) the defendant should not be granted bail on this type of offense; and (b) that the defendant is indeed more likely than not to have committed the murder of Jane Dunn. We have served on George Williams's attorney the affidavits of those expected to testify as well as photos of all evidence intended to be introduced. We have highly compelling statements, one of which includes an admission of the defendant himself."

The press corps taping the event murmured at the news of an admission.

Suddenly the TV reporter interrupted. "Howard, we have a disturbance at the back of the county's conference room. Let's see if our cameras can pick this up. Bobby can you rotate?"

Loud chanting could be heard, "Being black is not a crime … Being black is not a crime …" The camera showed twenty or thirty predominantly black people wearing bellhop red vests and punching freedom fists in the air in cadence with one another.

The chief, Patty, and Digger were glued to the live drama until a phone in the chief's office started ringing. Patty ran to get his private line.

"Chief Nickerson's line, this is Patty." After pausing to listen to the caller, she said, "Chief! FBI Agent Barnes is on your private line."

"Roger that, Patty, thanks," he said as he came into room and reached for the handset. Chief Nickerson here."

Digger, keeping an eye on the TV, moved over closer to the chief's door to listen to what the FBI had to say.

"Yeah, we're okay ... It was some sort of explosion under the truck ... Okay, well yeah. Well, your truck ... Branson called me screaming about the forfeiture notice ... I suppose you're right ... It was evidence seized as part of the commission of a federal crime ... No, we'd welcome your review of the scene. Come on down ... What's that? What about the Dunn girl and that truck?"

Digger leaned in.

"The DA here tells me that matter is wrapped up. The lab reports and coroner's report confirm deadly assault by George Williams. A Brigantine Hotel busboy confirms Williams boasted about planning to have sexual relations with her, and the DA's press conference, occurring as we speak, has indicated an admission has been made by the accused ... You have what? Lipstick? How do you know it's Jane Dunn's? ... No, the coroner never told me you had inquired or visited the morgue. In fact, there's a lot about your involvement down here that I seem to be the last to know. Does Sheriff McGeary and the DA know about this link? ... I think we better meet on it pretty quickly. Turn on your TV!"

"When are you coming down with your forensic guys? ... This afternoon? That's fine, we have it cordoned off. Our county investigators have been poking around. I'll make sure they do nothing invasive ... No problem, Barnes, anytime."

"No, really, it's not a problem. We are on the same side when it comes to catching the bad guys. Okay, see you soon. Goodbye."

Digger moved from the conference room toward the bathroom.

"Patty, get me Dr. Beebe on the phone, please. Then get McGeary. He is not gonna like what is brewing in Portland. Digger? Can you come in here please?"

Digger slowly turned back to enter the chief's office. "Sir?"

"The feds are coming down here in a couple of hours and are gonna start combing the tower for clues. Let the deputies out there know they're coming, and tell 'em not to touch anything. If the feds want to pay the overtime on this horror show, let's get out of the way. Next, I need you to clean up the conference room. Have it ready for them to use. Get rid of worthless papers. Move important papers to a drying area in the back.

The chief continued, "As you may know, they have an alternate theory on the Dunn murder that implicates our very own Charles Branson Jr., which I believe may coincide with some of your theories. I want to be briefed on every concept you have been wrestling with after you're done cleaning the conference room and alerting the county deputies out there."

"No problem, Chief. I should be ready for briefing in about thirty minutes." Digger stepped out.

"Chief, it's McGeary, line one," yelled Patty.

"Chief Nickerson here."

"Those aborigines hijacked our news conference! Did you see them in their little organ grinder suits? This has gotten out of hand. I have a mind to arrest the whole tribe! If they so ..."

"Sean, Sean! Listen to me. The FBI called. They place Chuck Branson and the Dunn girl together prior to her death!"

"Edward Nickerson! What in the devil's name are you talking about? The feds have nothing to do with this matter! And ... and ... so what if Chucky was with her before her death? I bet that girl was a regular pass-around pack! It means nothing! Nothing, I tell you. Now don't you throw off Butterworth with this nonsense. He's got a case to prove Wednesday, and news of this crap will just play into these monkeys' game plan! You know how the new administration in DC kowtows to the civil rights community! Heck, that's what got the president elected! I bet that's where these agents are getting their orders! Right from Rev Justice's organization!"

"Enough, Sean! Enough! They will be here in an hour, and they are taking over the investigation of the water tower explosion because the Branson truck was their evidence and subject to forfeiture. Your deputies are going to be sent home shortly."

"That's fine. The truck has nothing to do with the Dunn murder. More importantly, their messing with the Branson kid is going nowhere. Just a news flash for you, Ed ..."

"Why is that?" asked the chief defiantly.

"'Cause Butterworth cut a deal with the federal prosecutor, Ken Sussman, in exchange for Chuck's testimony."

"What's Chuck know about the Dunn murder? The chief asked incredulously.

"Ed, you're out of the loop, man! Chucky was Williams's cell mate, and Williams confessed to the murder! Chuck's turning state's evidence in exchange for dropping of the federal charges!"

"You are kidding me! Then why are the agents still investigating the water tower explosion if Branson is gonna walk?" asked the chief, truly bewildered.

"They shouldn't be! That's the point. Ed, I gotta run. Butterworth has got to call Sussman to get Sussman to call off the fed gumshoes ASAP. If Rev Justice catches wind of the FBI's activism, we're screwed!"

The line went dead.

The chief looked at the receiver, sighed, and slammed it down. "Pure politics … pure politics … I'll be daft!" he grumbled.

He looked at the date on his watch. "The primary is only a week away … no wonder he's getting all lathered up," he commented to himself.

Chapter 55

"Chief, you ready for that briefing?"

"Yeah, Digger, have a seat in my half-blown-up office. What do you think is going on?"

"I'm not sure, chief, but something smells about this case … literally." He pulled out a small notepad. "Remember, I knew Janie personally. Until yesterday I dated her best friend, Margie, also from Virginia. Margie has returned home, unable to deal with the traumatic events here."

"I'm sorry for her and you, Digger," the chief consoled half-heartedly.

"Thank you. My closeness with Margie allowed me to be close to the Brigantine employees, the dorm, et cetera. On the night of her murder, Margie and I were at Hartsons Beach with a couple of youth groups and a girl named Martha from the Brigantine. She said she had just been with Janie and that Janie was intoxicated and reeked of cheap perfume. I found out from my friend Rusty, the bartender at Ship's Pub, that later that evening Janie was kicked out of the pub and that she left her purse momentarily. When Rusty ran after her to give it to her, the purse apparently was soaked in this particular perfume. Rusty noted she was on foot and not driving."

He looked at his notebook and went on. "At about 2:00 a.m., Margie and I returned from Hartsons. I dropped her at the dorms and went home. Margie later told me that when she saw that Janie was not in their room, which reeked of Janie's perfume, she went outside to check the parking lot to see whether Janie's car was in the lot. She said that at about 2:15 a.m., she saw a man sneaking through the employees' parking lot with a sack on his back.

The next day we were all at the scene. At approximately 10:00 a.m., I was returning from the Brigantine pool area, where EMTs were tending to Margie. I came back toward the scene and saw Buzz having words with Chuck Branson, who was in his truck, holding up traffic. As I approached his truck, he saw me in the side view mirror, swore at me, and peeled out. I was close enough to get hit with a waft of perfume coming from his cab. I thought I recognized the perfume from time I spent with Janie and Margie. I asked Buzzy what the confrontation was about, and Buzz responded oddly, as if he was covering something."

"Next, according to press reports, a tip was called in at approximately 10:45 that an arrest would be made at the Brigantine. This is before anything was made public about a suspect. In my mind, someone was trying to publicize the arrest of a person for a purpose that served their interests. At approximately 11:00 a.m., George was arrested."

The chief interrupted. "That *was* odd that the press was on the scene of the arrest like that. Tracy Thomas later asked me how it could be true."

"Exactly, Chief! At approximately 11:15 a.m., I went to Janie and Margie's room to pack up Margie's clothes. I was hit with the same smell that came from Chuck's truck. The CSI guys showed me the empty bottle of Jontue perfume. With two suitcases of Margie's in hand, I left the dorm and walked by the bellhops' stand where I spoke with the older bellhops sitting and wearing their red vests. They told me that George and the rest of them leave their red vests on the back of their chairs for Larry the laundryman. I think how easy it would be to grab one and implicate someone.

"All of these factors started swirling in my head. But Buzz's behavior and the smell of the perfume from Chuck's truck put me on the scent—so to speak—of the night log. Buzz's entry looked altered. As you know, Patty found that it originally said that Janie and Chuck were together at about two in the morning. This to me is huge. Now it's a matter of connecting Chuck to the scene.

"And that is about all I know, other than that Chuck's truck and some of its contents got impounded. And I'm thinking tread analysis and fingerprints may be obtained. But then the truck is blown up before tests are performed.

"That's about the sum of my thoughts. What do you think?"

The chief squirmed in his chair a bit and said, "I find your rundown of the facts quite compelling. I feel for my good, old friend Charles Branson. But at this stage, it's not really what I think. It's what the sheriff and the DA think."

Digger quickly retorted, "I was fishing yesterday and ran into Jack over by Lands' End. The blues were runnin', and we parked side by side for a while and discussed this stuff. He told me don't confuse him or the case with cockamamie theories, but he gave me his personal phone number for whenever I get ironclad evidence on any case his office is working on … for what it's worth."

"Digger," encouraged the chief, "you do put some compelling strands of information together. Confirming what Buzz saw and what you smelled, the feds told me minutes ago that the Dunn girl's lipstick was found in the truck as part of their search and seizure procedure. But that still doesn't place Chuck at the beach, on the beach, on the tablecloth, with her."

"True, maybe not ironclad yet. But wait … hold on." Digger paused, staring intently at nothing. "Tablecloth? Tablecloth from the Brigantine, right?"

"Ayuh," the chief responded watching Digger's wheels turning.

"If my theory is correct, that tablecloth and the vest and the tobacco cup were added after the murder. Chuck would have parked with Janie in the parking lot. Let's assume he got out and went to that site. There would be no tablecloth. What would there be to sit on? A blanket? Or a towel? Perhaps a jacket?"

The chief, getting into the quandary, added, "A tarp, a slicka, or a poncho …"

CHAPTER 56

Agent Barnes and one other federal agent stepped into the police station. Patty jumped up, threw off her headset, to welcomed them and steer them toward the chief's office and the conference room.

"Would you gentlemen care for any coffee? The chief is right this way."

Patty knocked on the door, and Digger and the chief stood to shake hands with the federal agents. The chief introduced Digger, and Agent Barnes introduced Agent Mike Orringer, whom Digger recognized from the search of Chuck's truck on Ocean Avenue.

"Mike is the one who found the lipstick and had it tested through the coroner's office," said Agent Barnes. "We fondly refer to him as Agent Orange … just like the crap they used in Vietnam. He's got a scorched earth mentality when it comes to routing out bad guys."

Mike and Digger looked at each other, silently consenting not to correct any facts about who found what in Chuck's truck.

"Agent Barnes, can we brief one another a bit on this water tower explosion while Digger shows Mike the site?"

"Sounds good. Please call me Johnny." To Mike he said, "Run vectors from the epicenter and allow for secondary incendiary complications."

"You got it!" Mike responded and exited the office. The chief and Digger looked at each other, reacting to the demolition-speak.

"Sure glad you guys came down to help on this," the chief said.

"Our pleasure."

Patty appeared at the door with mugs and a pot of coffee. "This is what we call *cop coffee*, strong and ready to serve!"

Johnny Barnes laughed. "Sounds irresistible!" Patty poured two cups of black coffee without asking if they took cream or sugar.

"Have you heard from your US attorney on the Branson case?" asked the chief.

Barnes waited for Patty to finish pouring the coffee, smiling at her and waiting for her to exit before responding. "May I?" he asked, as he closed the office door.

"Of course. I'm sorry, Patty knows everything around here," the chief offered lamely.

"Sure," Barnes responded politely. "I guess I should ask you which Branson case are you referring to." The chief recognized this was going to get interesting quickly.

"Have a seat. Why don't *you* tell *me* which Branson case I am referring to? I seem to be the last to know what the heck is going on in the criminal cases in my own jurisdiction!" His voice rose dramatically, without any hint of anger.

"Yes, I don't mean to play cat and mouse with you, Chief. I just meant to underscore that we at the Bureau see two Branson cases. Sussman, the US attorney, may see only one drug case. And to be straight up with you, we did get a call from Sussman on the Branson drug case indicating a plea deal was in the works. Sussman requested us to hold up on proving our position on the drug charges. But the US attorney's office doesn't control the FBI's investigation of separate, distinct cases that may involve the same defendant."

"Fair enough, but what jurisdiction do you have over Branson's possible involvement with a non-federal crime such as the Dunn case? I *assume* that's the second Branson case you are examining ... correct?"

"Actually, it's a little more complicated than that. And I'm a little hesitant to discuss our angles, but I do need a local ally on this matter, so I am going to be candid and ask that this information not leave this room."

The chief, appearing a little fearful at this point, responded, "Of course."

"Civil rights violations are being alleged in the Dunn case. Our office has been asked to poke around the edges of the county's handling of the matter, and as you know, federal jurisdiction attaches under section 1984."

"Oh boy, this is what someone hinted might happen ... politics, pure politics!"

"Hold on! I'm not saying we're pursuing a formal civil rights violation case, just that because of the complaint we have jurisdiction to look around the edges of how that case is being handled. Frankly, I want nothing to do with it and am happy to stay out of it. But we need to be sure that we have answers when we are asked, as we will be, regardless of whether anyone's civil rights were violated.

"If we can trust one another, I think we all would rather see all solutions come at the hands of the local authorities. It's really the way it should be."

The chief nodded, accepting the honesty of that explanation while thinking of the locals running for election.

"I appreciate your honesty and deference to our locale," he said. "But I'm reminded of the statement of our famous senator to the south, in Massachusetts, 'All politics is local.' And we got a real political season upon us, Johnny."

The agent looked up toward the ceiling as if to seek divine inspiration for an answer to the chief's quandary. "Always siding on the side of truth is the best politics."

Agent Orringer came bounding into the station, knocked on the chief's door, and opened it before hearing a response. "I'm sorry to interrupt, gentlemen, but you got to see this out back. Your bike cop is forty feet up a tree wrestling with some object. I figure if he dies or gets injured and a workers comp case is filed, the chief may want to be a witness!" the agent added half-jokingly.

Both officers jumped to their feet and ran out of the station, with Patty right behind them. They trotted to the back of the property where they could barely see Digger in his dark uniform hidden by pine boughs up thirty or forty feet.

"Digger, what the heck are you doing up there?" yelled the chief.

"I followed the vector Agent Orange was describing and saw something."

Barnes asked his agent, "How the heck did he get up there? There are no branches for the first twenty feet!"

"He shinnied up it, hugging the trunk like a bloody bear! Shorts and short-sleeve uniform to boot!"

Patty giggled, and everyone else's mouths gaped as they looked up.

"Look out below. I'm not sure where it will land. And watch it ... it'll bounce!"

Everyone backed up about twenty feet.

"Is it clear below?"

"Clear," yelled the chief.

Branches started to snap and crack, and a big, black, charred tire hit the ground with a thud and slight bounce.

"I think there's some good tread on that baby," yelled Digger as he started to descend.

The ground crew circled around the tire. "Well I'll be!" said the chief.

"Not exactly how our forensic guys would retrieve evidence, but this works," added Agent Barnes.

Patty looked up. "Oh dear God ..."

Digger had commenced his bear hug shinnying operation in reverse to come down. It begged the question as to how a person, especially a man, could grapple a tree so closely and hump his way down to the ground.

The onlookers watched in silence until Digger was down and walking toward them, wiping his arms and thighs.

"What's the matter? Didn't you guys ever climb trees?"

"Yeah, apple trees and trees that had branches!" Agent Barnes quipped.

"It's a life skill I learned early. I think a tread analysis is in order," Digger said without skipping a beat and kneeling to examine the half-burned tire.

Agent Barnes leaned over to Chief Nickerson and whispered, "When you're done with him, will you promise to send to me?"

Chief leaned back to the FBI agent. "I'm keeping him as long as I can, Buster!"

CHAPTER 57

"Digger Davenport, what in the world did you get into?" his mother exclaimed, looking at the rash and scratches on his arms and legs.

"Aw Mom, it's nothing. I had to hug a tree today at work. Tree hugging and climbing is hard work!"

"Let me get some Solarcaine spray so those scratches don't get infected. Isabel? Isabel?"

Digger winced at the thought of Solarcaine freezing and stinging his abrasions.

Isabel, the Davenports' maid, came in from her quarters in the back, off the kitchen.

"Is a bell ringing? Is a bell ringing? I heard something!"

Digger smiled at Isabel's age-old joke using her name. Mrs. Davenport didn't.

"Isabel, could you please get the Solarcaine in the children's bathroom? Digger's been playing in the woods."

"Sure, Miss Meredith. Digger, what happened in the woods?"

"I was climbing a tree to track down evidence."

"You think dat bellhop did it?" Isabel blurted. "Thayz makin' a fuss this town has never seen before. I've never seen that many black folk in this state in my life."

"That's the case I'm working on, and we'll see what the evidence shows."

"I'm prayin' for you, Digger. I know with you helping, the right thing will be done."

"Thanks, Isabel, but people far more important than me are calling the shots."

"Deese politicians! And dey don't have to worry about the black vote like in da South. God help dat bellhop."

"Isabel, the Solarcaine please?" interrupted Mrs. Davenport.

"Yes'm Miss D," Isabel answered and waddled toward the back stairs to the children's end of the cottage. Digger caught his mother rolling her eyes at Isabel's comments.

Just then Dr. Davenport walked into the kitchen. "Hey, Digger, how goes the battle, young man? Whoa, what happened to you? Wrestling with Mrs. Milliken's cats again?" he said with a chuckle.

"No, I climbed a tree to fetch a piece of Chuck Branson's truck that may become very important in the Dunn case," he said encouragingly as if seeking to get his father's approval or recognition of his significance.

"It appears that Dunn case is all but concluded except for the obligatory marches of the minorities. I think this week's hearing will sew it up and quiet the masses," his father opined dryly.

"We'll see, Dad. It seems the feds have an interest and may be working with Chief Nickerson to explore other threads of evidence. Tomorrow will be a very important day to see if the threads amount to anything."

"According to what I hear on the TV, that's only one day before Butterworth's grand show, the Harnish hearing. I can't imagine he's exploring other theories the way he and McGeary are promising peace and prosperity through this hearing. It's like one big campaign ad. Did you hear that channel eight is going to cover it 'gavel to gavel' as they say?"

"Wait … I thought you couldn't have cameras in Maine's courtrooms."

"Maine, according to these incessant news reports on this case, passed some judicial rule this year that allows it for non-jury trials like this so-called Harnish hearing. Tracy what's-her-name from Channel 8 promises to give us the blow-by-blow coverage. She informed us shortly after the red vest gang invaded Butterworth's press conference that her station had applied for permission to film the hearing. The first time in the state's history, if you can believe that. Now like a soap ad, channel eight is running promos for Wednesday's coverage, stating that Judge Pendergast approved a pooling agreement for media coverage … all brought to you as 'a first in Maine by First Responders News 8!' Ugh."

Digger could think of only one word, *Wow*. Cameras in the courtroom had been a big debate in his Con Crim Pro class at UNYQ. The subject defied liberal-conservative labeling. It had become more of a right to know, media on demand type of debate.

Isabel came huffing into the room, "Hold still, honey. This is gonna sting," she said, aiming the spray at Digger's legs.

CHAPTER 58

"Oyez, oyez, all those having business in the Maine Superior Court of Lincoln County, Judge Francis Pendergast presiding, on this twenty-third day of August 1978, draw nigh for a determination of truth and dispensation of justice as Providence allows. Court is now in session!" the portly bailiff bellowed to a packed courtroom.

"Thank you, Gene. Ladies and gentlemen, we have a packed courtroom today with only one matter before us, the Harnish hearing requested by the state in the People of the State of Maine versus George Williams."

A rumbling grumble emanated from the audience.

"With a crowd of this size, I must remind attendees of some rules, such as no grumbling or making of any noise *whatsoever* or I will clear this room immediately. Do you understand?"

***

Back at Sow Hill, Patty, Digger, and the chief were watching the TV as most everyone in the State of Maine was. But they had all ears listening for the phones as well. They were waiting for a call from Portland. Agent Johnny Barnes would be calling to indicate whether the federal magistrate would approve a warrant for the search of the Branson home in connection with the explosion of the truck and destruction of the water tower. The tread analysis was completed on Tuesday, confirming that the tire on Branson's truck was indeed one of the tires leaving an impression at the beach parking lot during the relevant time frame. Sheriff McGeary, who had custody of the tread molds, had been informed on Tuesday that the remains of the tire needed to be tested. He initially had objected, but Chief

Nickerson convinced him using leverage that had to do with the campaign and interagency cooperation.

After confirming that the tread impression was a match, Agent Barnes and Chief Nickerson agreed to apply jointly for a warrant allowing Port Talbot police and the FBI to search the Branson home for evidence pertaining to the truck's explosion and any relevant evidence showing a relationship with Jane Dunn. The chief had balked about the federal warrant application mentioning Jane Dunn because he knew it would put his friends, Butterworth and McGeary, and his old friend Charles Branson, potentially in a deep and irreconcilable divide. Agent Barnes convinced him by assuring him that he would go on record as saying it was a federal requirement. "Blame it on the feds, Ed!" Barnes had said repeatedly.

Patty ran for the phone, which had been uncommonly quiet for a midweek day in high season. The calm was attributed to the local drama on TV. The cats stuck in the trees and cars parked on residents' lawns could wait.

"Port Police, this is Patty," she answered in a perky voice, standing at the chief's desk. "Just a minute, Agent Barnes."

The chief left the TV set, headed to his office, and grabbed the phone from Patty.

"Well?"

"Warrant issued. We are on our way," Barnes said in a deadpan voice.

The chief kicked his door shut. "Johnny, you mind if I stay out and let the kid go in with you guys? It'll be a good experience for him and it may help save some face here … You understand?"

"Chief, I understand completely. It'll be a pleasure working with Digger and showing him the ropes a bit. Who knows, he may show us something, too. By the way, I'm bringing our lab rat, Agent Forkel. He has the digit and blood cell signature for both Branson and Dunn if needed. Can he set up shop in your conference room?"

"Absolutely. Why, this is getting exciting!" the chief added gratuitously.

"Okay, here we come," Agent Barnes signed off.

The chief opened his office door, "Warrant issued! We are on. Digger can you come in for second? Excuse us, Patty," the chief said diplomatically.

"No prob, Chief. I'm watching a great TV show!"

The chief shut the door. "Digger, I have been really impressed with your cop skills and tact. I've asked Agent Barnes to allow you to go in on the search and possible seizure. He has agreed and looks forward to showing you the ropes."

Digger couldn't contain a beaming smile but controlled his voice and words enough to say in an even tone, "It's a great honor, Chief, thank you."

"Honestly, it gives me a little cover with my old friend Charles if I'm not there. You follow the feds' lead. The feds will no doubt be armed. You will not! You hit the dirt if that kind of thing develops, you understand?"

"I ... I can't imagine the Bransons would pull that kind of response, can you?" asked Digger hesitatingly.

"No I can't. Besides, the troublemaker, Chucky, is most likely already at the courthouse, waiting to testify."

"Do you suppose Butterworth will be willing to listen to us if we have ironclad evidence?' Digger said, looking at his watch. "I mean it's like the train is leaving the station right now."

"We will see, Digger. Trains can derail if they are going too fast or a small item is placed on the tracks. We will see."

CHAPTER 59

"May it please the court, my name is Jack Butterworth, Lincoln County district attorney, and I represent the people of the State of Maine. Today we intend to prove that George Williams should be held over in custody pending his trial for the assault and murder of Jane Dunn. We intend to show two things. One, we have sufficient evidence to conclude that it is more likely than not that Mr. Williams is indeed the perpetrator of this heinous crime, and two, that given the defendant's lack of ties to the community, the seriousness of the charges, and questionable employment, Mr. Williams presents a flight risk to this court and a danger to the community and possibly himself. It is for these reasons that he should be held in jail pending the trial and be denied any bail. Thank you."

Judge Pendergast looked over his bifocals at the defense counsel sitting next to George, who was in his orange jumpsuit and had shackles on his ankles and wrists. "Counsel?"

"Thank you, Your Honor. May it please the court, my name is Reverend John Justice, Esq. of New York State. I have been admitted to practice in Maine pro hac vice on the motion of Sanders and Smith prior to today's proceeding, and I would like to confirm that the court is in receipt of the pro hac vice admission order before continuing today."

"Reverend Justice, your reputation precedes you. Your temporary admission papers appear in order. Jack … er … Mr. Butterworth, do you have any objection to Reverend Justice proceeding?"

Jack leaned to his assistant DA and whispered, "Have you checked those papers?" The young attorney quickly answered, "All in order, sir."

"No objection, Judge."

"Please proceed, Mr. Justice," said the judge.

Rising to his feet slowly and turning around to ensure that the press pool's camera could identify him gave him a charge of animation.

"Judge Pendergast, it is an honor to be appearing before you, but I cannot say it is a pleasure while a truly fine man with no history of criminal activity in his entire life is shackled at his hands and feet and is expected to assist in his defense at this table today. I have appeared at criminal proceedings all across America, and I have not seen treatment like this, not even in the bowels of the South.

"I brought a dress suit here today and asked that Mr. Williams be allowed to wear it, but this request has been denied. I asked the cuffs to be removed and that request, too, has been denied. This man is innocent until proven guilty under our law in this great country. In this courtroom, however, he has been treated worse than his great-grandfather on the plantation! ... Not too long ago."

Murmurs were heard throughout the courtroom.

"Objection! Your Honor, the security of our community and the manner in which we take precaution is our business and not that of some slick orator from New York City!"

"Boys, boys, boys ... Will you both approach the bench, please? Also Bailiff please approach."

As the three men came up to the bench, a sheriff moved over to stand behind the defendant.

In a hushed tone the judge scolded, "Mr. Justice ... er ... Reverend, I really do appreciate your skills, but I will not take kindly to besmirching the reputation of this court." Turning to the DA before Reverend Justice could say anything, "Jack why didn't they let this boy, er, this young man get in a suit?"

"Well, uh ... uh ..."

The bailiff spoke up. "Your Honor, the suit was delivered ten minutes before the hearing, and we didn't have time to supervise his changing of clothes."

The judge's eyebrows gave away his response without a word.

"Why do we have him doubly bound?"

The bailiff again spoke, "Well, Your Honor, he is a murder suspect."

"You didn't have Johnny Winston doubly bound yesterday on that arraignment," said the judge to the bailiff, who was now looking down at his shoes.

"We are going to take a ten-minute recess, and that young man is going to come back here in a suit. And keep the shackles off while the young man is in the courtroom. You two," pointing to the attorneys, "I want to see you in my chambers now. Jack, bring your proof. We are going to have a prehearing conference."

"Yes, sir," the attorneys said in cadence.

"Ladies and gentlemen, the court is taking a ten-minute recess." To the court reporter he said, "Sally, can you set up in my chambers. We are going to premark some exhibits."

***

"So, Reverend Justice, have you had time to sample our lobster yet, or has it been all business?" asked judge Pendergast.

"No, Your Honor, I'm not a lobster person. It gives me an itchy throat. But baked stuffed haddock—now we are talking."

Jack, the DA, chimed in to keep them from getting too chummy. "Reverend Justice, the best baked stuffed is at your client's former place of employ, the Brigantine."

"Oh yes, I did note that during my investigation of this matter," said Justice, "among other items of interest."

"So Jack, what do you have tying George Williams to this crime?"

Sally interrupted. "Are we on the record, Your Honor?"

"Oh yes, Sally, thank you," replied the judge.

"Your Honor, the first exhibit is this red vest with George's name written on the inside. This was left by the defendant at the scene."

"Objection! Unless you were there, Jack, you have no idea how it got there!" interrupted the New York attorney.

Judge Pendergast spoke quickly before Jack could reply. "Reverend Justice, we are merely allowing the DA to present his evidence … like an offer of proof … in the best light to see what he has got. I'm not ruling on admissibility at this time. Sally, let's mark the vest as what? Exhibit A? Carry on Jack."

"Next we have the tablecloth from the Brigantine as Exhibit B. This is a dirty tablecloth that was presumably from the laundry area outside George's room at the dorms of the Brigantine and brought by him to the site of the murder."

"I object, Your Honor! There is no proof where that cloth came from!"

"Again, Counselor, we are just marking exhibits at this point. Once we are in the hearing, you can object to their admission. I remind you that in Maine, the proof at a preliminary hearing is like a civil trial. It is not beyond a reasonable doubt. Sally, mark that Exhibit B. What else do you have Jack?"

Chapter 60

"Hey guys, good news. The judge has recessed to allow the defendant to get on a suit," Patty announced, sticking her head in the chief's office.

"That helps buy time," Digger said. He stood and went to the chief's window, looking with a far-off gaze. "Chief, can I have a billy club with me?"

Patty caught the comment. "What the heck are you boys up to? Chief, I go to church with this boy's momma. He's not gonna be in harm's way is he?"

Digger spun around, not having realized Patty was still in the room. "Oh no, Patty, don't you worry about me. I just want the baton to keep me balanced. Everything is just fine," he said, walking to the door and backing her out of the office.

Blue strobe lights flashed against the walls of the police department. "It's Agent Barnes," Patty said. The chief looked at his watch. They flew! Three men entered the station, two in full riot gear carrying helmets, the third in casual clothes and carrying two black cases.

"Let me see, you must be the lab technician. I'm Ed Nickerson, Chief of Police for the Port," he said, holding out his hand.

"Brian Forkel. Nice to meet you."

Agent Barnes held up a black vest. "We brought an extra for the kid."

Patty shook her head and turned toward her dispatch area. "You guys save the world. I'll get the phones."

The chief showed the lab guy to the conference room and indicated where he could set things up. Then Agent Barnes led Digger and Mike Orringer into the chief's office and pulled out a map. "Here is Branson's house. Once Mike is in place here, Digger, you and I will go to the front door like a couple of Girl Scouts selling cookies," the agent said, pointing to the back door of the house on the map.

"Digger, you will not speak even if spoken to. I will be close enough to answer any question. If there is any gunfire or altercation, you hit the deck and crawl on your belly back to the car. Do you understand?"

"Yes, sir," Digger replied.

"Chief, what frequency is your radio on?"

The chief was at a loss.

Digger piped in, "We are at 45 megahertz spread spectrum analogue. How 'bout you guys?"

Agent Forkel yelled from the conference room, "That'll work! Let's test on channel fifteen."

The officers adjusted their sets, and the chief walked to the back to get one off the charger. He came back fiddling with the knobs. Digger gently took the radio from the chief, clicked a dial four clicks, and depressed the talk button. "Test, test, test." His voice came from every direction in the office.

"Patty! Test channel fifteen," Digger boldly called out.

"I'm with you, Ranger Rick!" Digger was not appreciating some of her sarcasm lately.

"Any questions?" asked Agent Barnes. There was silence. "Let's go."

CHAPTER 61

The bailiff stuck his head in the door of the judge's chamber. "Judge, the defendant is ready whenever you are."

"Thank you, Gene," responded Pendergast.

Jack continued with his exhibits. "We have the cup of spittle of Mr. Williams found at the scene as Exhibit C. We have the coroner's report as Exhibit D and a lab's report connecting the bodily fluid of the defendant intimately to that which was found on the decedent as Exhibit E."

Sally was busy marking the exhibit stickers attached to the plastic bags and documents containing the evidence.

"Cup of what?" asked the judge.

"Cup of tobacco spit, Your Honor. Many African Americans from the South spit tobacco into Styrofoam coffee cups with a lid instead of spitting on the ground."

The defense counsel piped up. "Again I object, Your Honor! This characterization of African Americans as cup-spitters is pure nonsense! I am an African American and have never seen such a practice. To be stereotyped as the DA so boldly proclaims as fact is downright racist and prejudicial!"

"You're right, Mr. Justice. Good thing no jury is involved yet. Jack, you're going to have to get more politically sensitive when the jury becomes empaneled."

"May I ask a question about the lab exhibits?" inquired Reverend Justice.

"Of course, sir," replied the judge.

"Jack, is the bodily fluid you previously mentioned the spittle found in the cup and possibly on the victim, or is there some other fluid of a different nature?"

"Here's the report. Read it for yourself." Jack roughly placed copies of Exhibit D and E in front of Reverend Justice.

The judge spoke up. "I think that was a reasonable question, Jack. What was the nature of the defendant's fluid found on the decedent? I mean do we have a sexual assault? Blood? Toenails? What? Make it simple for us, Jack."

"Page twelve of the report indicates that the saliva of the defendant was found in the mouth of Ms. Dunn."

Reverend Justice, who had been poring through the lab report, piped up again. "Don't you mean tobacco spittle, Jack? Not just saliva."

"Whatever," the DA said dismissively.

"What else do we have for marking?" the judge inquired.

"That's it for me, Your Honor," said the DA, beaming with a smile worthy of a toothpaste ad. "I will have witnesses introduce these items—you know, lay the foundation. I will also have other eyewitness testimony that will be offered."

"Who are your witnesses, Jack? And have you supplied their statements, if any, to Reverend Justice?" asked the judge.

"We have Sheriff McGeary as a witness to the items collected at the scene. There is no statement for him. We have two witnesses from the Brigantine, one witness from the laundry company, and we have one witness to an admission made by the defendant while they shared a jail cell. Their statements have been provided to the good Reverend. That's all I have."

"Counselor Justice, will you be introducing evidence or documents in rebuttal?" asked the court.

"I have nothing, Your Honor."

"All righty, then, let's get the show on the road." The judge glanced at Sally the transcriber. "That's off the record, of course."

"Yes, sir," she said obsequiously as she hit some delete buttons on her strange machine, which was perched on its little stand and pinched between her legs. Reverend Justice knew better than to say a word or react to the "show" comment as they exited the judge's chambers and walked back to the courtroom.

CHAPTER 62

Ding, dong! The door chimed at the Branson house, which was located within a thousand feet of Sow Hill. *Ding, dong* again.

"Who is it, and which door are you at?"

"Mr. Branson, this is the Port Talbot Police and the FBI, please open the door. We have a warrant for the searching of these premises," said Agent Barnes in a surprisingly soothing tone.

"That's crap! Perhaps you didn't get the memo. Sussman is standing down. My boy is cooperating. In fact he's at court now, helping you guys out. This must be a mistake!"

I am sorry, Mr. Branson, you must open the door or we are authorized by Judge Ambrewster in Portland to forcibly enter your home to conduct a search for specific items. If you would open the door, I will share the warrant with you."

"Ed Nickerson, are you out there?" yelled Mr. Branson.

"We have Officer Davenport with us from the Port Talbot Police."

"You send a kid to my home to mess with my constitutional rights? I'm calling my attorney."

"Mr. Branson, we will forcibly enter this home on the count of three. One! … Two! …" Johnny pushed Digger out of the way and began to square up on the door.

"Hold it! Hold it! I'm opening it!" Branson said as the locks clicked.

He opened the door halfway. "Let me see your warrant."

Johnny Barnes pushed the door all the way open and walked right in. Got any weapons or house guests, Mr. Branson?" Johnny asked as he handed the warrant to Mr. Branson and quickly moved through the first floor rooms checking for people.

"First floor clear," he spoke into his shoulder radio.

Mr. Branson capitulated. "No one else is here. I'm watching my son testify to help you guys out, and this is the thanks we get. Those politicians can forget getting reelected."

"Where are your guns, Mr. Branson?"

"In the den, locked in the cabinet, and under my bed upstairs."

"Where is the door to the basement and the back yard?" asked Barnes.

"Right there in the kitchen."

Barnes signaled to Digger to keep his eyeballs on Branson.

"Mr. Branson, have a seat, please," Agent Barnes said, pointing to the living room couch.

"You mind if I turn up the TV to hear how the Bransons are helping law enforcement in this community?"

"Digger, turn up the TV for Mr. Branson," Barnes allowed as he disappeared down the basement steps.

"You rich summah folk are all alike … stealin' the jobs from the hahd workin' locals. What? Daddy pay off a town selectman? You namby-pamby college boy. I think this job is too dangerous for you, you little candy-arsed, numbnut."

"You're not threatening a police officer, are you Mr. Branson?" Agent Barnes asked, coming back into the room with Agent Orringer right behind him.

"This is Agent Orringer, Mr. Branson." Barnes then spoke into his handset, "Mike, would you clear upstairs please? The basement is clear."

"Upstairs clear!" bellowed from the walkie-talkies. "Pistol from under the bed is secure," added Mike.

Agent Barnes relieved Digger from watching Mr. Branson. "Officer Davenport, please assist Agent Orringer in a sweep of the upstairs for the items in the warrant. Mr. Branson, do you have any questions about the warrant?" Agent Barnes asked in a kindly manner as he sat down next to Mr. Branson.

"Up yours!" Branson barked as he watched the droning court case on TV.

Mike joined Digger in Chuck's bedroom.

"First these," Mike said, holding out rubber gloves. "Then this," he added, pulling out a small flash camera. "And then this," he said as he pulled out a black garbage bag, "if we find anything of interest."

Digger nodded and went straight to Chuck's bed, which was loosely made with sheets, pillows, and a blanket. Putting on his gloves, he then made the bed a little better, pulling the blanket taut over the mattress.

Mike couldn't help but comment. "Digger, usually we destroy a room not clean it."

Without a word, Digger got on his knees at the bedside and whacked the bed in the middle of the taut blanket. A puff of sand bounced up.

Mike's jaw dropped. "Do that again!" Mike whispered as he, too, got down on his knees. Then Mike whacked the bed and more sand bounced. "I'll be. Looks like this blanket has been to a beach," Mike said into the walkie-talkie and added, "Let's carefully bring all the bedding with us. Johnny, I'll spot you. You need to come up here and see this." Turning to Digger, Mike said, "Show Johnny. I'll watch Branson."

"What'd you find?" Barnes asked as he entered the bedroom.

"Kneel down here with me and watch," said Digger. He whacked the bed. The perfectly normal, clean-looking mackinaw blanket flumed a cloud of sand for a second then returned imperceptibly back into the nap of the blanket.

"This has been to the beach all right." Agent Barnes started peeling the blanket off, folding it on itself to keep as much sand in it for analysis. As he lifted the corner of the blanket at the far foot of the bed, Digger held Johnny's arm still and pulled out his flashlight and shone it on the corner. The light illuminated a dark stain on the blanket.

Agent Barnes brought the stain up to his nose, whiffed, and whiffed again. "It's blood or I should retire! Run this blanket up to Sow Hill and get Brian analyzing it immediately. Then come right back."

Digger was rolling the blanket into the bag as on his way down the stairs when Mr. Branson caught a glimpse of it.

"Oh dear God, don't take Chucky's mackinaw! It's the only real thing he has to remember his deceased mother by. He will get it back, right?"

Digger didn't even acknowledge the comments as he left the house and let Agent Orringer respond.

"Yes, sir, it will be returned unless it is evidence of a crime."

"How can it be evidence of crime? His mother wrapped him in it as a boy and he wrapped her in it right until the time of her death from cancer."

"Did she bleed in the blanket at any time during her sickness?" asked Agent Barnes as he came down the steps.

"No, it was all internal cancer."

"Mike, would you resume the search in the same room?" asked Agent Barnes.

"How's the trial going Mr. Branson?" Barnes said as he rejoined him in looking at the TV.

CHAPTER 63

"Mr. Butterworth, the defense, having reserved its opening statement until its case-in-chief, means that you may call your first witness," directed the judge.

"The State calls Lincoln County's Sheriff Sean McGeary."

"Sheriff McGeary, raise your right hand and place your left hand on the Bible. Do you promise to tell the truth, the whole truth, and nothing but the truth so help you God?" recited the bailiff.

"I do."

"Have a seat there. And speak up, please, so I can hear over here," instructed the judge.

"Could you please tell the court, Sheriff McGeary, how long you have served Lincoln County as the sheriff?" asked Butterworth, commencing his direct examination.

"I have served the residents of Lincoln for over fifteen years, having been reelected three times in a row."

"Would you briefly describe your duties to the court?"

***

Charles Branson spoke up, yelling at his TV five miles away. "You harass citizens! You loser! You kiss babies and kill business!"

Agent Barnes started laughing. "I thought you were friends with Sean."

"Friends are as friends do! He hasn't done me right thus far."

Digger stepped into the Branson house. "Analysis is underway, sir."

Branson looked at the young kid, held up his middle finger, and said, "Analyze this, twerp!"

"Thanks, Officer Davenport. Join Agent Orringer upstairs to see if there are any other items that fit the bill."

"Yes, sir." Digger pivoted and bounded up the stairs, completely ignoring Mr. Branson's venting.

"How's it going, Mike?" asked Digger.

"We got this stuff: a can of gunpowder, and masking tape." Mike shrugged his shoulders. "Maybe it's tied to the truck."

"What did Agent Forkel say about the blanket?"

"He sent the chief to Brigantine Beach for sand samples and was doing some scraping at the blood on the blanket when I left."

Chapter 64

"I offer the red vest into evidence as Exhibit A," proclaimed DA Butterworth.

"Reverend Justice, do you care to voir dire?" asked the judge.

"No, and no objection to the vest coming into evidence," said Reverend Justice.

"The red vest is received into evidence as Exhibit A. Continue, Mr. Butterworth," said the judge.

"Sheriff McGeary, please describe what other items were found at the scene of the crime."

"We found a tablecloth that the deceased was lying on, we found an empty bottle of Jack Daniels whiskey, and we found a Styrofoam cup with a lid on it containing tobacco spittle."

"Handing you what has been marked as Exhibit B—can you identify this?"

"Yes, that is the tablecloth that belongs to the Brigantine Hotel that Ms. Dunn was lying on when we found her at the murder scene."

"I'd like to offer Exhibit B into evidence at this time."

"Any objections Reverend Justice?" asked the judge.

"May I voir dire?"

"Of course, counselor." The DA returned to his seat to allow Reverend Justice to have the floor with the witness to voir dire the witness, to determine if this item was exactly what it was claimed to be, namely a Brigantine tablecloth found at the scene under the decedent.

"Sheriff, please indicate to me where the tablecloth identifies its owner as being the Brigantine Hotel."

McGeary shot a quick glance to Butterworth to see if there would be any help in the form of an objection or otherwise coming from his attorney. None.

"It is the Brigantine's red that they use on all their tables, and this is the cloth the Dunn Girl was found on. Those are my initials on the chain of custody certificate for the evidence locker."

Reverend Justice pressed in, "So if I understand you correctly, there is nothing on this item that identifies it as being from the Brigantine. Is that correct?"

"Uh, ah … that's correct," McGeary admitted.

"Judge, based on my voir dire I am going to object to the tablecloth being introduced into evidence."

"Mr. Butterworth?"

"Your Honor, we have another witness who can attest to the fact that this tablecloth is from the Brigantine. I would like to reoffer the exhibit as simply the tablecloth upon which the decedent was found."

"I will sustain the Reverend's objection that the tablecloth is not being admitted as the Brigantine's. Now the DA is simply offering it into evidence as the cloth upon which the decedent was found. Do you have any objection, Reverend Justice?"

"Yes, Your Honor. I fail to see the relevance of some tablecloth to the issues before the court, namely, did my client commit this crime?"

"I agree with Reverend Justice. His objection is sustained. Exhibit B is not received into evidence. Proceed Mr. Butterworth."

There were nearly imperceptible murmurs in the courtroom. The judge looked up at the crowd like a good hunting dog about to point.

"But Your Honor, all we are saying is that this tablecloth was at the scene." Butterworth hung tough.

"Jack, if you have a witness that can tie this exhibit to the defendant, then I'll listen. Move on, counselor."

Without skipping a beat, Jack said, "Thank you, Your Honor," and turned to the witness and asked, "Handing you what has been marked as Exhibit C—can you identify this?"

"Yes I can," said the sheriff.

"What is it?" Asked the DA

"That is the defendant's cup that he used for spitting tobacco chaw," answered McGeary.

"Objection! The reply assumes facts not in evidence!" shouted the Reverend.

"Sustained," said the judge.

"Sheriff, let me ask you this way, when did you first see this item?"

"At the scene of the murder on the beach. Our forensic team picked it up and analyzed it," answered McGeary.

"Objection. Hearsay, Your Honor."

"Sustained as to the actions of the forensic team, but I'll allow the statement he saw it himself on the beach. Continue, Jack."

"What did you observe regarding this cup?"

"I watched as it got placed into an evidence container and I saw it get sealed and removed from the murder scene. I personally observed the lab analysis ..."

"Hold on, Sean ... Sheriff." The DA turned to the judge. "I have no further questions of this witness."

The sheriff looked bewildered at the DA. The cameras and audience picked up on the dissension.

"I'd like to call as my next ..."

The judge gently interrupted the DA. "We are going to let Reverend Justice cross-examine the witness."

To the sheriff, who was already starting his high-in-the-saddle law-enforcement stride back to his seat, he said, "Sheriff, you may remain seated," and to the defense counsel he asked, "I assume, Mr. Justice, you would like to cross-examine the sheriff?"

"Yes please, Your Honor," the attorney responded like he was being offered another helping of stuffing with gravy at Thanksgiving.

CHAPTER 65

"Agent Barnes, channel twelve, please." Patty's voice echoed throughout the Branson house from the officers' radios. Barnes stood up from the couch where he was sitting with Mr. Branson and moved into the kitchen but within view of Mr. Branson.

"This is Barnes."

"Forkel here; this blanket is a goldmine! But it's going to take time. My sand samples match. I'm working on the blood smear slides for a match. I also got what appears to be female brown hair, root follicle and all! But I need a sample of Dunn's hair. Between the sand and the blood match, we could be 85 percent sure that the Dunn girl was on this blanket on that beach and bled. My makeshift lab isn't able to analyze the blood samples any better than an eighty-five percent probability. If we add the hair match, we are at 100 percent. I need hair from the corpse, and I need a witness with me to observe chain of custody as I perform these tests in the field ... right? We *are* on a time crunch, right? Or can I send this stuff to the Virginia labs?"

"If we delay, an innocent man will probably be in jail for a long time, although watching the DA on TV, I'm not impressed."

"Oh, that's rich, I'm freaking out up here under a time crunch and you're watchin' the boob tube."

"Hey, hey, it's part of keeping the suspect at peace and keeping him from calling in a bunch of sharks. Looks like you got to get over to the morgue, right? Zip and mark your samples, including the blanket. I'm sending you and Boy Wonder over to the morgue. If and when you have a match, give me a ring. And be ready to take the stand to testify."

"I was born ready," Forkel replied.

"Put the chief on. I'm gonna stay here with Mike, making friends with the lobstah mobstah."

"Okay, hold ... Chief Nickerson, its Agent Barnes."

"Nickerson here."

"Chief, Brian has got to get to the morgue to do a hair sample analysis and needs a witness to corroborate chain of custody during the process. Again I think Digger is the best to send. Mike and I are gonna piddle around here and try to keep Mr. Branson off the phone to his lawyers for as long as possible. Brian is quite capable of walking into the courtroom and taking the stand to back up his scientific mumbo jumbo if we should get so lucky."

"Sure. They can take my cruiser so you guys aren't stranded. I'll hold the fort here. Lord knows with an office blown to crap, this is where I need to be! Any evidence of explosives down there?"

"Just some duct tape and gunpowder for repacking shotgun shells. But we're still only on the second floor. I'll send Digger up. Brian will signal us when he's done checking the hair."

"Roger that."

CHAPTER 66

"Sheriff McGeary, where did you go to college?" asked the defense counsel in a nonchalant tone.

"Objection, irrelevant!" said the DA, pouncing on the question, which startled everyone.

"Overruled. Direct examination of this witness addressed the witness's background and experience," admonished the judge. "Continue, Reverend Justice. Er, Sheriff, please answer the question."

"I did not attend college."

Ever-so-faint whispers were heard in the courtroom. This time the judge did not look up.

"Where did you get your high school diploma?"

"The State of Maine granted me an equivalency degree in 1965. I dropped out of high school to help my daddy on the boats," McGeary added quickly, hoping to garner some sympathy while having this gaping hole in his resume broadcast to the world during the last week of the primary, which, in this neck of the woods, could seal the election.

"I understand, Sheriff," the defense counsel responded soothingly, using the pastoral voice that he usually reserved for church matters he was actively involved in.

"Your Honor, may the witness be instructed to answer only the question asked? I asked where the degree came from, not why," Reverend Justice inquired of the bench.

The judge turned to Sheriff McGeary, "Do you understand the difference? Please confine your answers to the specific question, okay?"

Sheriff McGeary looked at the judge with a beet-red face and sweat forming on his brow and quietly assented to the instruction by nodding his head.

Reverend Justice, not letting go of the simplest screw-ups, turned to Sally the court reporter and added, "Let the record reflect the witness has nodded his head in agreement with the judge's direction."

Sally looked to the judge, who nodded approval of the attorney's instruction. After all, instructions regarding the record should come only from the judge, but attorneys have long attempted to take over simple instructions for expediency's sake ... or because of ego.

"Sheriff, on direct exam you said that certain items of evidence were taken from the scene is that correct?"

"Yes."

"A cup?"

"Yes."

"A tablecloth?"

"Yes."

"A red vest?"

"Yes."

"Did you take tire tread molds from the scene?"

"Um, yes."

"Were there tire impressions in the vicinity that you deemed important enough to take impressions of?"

"As a precaution, we gather all kinds of evidence," the witness added noncommittally.

"I will repeat my question, were there tire impressions in the vicinity that you deemed important enough to take impressions of?"

"Yes."

"To your knowledge, did the decedent have a vehicle at the scene?"

"No, she did not."

"To your knowledge, does the defendant, George Williams, own a vehicle?"

"According to our records, he does not."

"And yet you took tread molds?"

"Yes."

"As you sit here today, do you have any vehicles, the tires of which match those molds?"

"Not to my knowledge," the sheriff said, adjusting his position in his chair and reaching for the cup of water on the railing with a slight tremor in his hand.

"Directing your attention to the arrest of George Williams, were you present?"

"Yes."

"Where did the arrest occur?"

"At the Brigantine employee dorm."

"Who was present?"

"I was there, we had two deputies, at least two Port police officers, and the chief of police. There were some press personnel and perhaps some Brigantine personnel."

"What time did the arrest occur?"

"At approximately 11:00 a.m."

The district attorney spoke up. "Your Honor, I am going to object to this line of questioning. It is completely beyond the scope of my direct examination and irrelevant."

"Overruled. Reverend, get to your point, please."

"Yes, Your Honor," obliged the defense counsel.

"What time that morning did you reach the conclusion to bring in George Williams?"

"At approximately 10:30 a.m."

"Between 10:30 and 11:00 a.m., did you or anyone that you know of brief the press regarding having a suspect in mind at the Brigantine?"

"Not to my knowledge."

"Were you surprised to see such a large press gathering outside the Brigantine dorm at the time of the arrest?"

The sheriff looked quickly over at the DA to see if there would be any help avoiding this line of questioning. The DA kept his head down, looking at his yellow legal pad.

"Yes. I was surprised to see press present."

"Did it appear that the press had been tipped off?"

"Objection!" said the DA, pouncing on the question.

"Sustained. Calls for a conjectural conclusion." The judge seemed to enjoy teaching his audience Trial Practice 101.

Reverend Justice continued without missing a beat. "Did there come a time when you were told that the press *did* receive a tip at approximately 10:45 a.m. that morning?"

"Yes, I did."

"Who told you they had received a tip?"

"Tracy Thomas of Channel 8 News."

"When did she tell you this?"

"The following day during a press conference."

"What did she say?"

"Objection, hearsay!" the DA stood to say.

The defense counsel quickly responded as if waiting for this moment. "We are not offering Ms. Thomas's statements for the truth of the matter asserted within her statements. We are simply offering those statements as a basis to examine the mental state of this witness in his decision to arrest and prosecute my client."

"The mental state of this witness is not in issue, Your Honor. The decision to arrest and charge and incarcerate involves many government personnel."

"I will allow the witness to answer," said the judge. "After all, we don't have a jury to be confused over the nuances you raise. Please answer the question, Sheriff."

"Tracy Thomas informed us that her station received an anonymous call fifteen minutes before the arrest."

Murmurs came from the audience.

"What else did Tracy say?"

"I don't recall her saying anything else."

"Didn't she say ..." and the defense counsel looked down at his notes with a slight pause and commenced to read what he made sound like a script, "'Is it possible that the only person who could call in the tip was the real murderer trying to frame George Williams?'"

The murmurs started to crescendo and culminated with Judge Pendergast cracking the gavel down. "Order. Order!"

"I don't recall her statement that specifically."

"But you do recall the gist of her inquiry asserting the possible framing of George because of the details of the tip?"

"We get a lot of crazy ..." Reverend Justice interrupted the sheriff quickly and forcefully. "Yes or no?"

"Yes or No, what?" the witness played coyly.

"Your Honor, may I have the question read back to the witness?"

The judge assisted in the game. "Sally, would you please read back the question for the witness?"

Sally nodded and reached into the little rectangular box mounted on the front of the transcribing machine and lifted toward the ceiling the long ticker tape with strange code on it and commenced to translate in a loud and clear voice. "Question from Mr. Justice, 'Is it possible that the only person who could call in the tip was the real murderer trying to frame George Williams?' The court, 'Order. Order.' Answer from the witness, 'I don't recall her statement that specifically.'" And then Sally added with a smile, "Oh, here is the last question of Reverend Justice, 'But you do recall the gist of her inquiry asserting the possible framing of George because of the details of the tip?'" Sally paused. "Back on the record, Your Honor?" Sally asked as a means to stall for time as she returned her tape to the steno box.

If the sheriff was playing a game at not remembering the question, he lost. Having Sally try to find the right question caused her to reread the most damaging concept, George was framed.

"Yes please, Sally. The witness will answer the question with a yes or no," instructed the judge.

"Yes, I do recall that is what she was trying to say."

"Did you subpoena the station's phone records?"

"No."

"Did you inquire of any other press company as to whether they had received the tip, too?"

"No."

"Did you contact the phone company in an attempt to track down who could have had this information and shared it with the press?"

"No, I did not."

"Are we to understand that an officer of fifteen years on the force is presented with credible evidence of a frame job, but you did absolutely nothing to check the legitimacy of the lead?"

"Objection!" the DA shouted, jumping up.

"Grounds, counselor?" asked the judge in a toying tone as if to say, "What are you going to with this one? It's a tough question."

"It's an unfair question in that it mischaracterizes the nature of the alleged tip and assumes a fact that is not in evidence that there was a tip at all!"

"I will allow the question. The witness may answer."

"We didn't check further into the statements of Tracy Thomas or any other member of the press."

"I have no further questions of this witness at this time," the defense counsel said as he returned to the defendant's table.

The judge looked over his bifocals down at the DA. "Any redirect?"

"No thank you, Your Honor," responded Butterworth plainly, which was a tremendous concession that he could not rehabilitate any damaging testimony obtained from the sheriff.

The judge looked at his watch. "The court will recess for thirty minutes for lunch," and tapped the gavel once. The room surged with a cacophony of voices discussing thoughts and impressions of the morning hearing.

The sheriff leaned over to Butterworth as he returned from the witness stand. "What the heck? Man, that was painful!"

Butterworth reassured McGeary, "Hey we're just warming up. This case is about the forensics and the admission in the jail cell anyway. And that's next."

"No, this case is about me getting reelected, and he made me look like crap up there!"

"You'll be fine, Sean." Both men looked through the double doors of the courtroom to see the frieze lights on and the clamoring of the press talking with Reverend Justice at the center of it all.

"How 'bout we issue some 'no comments' till we get through this day?" the DA suggested to the sheriff.

"Ya think?" the sheriff responded in a sarcastic tone.

CHAPTER 67

The morgue for Port Talbot consisted of Reilly's funeral home not far from the courthouse and the county building. Digger had agreed to meet Agent Forkel there. He preferred to ride the bike through town. It was far quicker in the summer.

"Hello, I'm Agent Forkel of the FBI, and this is Officer Davenport of the Port Talbot Police Department. We are here to look at the body of Ms. Dunn," the agent said pleasantly but officially as he handed his badge to the receptionist at the funeral home.

"Of course, gentlemen. Let me get Mr. Reilly. I know Dr. Beebe is over in court and unavailable all day. Just a second."

The receptionist reached for the phone. "Mr. Reilly, can you pick up please? … Hello, sir. I have the FBI here regarding the Dunn girl … Thank you." Looking up, she said, "He will be right here."

"Digger, really nice to meet you." The funeral director held out his hand to shake Forkel's and Digger's hands.

"Hi, Mr. Reilly." Forkel started by handing him his ID and showing his FBI badge. "We are in somewhat of a hurry on federal business and need to see the body of Ms. Dunn, please."

Reilly looked toward the receptionist, who was soaking this drama up as well as keeping an eye on a small TV that was tuned to the court proceeding and the blather of the news reporters during the lunch break.

"Here, step into the conference room for a second." Reilly shut the door. "Sheriff McGeary told me not to let anyone have access to that body without his permission." He said to Digger, "You know how small this town is. I'll lose the morgue rent."

Digger Davenport spoke up. "I certainly understand, Mr. Reilly, but two things: If this matter goes the direction I believe it will, McGeary won't be your concern. Second, this is the FBI. For the morgue to refuse access to the FBI would probably cause a world of hurt more than McGeary can muster even if he *is* reelected."

Forkel tipped his head toward the kid, signaling, *Who can argue with that logic?*

Reilly motioned the officers through the only other door of the conference room, which brought them to a room that appeared to be wall-to-wall stainless steel. One wall was outfitted with square doors floor to chest height. Each square had what looked to be old style refrigerator handles.

"The poor dear is right here," Mr. Reilly said, opening the door and pulling out a large metal tray with a gray, naked body on it. The tray rolled out with ease like a file cabinet drawer on wheels. Mr. Reilly picked up a clean sheet and draped Janie's naked body. "Excuse me," he said as he fussed with the sheet.

Digger quietly uttered a thank you. He had turned a shade of gray similar to Janie's.

"Officer, better get used to corpses if you're gonna be in this line of business," said Forkel.

Mr. Reilly spoke first. "I think Digger Davenport has seen a few bodies. Aren't you the boy who hauled in the chef, who as I recall was also from the Brigantine?"

Digger just nodded. Forkel double took a glance at Davenport. "You do have some experience, then."

"Gentlemen, carry on. I'll be on the other side of that door. Agent Forkel, may I get a copy of that ID for my records?"

"Absolutely," he said, handing over the ID. "May I set up a microscope on this table here?" Forkel asked.

"Sure. If I could reach Dr. Beebe, I'm sure he'd let you use his equipment over there. But everyone is incommunicado during the hearing at the courthouse up the road."

"This will do, thanks."

Reilly left, and Forkel peeled back the sheet fully. Digger looked away. "Davenport, check this out. You can see she was crushed. This portion of her torso is completely caved in."

Digger just gave a weak "um hum" as he stared out the frosted windows at nothing.

"She doesn't look at all like a rape victim."

The lab rat is getting too much into his specimen, thought Digger. "What about the hair? Is there a match?" he said, looking at his watch. "We're on a deadline. They're back from lunch by now."

"Keep your shorts on, Poindexter! Here we go, I need only one strand with the root follicle intact. Observe."

Digger watched as Forkel, wearing rubber gloves and using tweezers, singled out one or two strands of hair at the crown of Janie's scalp, twisted the tweezers around like wrapping spaghetti on a fork, and yanked. Janie's head and body stayed completely still like a rock when Forkel tugged the hairs out.

He held the specimen up to the light. "Perfect follicle and all!"

He moved over to the microscope and placed the specimen in a glass jar that he pulled from his briefcase and which itself had been in a sealed wrapper.

"I have three follicles and am leaving two in the evidence jar and preparing a slide with the third, okay?"

"Roger that," Digger replied as he re-covered Janie with the sheet.

"What, are you squeamish about naked women?" Forkel asked as he started to squint into the microscope and turn its knobs.

"Not really. It's just that I don't have a thing for *dead* naked women, and this particular girl had been a friend of mine and best friend of my girlfriend."

"Oh geez, Digger! I didn't know that! Barnsey never told me you had ties to the decedent! I am really sorry to be poking around someone you knew and cared for. I just approached this like so many corpses in my past."

"You're cool, man, don't worry." He paused. "How's it look?" Digger asked him, looking at his watch. Digger sensed that it was getting close to when everyone in court would return from lunch.

"Come see for yourself. I have three slides here."

"Three?"

"Yes. Tell me what you see. Slide 1?"

Digger adjusted the knobs slightly. "Okay."

"Got the cell wall pattern? The color? The width?"

"I think so," replied Digger, still squinting into the scope.

"Slide 2!"

Digger looked up to refocus his eyes and then back down over the scope and adjusted the knobs. "Whoa, what is this, animal fur?" Digger exclaimed.

"No comment. Slide 3?"

"Okay," said Digger, looking down again. "That's slide one."

Here is slide one. Take your time; be sure," Forkel said soothingly. "People's freedoms for many years are at stake."

Digger kept comparing slide one and three. "These are identical."

Like a professor, Forkel asked, "What does slide one say there in the corner?"

"Branson blanket."

"And slide three?"

"Dunn corpse!"

Digger looked at the notation on slide two. "Who or what is BIF?"

"Brian Ian Forkel."

"That's *your* hair? Gnarly dude!"

"It's my Irish heritage … definitely twisted. We are done here."

Just then they heard a commotion out in the hallway.

"I know Nickerson is here. That's his car out there!" bellowed an angry voice. The door banged opened and Sheriff McGeary stood with his hands on his hips, not far from his service revolver.

"How would you boys like a tampering rap that will end your careers before they even start? Dispatch, I need backup at the Reilly funeral home pronto!" McGeary bellowed into his two-way radio.

Digger slowly reached for the transmit button on the radio box on his belt by the back of his hip and slid it up to the on position.

"My name is Agent Brian Forkel of the FBI, and I am conducting a forensic examination in accordance with federal law and procedure."

Digger spoke up, "Sheriff McGeary, this examination has just confirmed that Jane Dunn's hair and blood have been positively identified on a different suspect's personal property."

"Shut up, you piss-ant! The case is wrapped up, or will be in an hour or two. And you boys can just chill out here while my deputies secure this area."

Forkel spoke next. "Are you saying you plan to detain us? Sheriff?"

"Exactly. Evidence tamperers are nothing but common criminals," he hissed back as he released the snap on his weapon's holster and drew his weapon.

"Sheriff, please return your revolver to its holster," Digger responded so whoever was monitoring the radio would get a picture of what was going on.

The phone started to ring at the funeral home and stopped. The pretty receptionist came around the corner. "Sheriff McGeary, it's for you."

The sheriff turned her way, and Forkel leaped at the sheriff and took him down to the ground, knocking the pistol out of his hand. Forkel had him pinned momentarily.

Digger jumped into the action by diving for McGeary's handcuffs on his belt. He caught one of the sheriff's arms as it was swinging toward Forkel and snapped it into one cuff. Forkel was able to get his knee on the neck of the sheriff and pull the other arm around, which Digger assisted into the other cuff. Forkel stood up while Digger lay in a cross-body block on the sheriff's thumping and kicking body. Forkel retrieved the Glock pistol, which had skittered across the floor, and put it in his waistband. He approached the writhing sheriff and yanked his radio off his waist.

"Dispatch, this is FBI Agent Brian Forkel, DOJ ID 33578, Portland Office. Under interagency protocol, I am directing that the last order of Sheriff McGeary be rescinded and that all deputies stand down. Over?"

"Connie, don't you listen to him! He's nothing but a common criminal! We have state's rights!" McGeary yelled in the background as Forkel stepped away from the sheriff into the conference room next door.

"Over?"

CHAPTER 68

"Call your next witness, counselor," the judge said to the DA. The judge looked at his watch. "Is this your last witness?"

The sheriff had testified. The biochemist and the coroner went quickly, and the Brigantine busboy, Jerome, had testified with very little cross-examination.

"Yes, Your Honor, this is our last witness. I'd like to call Charles Branson Jr."

Chuck stood up from the bench in the audience area directly behind the DA's chair and walked toward the judge to be sworn in.

Precisely at that moment, Digger came walking through the double doors with a briefcase in each hand and sat in Chuck's now vacant seat.

The audience murmured as the police officer strode down the center aisle of the courtroom. The judge did his best to ignore him.

"Raise your right hand and place your left hand on the Bible."

While the witness was being sworn in, the DA turned around to see what the commotion was behind him.

The two leaned toward each other. "Jack, remember you told me that I should do whatever it takes to bring you ironclad evidence before anyone else? You're gonna want to see this stuff right away before this particular witness testifies." Digger nodded toward his briefcases.

"Where's Nickerson?" hissed Jack, as if this kid didn't have the clout to be discussing the subject.

"He is in a constitutional showdown with Sean McGeary and the FBI at the morgue … weapons drawn."

Butterworth's eyes got as big as saucers.

"DA Butterworth, your witness is sworn and ready for you to proceed," the judge announced impatiently. "I have done my part, and now it is time for your part," the judge added to humor the crowd.

"Yes, thank you, Your Honor. I am sorry, but I need to request a brief recess."

"You got eight minutes, counselor," barked the judge, looking at his watch and smacking the gavel. Digger looked to his immediate right. It was Chuck's attorney, Peter Coffey.

"Hi, Mr. Coffey; Digger Davenport, University of New York. I'm a friend of your son, PJ, and I attended your lecture on Con Crim Pro last semester. Very interesting stuff. I think it was on perjury."

Coffey wrinkled his face, not remembering that perjury was the topic. "Nice to meet you again. I think we met there, right? The seminar was on search and seizure, I think."

Before Digger could answer the question politely, the DA had grabbed him by the arm and said, "Excuse us please. We need to talk, yes?"

Digger doubled back and grabbed the two suitcases, and they pushed their way through the crowd, which had now filled the aisle. Out in the front hall, Tracy Thomas came click-clacking over in her high heels with a microphone at the ready.

"Hey, Digger, what gives?"

Butterworth leaned in and barked, "No comment!" and continued to strong-arm Digger away to the first attorneys' conference room in the hall.

"Speak to me, Bike Cop!" Butterworth demanded.

Digger stated it plainly. "George Williams didn't kill Jane Dunn. Chuck Branson did ... and probably blew up the water tower, too, but that is beside the point."

The DA threatened Digger, "Let's have the ironclad evidence now, and it better be good or you will never get a job in the law, period. *Never!*"

"Before I begin, let me give you a heads-up. Sheriff McGeary has not been informing you of certain developments in this case and sits at this moment in handcuffs on the lab floor of Reilly's funeral home, surrounded by FBI agents who are themselves surrounded by deputy sheriffs. Shall I continue?"

"No. Hold please." The DA stuck his head out of the conference room. "Willy! Get in here! ... This is my assistant DA, William Wentworth. This is Digger Davenport, Port Police." The two shook hands.

"Willy, Digger is going to brief me on some evidentiary developments in this matter, and I need you to call Reilly's funeral home or drive over there and find out what is going on and brief me ASAP. Don't talk to the press!"

"Of course. Right away, sir." He departed at a run.

The DA slammed the door shut and spun around to Digger. "What has McGeary withheld from me?"

"The fact that the tread molds from the beach confirm that Chuck Branson's truck was the vehicle at Brigantine Beach."

The DA rubbed his forehead. "He just testified to the contrary ... unbelievable! What else?"

"The fact that the Port Talbot police night log confirms that at approximately 2:00 a.m. of the morning of the murder, Port police officer Brian "Buzz" Edwards placed Chuck and Jane together in Chuck's truck stopped on Ocean Avenue. A copy of the log entry is in here." Digger pointed to one of the briefcases.

"Chief Nickerson shared these developments with the sheriff. Now for the ironclad stuff." Digger pulled his small notepad from his top pocket.

"Oh God, there's more?" the DA said quietly. He sat down in one of the cheap chairs provided by the county for the small attorney conference rooms.

"FBI forensics, working in conjunction with a biochemist from Portland, Sanford Reims ..."

The DA interrupted, "Yes, Sanford, my witness who just testified this afternoon. Go ahead."

"They confirm that the lipstick case found in Chuck Branson's truck as part of its impound procedure on the drug bust was Jane Dunn's." Opening one of the suitcases, Digger pulled out a large envelope that had the certified report of analysis, the lipstick case itself, and its chain of custody log, with Digger's signature as the last entry.

Jack looked at the log to the name just above Digger's at 11:30 a.m. "Where's Agent Barnes?" he asked as he looked at his watch.

"He probably has his weapon pointed at McGeary while McGeary's deputies have their weapons pointed at the FBI. And we are here."

The DA shook his head in disbelief. "You *are* kidding me, please?"

"Not really, sir. They were at a standoff and allowed me to sneak out the back door to show you this evidence in hopes that it will avert disaster.

"Let me lay the big clump of iron on you." Digger reached down and opened the other case. It sprung wide open, revealing a beautiful mackinaw blanket.

"Let me guess, Chuck Branson's blanket with proof that it was at the Brigantine beach."

"Exactly sir, but with some hitchhikers on it. Besides Brigantine Beach sand, first, Jane Dunn's hair." Digger offered a separate envelope with plastic bags and a handwritten report and certification.

"Who is Agent Forkel?" the DA asked, studying the documents.

"They refer to him as 'the lab rat.' But the way he decked McGeary I'd say he's more like Dr. Jekyll. It was sick."

"Stop. This is too much. What else was attached?" asked the DA, recomposing himself for the battle at hand.

"Second, Jane Dunn's blood in a fairly large stain here on the corner of this blanket." Digger pulled the plastic bag from the case and showed the DA the distinct dark spot. "Here's the certified analysis."

A rap on the door interrupted their discussion. It was the bailiff. "Jack, the judge is on the bench, Branson is in the hot seat, and everyone is waiting for you."

"Coming, Gene! One minute." The DA looked down in silence, thinking.

Digger broke the silence, anticipating the DA's thoughts about Chuck Branson.

"It's not a custodial interrogation. He has promised to tell the truth and cooperate as part of turning state's evidence, right? No Miranda, no right to counsel. He could plead the fifth if he knows to."

"Maybe he can identify this," Digger said, holding up the blanket. "His dad told us his mom gave it to him, and it was special. I guess that's why he kept it on his bed and never washed it."

The DA slapped his own forehead as if he had gotten a fresh revelation. "Hot seat, all right," he muttered as he got up, and walked out of the tiny conference room. He turned back toward Digger, who was packing things up.

"Give me the suitcase with the blanket and the night log. You keep the other stuff."

Digger stood up and handed the heavier case to the DA. They headed down the hall toward the courtroom shoulder to shoulder.

"I hate being played for an idiot," the DA whispered to Digger, referring to Chuck's attempt to implicate George Williams. Just then Willy Wentworth, the assistant DA, came running into the front hall of the courthouse.

"Mr. Butterworth, it's unbelievable! Three deputies are outside the funeral home, waiting in their cruisers for instructions from McGeary. And two FBI agents are playing cards inside the mortuary while McGeary is sitting on the floor. They all say they are waiting for you to wrap up this case, which they say will settle the jurisdictional dispute."

"Thanks, Willy. Let's see how this goes. Please go back to them and tell them it will be resolved shortly and to keep their cool."

Chapter 69

"Please state your full name for the record," the DA asked, displaying a peaceful demeanor.

"Charles Langford Branson Jr."

"Where do you reside?"

"Sixty-six Benson Creek Lane, Port Talbot, Maine."

"How are you employed?"

"Branson Seafood Distribution Company."

"Have you agreed to testify today under an arrangement with the district attorney's office?"

"Ah, yes."

"What is that arrangement?"

"Ah … well, uh … uh … I agree to tell you what I was told regarding the murder of Jane Dunn, and you will give some consideration of that cooperation regarding my criminal charge for possessing pot."

The audience began to murmur. The DA pressed on unfazed.

"Have I or has anyone from the government made any specific promises to you regarding a sentence or any other specific deal?"

"No. I wish."

The audience tittered and snickered at the witness's honesty.

"What have you promised to do here today?"

"Tell the truth."

"Are you here under any compulsion?"

"No."

"Subpoena?"

"No, I don't believe so."

"You are here on your own free will and not under any government requirement?"

"Yes."

"Do you know George Williams?"

"Yes."

"How do you know him?"

"I knew of him as a bellhop at the Brigantine and got to know him a little better when I was placed in a jail cell with him four days ago."

"Please explain to the court why you were put in jail on that occasion."

"I was charged with possessing marijuana in my truck."

"Was that the same truck Buzz Edwards stopped you and Jane Dunn in the night before?"

"Ah … uh, yes," said Chuck tentatively.

Pretending to be reading from a report, the DA asked matter-of-factly, "So if Buzz Edwards said it was a 1977 Chevy four-by-four that you and Jane were in, would he be correct?"

"No, Buzzy would not be correct. We were in my Dodge Ram 454 Hemi." The crowd laughed. The laughter seemed to buoy Chuck's spirits.

Out of the corner of his eye, Digger saw Chuck's attorney, Peter Coffey, turning through some pages of his yellow pad looking like he was trying to find this information.

"So is it fair to say, rightly or wrongly, a few days later you got busted in this truck?"

"That's the short of it. Yes sir."

"And you got put in jail next to George Williams, and your truck got impounded."

"That's correct. I do dispute the charges."

"Did you talk with George about Janie?"

"Yes I did."

"Did you tell him that you were with Janie earlier that night in your 1977 Chevy?"

"I said Buzz got it wrong. It's a Dodge. No, I didn't discuss that." Chucky was looking uncomfortably confused.

The DA backed off. "Who is Buzz Edwards, anyway?"

"He is a friend of mine and a policeman for the Port."

"So that night when he pulled up and saw you with Jane Dunn at 2:00 a.m., did you greet one another as friends? Or was it on police business?" the DA asked, again like he was looking at an official report.

"What are you reading from? Did he report that? It was friendly! We just said hello. We hadn't done anything wrong. I was just giving her a ride."

The DA added nonchalantly, "Did Janie say anything to your buddy, Buzz?"

"No. She just waved, I think. She thought it was pretty cool to have a cop as a friend."

Chuck was answering the questions with a nervous tremor in his voice, seemingly hoping this line of questions would end soon.

"So you had picked up Janie on Ocean Avenue and were headed toward the Brigantine? Right?"

"Uh, uh, yes."

The DA brought the subject back to George. "While in the cell with George, did you say anything about going to the beach with Janie that night?" As he asked the question, he slowly opened the large plastic bag containing the cream-colored mackinaw blanket with the classic yellow, red, and black stripes and placed it on the counsel's table, allowing the blood-stained corner to hang down in only Chuck's and the judge's view. Interrupting his own question, the DA asked the court for a moment to find something. The judge granted the brief interlude. The DA took a few moments pretending to look in his files for something.

During this time, Chuck looked very upset and started to squirm in his seat and began looking at the judge, at the bailiff, and at the exits, staring almost in a trance at the blanket.

The DA came back. "I'm sorry, Mr. Branson, let me repeat my question. While in the cell with George, did you say anything about going to the beach with Janie that night?"

"What? What? No, I didn't discuss that." Chuck spoke slowly as his eyes seized on the blanket.

"Didn't you talk to George in the cell about"—the DA picked up the blanket and started walking toward the witness—"being on the beach with Janie?"

Chuck was getting paler the closer the blanket came to him.

The DA shook the blanket, and sand fell visibly from it.

Chuck took a deep breath and recoiled back in his seat.

"Your blanket still has the sand in it. Didn't you talk with George about this?"

"Uh a a ..."

"Chuck, can you tell me what this is?"

In a barely audible whisper Chuck said, "It's my momma's blanket. It's my blanket, too."

The DA held it out for him to touch.

Chuck reached for it, briefly touched it, and then let it go looking at it like it was a loved one being lowered into a grave. His eyes darted from side to side. He rocked back and forth taking deep breaths with a very sad countenance. Chuck had a foreboding look on his face.

George Williams, sitting at the defendant's table, leaned over to his attorney to inquire what the heck was going on. Reverend Justice put his hand on the defendant's arm as if to say, *Shush, not now. Wait.*

The judge caught the eye of the bailiff and raised his eyebrows toward the witness. The bailiff slowly started to position himself closer to the witness.

The DA still held a portion of the blanket, the portion with the bloody corner. The DA raised the corner in front of Chuck's eyes and asked, "So in the cell with George, did you talk about how Janie had bled on your momma's blanket?"

Peter Coffey was still thumbing through his notes in his legal pad, trying to find the part where Chuck had been with the Dunn girl. He couldn't find this part of the discussion that occurred with George in the cell.

"Did you discuss this blood on your momma's blanket?" The DA repeated strongly while he waved the bloody corner incessantly in front of Chuck.

Chuck was obviously weighing his answer and his options.

Finally after a brief delay, Chuck jumped to his feet. He had had enough.

"She shouldn't have died, all right? She just busted underneath me like an eggshell or something! I didn't kill her!" he said in a loud voice. "She just died!" he added quickly and softly.

Tears were now streaming down his face. "How'd you get my momma's blanket?" he asked angrily. He pointed at Digger. "You took it from my bed! Didn't you?"

Chuck started to come out of the witness box toward Digger.

"Mr. Branson, sit down! Bailiff! Secure the witness!" yelled the judge.

Gene, the bailiff, swooped in front of the witness with his hands in the air, telling Chuck to stop and calm down. "Now, now, Mr. Branson, sit down!"

"You took my blanket didn't you, you pig!" Chuck shouted at Digger.

Chuck threw a punch with his right fist to the bailiff's rotund stomach and followed with a left karate style hatchet chop to the back of the bailiff's neck as Gene was bending over from the blow to his gut. The bailiff crumpled into a large lifeless pile on the courtroom floor. Chuck knelt down, trying to get at the bailiff's revolver.

"He's trying to get his gun!" someone yelled.

Digger jumped up onto his bench seat with his police baton out, stepped onto the railing that separates the attorneys' tables from the audience, made a huge step onto the DA's table, and then used the table to launch a giant leap onto Chuck, who was fumbling with the bailiff's holster. Digger whacked the back of Chuck's head with one quick strike of the billy club, and Chuck immediately slumped over the bailiff.

Digger stood up stepped over the mass of tangled humans. He pulled the bailiff's pistol out of its holster and tucked it into his belt, just like he had seen Agent Forkel do at the funeral home. He knelt over the bailiff and pulled the bailiff's cuffs out of their case, which was attached to his belt, and scrambled over Chuck's body, which was starting to move. Digger yanked Chuck's motionless arms behind his back and clipped them into the handcuffs.

Digger stood up and unclipped his radio. "This is 19. We need immediate backup and an EMT at the courthouse! Like *now*, Patty. Please!" He looked up at the courtroom audience, which was staring aghast in silence at him and at the scene that had just occurred in the span of thirty seconds. The audience started to clap and then stood to its feet, including the judge and attorneys at their tables, and gave Digger a standing ovation.

Three sheriff's deputies came pushing down the center aisle just as both the bailiff and Chuck were to starting moan and groan and move on the floor.

The judge started to gently rap the gavel. "Let's settle down here, folks … settle down. Deputies, remove Mr. Branson to the holding cell. Gene, are you okay?"

The bailiff was starting to stand with Digger's assistance, and Gene gave a high sign to the judge. The crowd erupted in another round of applause for the bailiff.

The deputies were dragging Chuck, who by this time had regained his faculties and began kicking and screaming. "I'll get you, Davenport! You're a dead man! I'll get you … you pig!"

The screaming echoed down the interior hall of the courthouse all the way back to the holding cell area.

"Order in the court! Order in the court! Settle down. Settle down. Take your seats!" the judge called out in a calm but firm tone while repeatedly smacking the gavel. The audience quieted down and retook their seats. A deputy returned to help Gene out of the courtroom. Digger picked up the blanket and brought it back to the DA's table and returned to his seat.

"Counsel, please approach the bench, including you, Mr. Coffey."

The judge first addressed the DA, somewhat annoyed. He hissed in an urgent whisper, "I take it you rest, Jack? What the heck just occurred here, Jack?"

The DA wasn't going to be intimidated by the judge and stated matter factly, "Actually, Judge, when we go back on the record, I plan to withdraw the charges against George Williams and herewith file a prosecutor's information against Chuck Branson for the murder of Jane Dunn."

The Judge asked Peter Coffey, Chuck's attorney, for comment. Coffey said, "Your Honor, when we go back on record, I would like to assert my client's Fifth Amendment right against self-incrimination, nunc pro tunc."

"What do you mean assert the right nunc pro tunc? You can't assert them 'now for then!'" hissed the judge, translating the Latin phrase. "In fact I doubt you can assert them at all!"

"Reverend Justice? What say you?"

"Your Honor, we of course waive our right to cross examine the witness."

The DA guffawed slightly.

"What a surprise!" the court added with some sarcastic levity.

The defense counsel said, "And we join in the district attorney's motion to withdraw the charges against George Williams."

The court looked over their shoulders, "Is that the Ocean Avenue Davenports' kid?"

The DA responded, "Yes, that's Digger, a sophomore at UNYQ. He's the bike cop in the Port for the summer."

The judge slowly shook his head. "Unbelievable! Okay, let's wrap this debacle up with your statements for the record."

"Back on the record," the judge announced as Sally and the counsel returned to their places. The announcement brought instant silence to the courtroom.

"Mr. Butterworth?" The judge invited the DA to state his position first.

"Thank you, Your Honor." The people of the State of Maine withdraw all charges against George Williams."

The courtroom erupted in pandemonium and several press people darted quickly from the courtroom.

The judge smacked the gavel repeatedly. "Order! Order!"

When silence was achieved, he asked, "Anything else from the DA's office?"

"Yes, Your Honor. Based upon the sworn testimony of Charles Langford Branson Jr., today I herewith file a prosecutor's information charging Mr. Branson with the murder of Jane Dunn of Richmond Virginia."

The courtroom immediately started to rumble. The judge smacked the gavel several times.

"Mister … err, Reverend Justice?"

"Thank you, Your Honor. George Williams waives his right to cross examine that last witness," the reverend said, slightly turning to the audience and raising his eyebrows, signaling this was a sarcastic and a humorous gesture.

The courtroom bubbled forth with giggles and sighs.

The judge, too, smiled. "Anything else counselor?"

"We join in the State's motion to withdraw the charges."

"Mr. Coffey, counsel for Mr. Branson?"

"Thank you, Your Honor. As counsel for Charles Branson Jr., I hereby assert his Fifth Amendment right against self-incrimination, nunc pro tunc; request that his statements which were obtained under false pretenses be struck from the record; and request that he be released on his own recognizance at this time."

To this, the audience moaned and hissed. Someone shouted out from the center of the audience, "He's a two-bit thug!" Someone braver stood up, looked the judge right in the eye, and said, "Frank?" addressing the judge by his first name, "You know he's a plague on the Port! Dollahs to donuts he blew up ouah watah towah, yes sah!" The crusty elderly gentleman sat down immediately. The crowd nodded and voiced approval of the statement.

The judge smacked the gavel several times and directed his comments to the brave soul who stood. "Charlie, this isn't the *Phil Donahue Show*, where the audience gets in the act!" Then to Sally the reporter, "Statements of the audience are to be struck from the record."

The court spoke. "These are the rulings of the court. The request to withdraw charges against George Williams is granted. The filing of the prosecution information against Chuck Branson for the murder of Jane Dunn is hereby recognized, and arraignment will be this Friday at 9:00 a.m.

"As to whether the statements of Charles Branson can be retracted by his counsel's assertion of a Fifth Amendment right, I am requesting the DA and Mr. Coffey to brief the matter for my review and ruling at a later time."

Upon collecting his thoughts, he said, "Finally, the court wishes to officially recognize the bravery and wise police work of Digger Davenport of the Port Talbot Police Department. I believe, Officer Davenport, that your heroic actions saved the lives of people in this courtroom. There was no doubt that Mr. Branson was trying to obtain the bailiff's pistol until you acted. We all are grateful and thank you."

He started another round of applause for the young cop. Digger stood and turned toward the crowd and gave a quick wave with a smile and sat down again.

When the applause died down, the court leaned into the microphone and declared, "Court is adjourned!" The judge smacked the gavel one final rap.

CHAPTER 70

After court adjourned, Digger stayed with the DA to repackage the evidence and take custody of it for the upcoming proceedings. Mr. Coffey leaned over to Digger and said, "Even though you just sunk my client, thanks for your bravery," and shook his hand. "You knew I didn't speak on perjury didn't you?"

Digger simply responded, "You can come speak on it now!" They both shared a quick laugh.

Jack made a quick exit out the bailiff's door of the courtroom to check on Gene and run to Reilly's funeral home. By this time, there were no deputies out front. At the sheriff's request, they had been dispatched to the courthouse. Inside the lab room of the funeral home, the sheriff was sitting in a chair, hands behind his back, completely kowtowed. Agent Barnes stood, introduced himself, and shook hands with the DA and began to explain the situation. Jack held up his hand asking Barnes to stop.

"May I have a minute with my friend alone? And may I have the cuffs key?"

Agent Barnes nodded and gestured for Forkel to follow him into the conference room next door. Barnes added, "I don't know where the key is."

The sheriff said quietly, "I got the key. They're my cuffs, for gosh sakes! Key's in my right breast pocket, Jack."

Jack approached his buddy of many years, reached into his shirt pocket, and started to snicker, then giggle. The sheriff whispered a swear word and started to snicker and giggle until they were both laughing outright while Jack worked at the lock to set his friend free.

When they calmed down, Jack asked, "Whose detective work caught those tire molds?" The sheriff, immediately catching the thrust of the next campaign angle, said, "Mine! By cracky!"

"Who oversaw the collection of the key evidence at the morgue?" Jack added with a wry smile, looking around the room.

Jack stopped walking in the direction of the conference room, paused, and burst out laughing again. He answered his own question. "Why none other than our sheriff! *He* did it ... with his hands tied behind his back!"

The DA and the sheriff debriefed with the federal agents, and then with Mr. Reilly of the funeral home on the nature of the sheriff's "concern" and the collection of evidence under his "watchful eye."

Back at the courthouse, about a hundred people, largely African American, donned red vests and exited the building singing "We Shall Overcome."

Reverend Justice, wearing an extra-large red vest over his suit coat, stood shoulder to shoulder with George Williams and spun gracious platitudes about Maine people and Maine justice.

Digger had left the courtroom through the bailiff's door. The EMT arrived while Chief Nickerson was talking with Gene. He slapped Digger on the back. "Ya done good, kid, ya done real good!"

Gene added as he rubbed his neck, "So I hear! Thanks." Digger handed him his service revolver and said, "Gene, if you hadn't taken him on like a bulldog, this would be a different day we're having!" Gene rolled his eyes. "Thanks for the bull crap, son, but keep it up. I got three years before my pension vests. Keep it up." They all laughed.

"Chief, you mind if I keep carrying the police baton?" Digger asked, resting his arm on the black billy club attached to his belt.

"Absolutely, you've earned it!" The chief said, beaming.

"Oh, another thing, can you sign off on these pieces of evidence and take 'em back to the locker? It was quite a feat riding the bike to the courthouse with them." Digger nodded toward the glass exit door. On the other side was his parked bike, with bungee cords still dangling from the back rack.

The chief looked at the bike, back at the suitcases, and then at Digger. As he was about to speak, Digger interrupted. "You don't want to know, trust me!" They all laughed. Digger certainly didn't want to explain the constitutional showdown that occurred and how had to sneak out on his bike with the evidence.

Digger left the courthouse and was mounting his bike when Tracy Thomas came around the corner of the building.

"There you are—the hero of the day!" Digger looked around, pretending to be confused as to whom she was addressing.

"Yes, *you*, Digger Davenport—Badge 19!" she said as she sidled closely up to him.

"Where's the microphone?" he said sarcastically, looking all around her. He leaned in close to her and looked down. "Are you wired?"

"Oh, I'm wired all right!" she said. "But that's strictly off the record."

Next in the series…..

The following summer in Port Talbot there are more crushes and alas, more crimes. Digger Davenport is rehired and befriends a gorgeous gal who is in the Port on a sixty foot wind-jammer sailboat as part of the Upward Bound summer program. The program is the attitude adjustment experience for the rich and famous' college and prep school kids; a sink or swim proposition. Unfortunately not everyone swims. One unfortunately hangs. Digger doesn't think it is suicide. Join Digger in the next Bike Cop thriller: **The Son is over the Yardarm** available Fall, 2018.

Also available from the author….

Also don't miss the author's series on legal how-to's! Completing years of a successful radio syndication as *The Proverbial Lawyer*, Bruner pens a booklet series where *The Proverbial Lawyer* addresses common legal needs by combining ancient biblical wisdom with current legal principles. Visit www.theproverbiallawyer.com for more information.